THE
JOSIAH
FILES

THE JOSIAH FILES

LINDA · HALL

THOMAS NELSON PUBLISHERS
Nashville

Published in Nashville, Tennessee, by Thomas Nelson, Inc., Publishers, and distributed in Canada by Word Communications, Ltd., Richmond, British Columbia, and in the United Kingdom by Word (UK), Ltd., Milton Keynes, England.

Scripture quotations are from THE NEW KING JAMES VERSION. Copyright © 1979, 1980, 1982, Thomas Nelson, Inc., Publishers.

Library of Congress Cataloging-in-Publication Data

Hall, Linda, 1950–
    The Josiah files / Linda Hall.
        p.   cm
    ISBN 0-7852-8252-1
        1. Twenty-first century—Fiction.   I. Title.
PS3558.A3698J67   1993
813'.54—dc20
                                                    93-24269
                                                    CIP

Printed in the United States of America

1 2 3 4 5 6 7 - 98 97 96 95 94 93

To Rik
— For always being there

ACKNOWLEDGMENTS

— A special thank you to Phil Gagnon of Christian Challenge Ministries, and to the others at the Christian Research Institute, Calgary, who loaned me stacks of books, sent me dozens of articles, and answered hundreds of my questions regarding the New Age and occult.
— To Wendy and Ian, thank you for being the really special kids that you are. I love you.
— To my parents, Bob and Edith Mignard, thank you for your faithful prayers.
— To my Monday night Bible study group, thanks for praying me through this.
— And finally, to all my friends in the Alberta Christian Writers' Fellowship, thank you for your support and encouragement.

December 24, 2195

1

Dr. Clave Hammill stood slowly, his heavy gold robe falling in neat folds about him to the floor. He stroked his well-trimmed beard and stared down from his high loft into the spacious auditorium. Every seat was filled. Old faces. New faces. People for him to greet following the service.

Frown ridges formed between his thick brows. He fought his despair, picked up the silver tray with the small loaf of bread, and lifted it high above his head. For a few moments, he gazed wide-eyed at the high-arched ceilings, trying desperately to see beyond the rows of crystal, laser-lit chandeliers, and the holographic sculptures that ringed the dome.

His voice sounded controlled, deep, as he said, "This is the body, the body of all humanity. For we are one body—God. And God is in us and we are in God, for we are God."

Bringing the tray down, he broke off a piece of bread. His church clients each took the small pieces of bread which had been distributed earlier. "Take this and eat of it," Clave said.

Even as he touched it to his lips and placed it on his tongue, the bread seemed to turn sour in his mouth. He looked down again on the hundreds of people before him. Ordinarily, this crowd would cheer him. Normally, the faces of his clients looking up at him, trusting him, gave him special satisfaction. Tonight he should feel particular pride. This was Winterfest Eve. Already it could be expected that less committed clients would be enjoying themselves in the Safe-Drugs and Pleasure

Parlors or be in their personal living quarters sitting comfortably around decorated Winterfest trees. Yet they chose to be here, to listen to his lecture, to partake of the Sacrament under his authority.

He glanced toward the far wall to a group of teenagers. They were all wearing the waist-length, orange-braided wigs which were the rage right now. What will they think of next? he thought. He started to repeat the words, "For we are one body."

He caught himself—aware now that he was stumbling through the ritual. It was not his usual fast-paced, confident program. His gaze settled on his wife, Diona. He sought her reassurance, but she seemed puzzled as she looked up at him. Everyone around her was meditating. Her friend Kara sat beside her, her head bowed, her long hair hiding her face. It was obvious to Clave that Diona was not centering in and meditating on the bread and wine. She was worried about him.

Did she know that tonight he felt little pleasure?

Six years ago this church was foundering, on the brink of being shut down by World Order Church headquarters. Then Clave arrived. He spoke forcefully and eloquently about the God-potential within each person. His dynamic lectures and personal charisma became the talk of Sector 44 of the Northern Hemisphere. People flocked to hear him.

Within months, they were constructing a sleek chrome cathedral with all of the amenities and robot help of only high-priced establishments. Attendance rose. Clave was the guest on a number of holovision talk shows. Excerpts from his lectures and from his self-help series of books were often quoted in the news. And a year ago he was voted *InterPlanetary News* magazine's Man of the Year.

Success surprised even Clave. It troubled Diona. Up until six years ago, Clave had served as a small town church director in a backwater community in Sector 5. But something happened to him when he was assigned the directorship in this urban and highly industrialized area. One morning he looked into his mirror and decided that he would succeed. "I can be somebody because I am somebody," he told the bearded face which stared back at him. "I am somebody. I am God. And I can change the world."

On the recommendation of the WOC's Supreme Advice Board, Clave visited Sister Morag, a noted spiritualist and trance channeler. She received her guidance and counsel from Jason the Seer, the Ascended Master, who spoke through her. Jason had been reincarnated for the last time; he was now one with the Mind of God. Through Sister Morag, Jason suggested lecture outlines and courses of procedure for Clave. He urged Clave to start wearing gold rather than the traditional purple. It was as if he, Dr. Clave Hammill, Doctor of Humanities, was being singled out for some special purpose, some mission. That is why tonight, as he strode across the deep red carpet of the loft, he felt confused. Was this the culmination of six years of promise?

Several times in the last hour he had forced himself to pause mid-sentence, bow his head, and refocus, centering his mind, willing waves of peace to wash over him. But somehow his thoughts would not leave the two-page letter which lay folded in thirds on his desk. It was written—rather than imaged—which bespoke its importance. When he retreated to his office following the service, he would go over it again, point by point.

In front of him, the people grew restless. Diona's eyes searched his once more. He averted her gaze and nodded to the men standing nearby. Small containers of crimson wine were passed to his clients by lavender-robed assistants. Clave raised his own silver chalice, his hand trembling.

"This wine represents the blood," his strong voice thundered down into the grand sanctuary, "the blood that flows through all humanity: humanity past, humanity present, and humanity to come. This blood is life, and life is God."

He stole another glance as one of the assistants passed a crystal cup of wine to Diona. Clave watched her stare into the swirls of red liquid she held. Swirls of light. Swirls of God.

Swirls of heat. Swirls of love. He ached for her. He imagined her struggle, her faltering determination to meditate. He knew her so well. She would be determining to love him more so that the spirit of her love, her goddess love, would pass through her and into him and heal him.

"This blood is life, and life is God," he repeated. "Drink it, all of you, and become as God."

Even though Clave had presided over the Humanity Celebration Sacrament more times than he could count, this part of the service was especially meaningful to him. He would talk about the glory of humanity—the art, the culture, the architecture, the music, the technology, the science. Man was truly a creature like no other. But tonight, as he bowed his head, spidery tendrils of pain weaved their way through his forehead.

His headaches had started a year ago. Two days after last Winterfest, he had visited Sister Morag. This time Jason had an ominous message for Clave—begin rounding up Sector 44 clientele for the Elevation Sacrament. During Elevation, the elderly, the homeless, the injured, and the disabled were given euphoria-producing drugs. They were then laid in comfortable lidded beds and placed inside a small room opposite the loft. During a corporate incantation, the director would activate the terminator and the sleeping spirits would be reincarnated into higher life forms. When the ceremony ended, the bodies were removed and cremated. He had left that session with Morag feeling drained, exhausted. Even though Elevation was one of the assigned Sacraments, he avoided it. Was that the reason for the letter now?

Clave lifted his head slightly, his gaze drawn to the Elevation Suite halfway up the opposite wall. Its arched door was inlaid with brass faces—smiling faces, laughing faces, contemplative faces, the avatars of a new age. Surrounding the door in gold leaf were half moons, animal heads, pyramidal shapes, and figurines of gods and goddesses.

Elevation, according to the WOC, was considered the paragon of all sacraments. To go willingly into the Elevation Suite would most certainly guarantee one the position of Ascended Master much more quickly; it was a position that all would eventually obtain, although for some, the journey was prolonged, requiring many, many lifetimes to achieve oneness with God.

Tonight, the little faces and figures looked like gargoyles, sneering sentinels at the doorhouse of death. Even though the computer-controlled thermostatic unit kept the sanctuary at an even temperature, the loft felt hot. Grimly, Clave wiped his forehead with the back of his hand. He continued reading from his lecture notes which were neatly and precisely scrolling on the small computer screen in front of him, no faster or slower than he needed. Voice activated, if he spoke faster, the words sped up. If he slowed, so did the display. He read, "And if we truly know that we are God, one with His mind, then our potential is limitless. What limits us is our own fears, our own tears. Think about these things, my friends."

He searched the faces in front of him. Once again, he saw Diona studying him intently. She was frowning.

"Think about them the next time you see the word *failure* written across your life. Think about them the next time you are tempted to say, 'I can't.' Remember the cup, the wine which represents the blood—the common blood which runs through the veins of all humanity, past lives, present lives, future lives, all intertwined within the mind of God! There is no such thing as 'I can't' to God."

Clave raised both hands, brought them down slowly, and bowed low. The service was over. Soft, repetitive tones of music filled the auditorium. People sat quietly. Some meditated. A few fingered crystals and other aids to meditation until the music gradually stilled. One by one, they got up from their chairs and headed to the Winterfest celebrations in their home sectors.

His wife, Diona, stood in the back, smiling, shaking hands, and wishing Merry Winterfest to church clients as they bundled impatient children into coats and boots. From his loft, Clave watched them laugh, wave, call to each other, and hurry out into the cold. Diona seemed to be waiting for him to come, but Clave could not greet his clients on this Winterfest Eve. His face, inscrutable from the safe distance of the loft, would be discernible at close range. Instead, he descended the back way and walked down the corridor, his golden cloth slippers making no noise on the padded floor. Diona would be settled in their living quarters wrapping up last minute gifts and fussing over tree decorations before he got home. After twenty-three years of marriage, she knew how much he needed to center himself after each lecture, especially after the Humanity Celebration Sacrament.

A quick handprint on the computer sensor lock, and he was inside his office. He pulled off the heavy robe and hung it on a hook by the door. A flashing blue light on his desk panel indicated that he had received two messages during the service. He would get to them later. He sat down at his desk and unfolded the heavy vellum sheet and spread it out in front of him. The letter from Edward, World Order Church General Director for Quadrant 3, had arrived by interplanetary courier just that afternoon. In essence he was being asked to consider a move to Mars. No, *asked* was the wrong word. *Strongly urged* was better. *Forced* was even better. There were no WOC's in Sector 7, Mars, and with a population of more than 40,000, it was time that a WOC was established there. Headquarters felt that Dr. Clave Hammill would be just the person to get the job done.

"The Supreme Advice Board," he read again, "has carefully reviewed your performance and commitment to the World Order Church in Sector 44, Quadrant 3, Northern Hemisphere, Planet Earth, and has determined that you are the most qualified individual to direct the new World Order Church on Sector 7, Planet Mars."

Clave knew all about Sector 7, Mars. It boasted the highest crime rate in the galaxy; it was the dirtiest, the poorest, the place criminals were sent, a place of social and political unrest. The most unlikely place for a WOC. Centuries ago the term "Third World" had been coined to refer to underdeveloped nations on Earth. Today, the term Third World was still used. It referred to poor and crime ridden worlds of the galaxy. Sector 7 was definitely a Third World.

"Most qualified," he read again. It was a slap in the face as far as he was concerned, a punishment for bad behavior. But why? Was it because he only reluctantly performed the Elevation, only when clients were very infirm and had requested it themselves? But nowhere was it a popular Sacrament. Did they know what Jason the Seer was demanding? What had Clave done wrong that they would make the "Man of the Year" leave this successful church for the galaxy's ghetto?

He scooted his chair over to his messaging unit. He had two, an audio message from Sector 45 and an interplanetary image message from Mars. He took the audio message first. It was his sister reminding him that she and their parents would be arriving for Winterfest about 1000 hours the following morning, and could the whole family wait and open their gifts together then?

For a moment he allowed himself to think about his family. His unmarried sister, Katron, a highly successful laser engineer, spent her days in front of large screen computers and imagers. No doubt she would pack along the latest in laser gimmickry as Winterfest gifts for everyone.

She lived with their parents. Clave frowned. They would be the first to go in Elevation. If Katron understood this, she never talked about it. She had no use for religion of any kind. As far as she was concerned, death was merely annihilation, not reincarnation. Science and only science had been the salvation of humankind, she said. For the sake of family peace, Katron and Clave never argued religion.

He spoke the command and the computer accessed the image message. The face of the High Priestess filled the screen: narrow, arched eyebrows, high, gaunt cheekbones, red lips, black hair pulled tightly up under a glittering headpiece. He watched the thin lips begin to move.

"Dr. Clave Hammill, I hope you will give Edward's letter serious consideration. Edward and I are on Mars now. I am happy to report that we have secured property in Sector 7, and the newest World Order Church in the galaxy should be ready to inhabit in about six months time. Do consider taking on this position, Clave." The screen went blank.

The High Priestess. He had never met her in person. His World Order Church was the largest WOC on Earth, and yet she had never set foot inside it. His dealings were always with Edward. Edward took the weekly reports. Edward collected the weekly client membership dues—accounting for every penny. Edward arrived unexpectedly for spot checks and evaluation. Edward coached him on proper holovision talk show protocol. Edward made sure his pay was credited to his account. That the High Priestess would contact him directly meant that the message was of utmost importance. And he'd better not ignore it.

"Review," he spoke to the screen. Again, the face and voice of the High Priestess. Again, the thin arched eyebrows, the blood-red lips.

"Dr. Clave Hammill, I hope you will give Edward's letter serious consideration. Edward and I are on Mars now. I am happy to report that we have secured—"

"End," he said. The shrill voice stilled. The monitor face went black. His answer must be a resounding "yes." He knew how uncomfortable they could make it for him if he refused. He had seen it happen with other WOC directors. Clave frowned and rubbed his aching forehead with the heel of his hand. How could he face Diona with the news? What a nice Winterfest gift, "Hi, honey, we're moving to Mars, Sector 7. Merry Winterfest!"

Outside the window stood an ancient stone church. The high intensity spotlights which encircled his own building illuminated this old one as well. He could see it clearly through the darkness. It was a view he had looked at and contemplated many times as he prepared his weekly lectures. Built of large, rectangular gray stone blocks, it must have been an imposing structure at one time. Now it was dwarfed and squat beside the high, shining steel towers and pinnacles of Clave's WOC. The old structure was on World Order Church property and, therefore, owned by the WOC, as all ancient church properties were. Heavy wooden doors, facing a road no longer used, were shut and locked, their hinges discolored and caked with rust. Rows of large oval windows along each side of the building were overlaid with ancient, rotting timbers. No one had stepped inside the building in nearly a century. He was surprised that no one had torn it down and used the land for something else by now.

A cross made of heavy timber, one wing partly broken off, still reached crookedly toward the sky. The cross, an ancient symbol of death; a religion based on death. How bizarre, he thought. He prided himself that his religion, his spirituality, was based on life.

Yet, there was something about that old solid structure that drew him. What kind of a person directed it so many centuries ago? What were its clients like? Did that director have as much trouble collecting the monthly client membership dues as Clave did? Did he dread filling out the weekly inventory forms? Did he constantly feel that he was under observation and indiscriminate scrutiny by the High Priestess, or whoever it was who headed up the Church then? Did his failures outweigh his successes?

Often Clave had wanted to go over there and refurbish that building, to re-carpet the floor, polish the stones, and re-hang the front door. He would tear down the cross, get rid of it. That would be the first thing he would do. Then he would commission a brand new chrome statue of the Universal

Trinity—Gaia, goddess of the Earth; Diana, the Moon goddess; and Mars, the god of war—to take its place. But in the past six years he had done nothing. If he wanted to do something now, he only had six months left, he thought glumly.

He picked up and fingered a heavy milky-white crystal, a gift from his wife a few Winterfests ago. It was supposed to impart emotional and physical health. He placed the rock against his throbbing temple. Aside from providing a momentary coolness, it did nothing.

The wind was picking up. The old broken cross strained against the front stones of the church. Snow had been forecast; maybe they would have a white Winterfest after all. His daughters were flying in tonight: Dierdron, from her teaching post on the Moon, and Nori, from Sector 53 University. He looked forward to seeing them again. There, think about tomorrow and family. Think about Winterfest, a time of good-will and peace toward all. Maybe on the way to his living quarters he'd even pick up a few things.

Clave laid the crystal back on his desk, fumbled into his thick great coat and headpiece, wrapped a red, plaid scarf around his neck, and headed out into the night.

2

Outside it was dark. The heavy metal door closed behind him and he heard the computer sensor lock click into place. A sleety wetness, which couldn't quite make up its mind whether it wanted to be snow or rain, was leaving slushy, gray puddles along the sides of the walkways. Under the road lights rivulets ran crookedly down the street like veins on an old man's hand.

Clave liked the walk home. Aerocars could roar above him, and hovercars could zoom past him, but he preferred to walk the four blocks from his church to his living quarters every day. Tonight, however, the streets were slippery, the night was damp, and the wind flip-flapped the ends of his scarf. He pulled his headpiece more snugly down over his ears and fastened his coat up to his chin. It was going to be a cold one, he thought.

He willed his head not to ache as he sloshed down the back alley next to the gray stone building. A large, flat, square structure in front was, presumably, some sort of old signage, but the information it had once proclaimed had been obliterated by time and the harsh northern winters. Clave tried to imagine what it had said. Had it talked about meetings within its walls? Had it reminded clients to pay their dues? Or did it hold quaint little messages of good cheer to the passersby?

On the main highway the mall was still open. Inside, an octophonic sound machine surrounded shoppers with Winterfest carols. Shimmering lights and glittering Santas were strung along the walls and entertainer robots in red suits and white pompons glided throughout the mall handing out colorful neon suckers to children and reminding customers that they had only two more shopping hours until Winterfest.

"Dr. Hammill, Dr. Hammill! Merry Winterfest, Dr. Hammill!"

Clave recognized both the high pitched voice and the frantic hand waving. He turned and walked into the jewelry store.

"And Merry Winterfest to you, too, Risa," he called as he made his way past the display cases featuring expensive watches, rings, and crystal pendants, and to the back counter where the thin, bird-like woman stood, smiling widely.

"I have three very special ladies waiting for me when I get home," he told her. "So I'm looking for three very special gifts. Do you have anything that might fit the bill?"

Normally fidgety, Risa became still, a concerned look crossed her face. "Dr. Hammill, you don't look so good. Is something wrong, Dr. Hammill?"

Clave backed away.

"I mean, you look like you seen a ghost or something. Ain't none of my business, but you okay?"

"Fine, fine, just a bit of a headache is all," he said touching his forehead. "When I get out of this noisy shopping center and back to my own living quarters with my feet up and a piece of Diona's great fruitcake, I'll be fine."

Risa smiled wanly.

In the end Clave purchased three identical half-moon crystal pendants. Risa wrapped them up for him. He dropped them into the deep pockets of his heavy, gold coat.

On his way out, Clave stopped in front of one of those computer "Design Your Own Chocolates" booths. After keying in his Personal Debit Number (PDN), he began tracing out shapes on the screen. His wife would get a kick out of the teddy bears, lopsided Santas, and uneven heart shapes he was drawing. When a female computer voice told him he still had one more to go, he drew a cross. He didn't know what possessed him. He didn't know why. And when the chocolate candies were dispensed into the little box he held, he stared for a long time at the little chocolate cross which lay at the top of the box.

Outside the night was even colder. Or perhaps the warmth of the mall just made it seem colder. He wrapped the scarf securely around his neck and carrying the box of chocolates, he set out toward his living quarters.

In the distance at the top of the hill he could see the lights of his impressive living quarters, the spacious grounds surrounded by heat sensitive fencing and protected by Dos, his golden retriever.

Maybe it was because he was staring at his living quarters and not at the ground in front of him that his right foot suddenly went out from under him. The next thing he knew he was seated on the sloppy, wet walkway, his headpiece a few feet from him, upside down in a puddle. The box of chocolates, thank the gods, was still in his hands. But how many pieces they'd broken into, he wouldn't guess. He felt in his pocket; the three small packages were still safe.

"Drat!" he said, slowly rising and brushing grimy, wet splotches off his robe. Nothing broken, nothing bruised, just my dignity, he thought. And then he paused. When he fell, he had faced a dark warehouse, one of many along this avenue with stairwells descending below street level. He could have sworn he saw the glow of lights. Or was it just the road lamps reflecting on the walkway? He crouched down to get a better look. Sure enough, in the lower window there was a dim string of tiny, white Winterfest lights. He peered more closely. They were strung in what appeared to be a very small cross. The sight stunned him. He stared at that cross until the biting wind stung his face and ears and forced him to get up and get going. Still staring at that window, he brushed off his headpiece, snugged it over his ears, tied the scarf under his chin, and began trudging slowly toward his living quarters.

✝ ✝ ✝

Down the dirty stairwell, behind the grimy, shuttered windows with one small lighted cross, a little group of believers sat in a circle holding hands, their heads bowed. Inside, the room was well lit, warm, and cheerful. A large wooden cross hung against the far wall. On a table beneath it were a loaf of bread and a pitcher of wine. To the right were a couple of computer terminals, an image screen, and two household robots. Two cloth banners were hung on the shuttered window. "Maranatha! He is coming soon!" proclaimed one, while "Look up, your salvation is at hand!" was embroidered in bright strands on the other. Someone had even fashioned a holograph of three crosses on a hill which revolved on a stand between the banners.

A doorway at the back led into a large room that was brightly lit as well. Long tables were spread with the remnants of a turkey feast. It was clear that this group had eaten a traditional Winterfest dinner. But they didn't call it that. They had a different name for it.

Men and women clad in the blue shirts and trousers of the working class sat in the circle holding hands with men and women in the purple robes of the academia and with those in the brown uniforms of the unemployed. An elderly gray-haired man sat in a computerized wheelchair, obviously fashioned by someone from the group, since wheelchairs and paraphernalia for the disabled were no longer manufactured. He seemed to be the leader of the little group. Children in white sat on laps. The very young ones looked around with their thumbs in their mouths, while the slightly older ones bowed their heads in imitation of their elders.

They met like this every evening. Every evening they shared the bread and wine. Every evening—for a year now—they held hands and prayed.

3

Clave walked into the warmth of their living quarters and hung his coat and scarf by the door. "I'm home, Diona," he called. "Where are you?"

"In the kitchen."

He caught the cheer in her voice and felt comforted. He forced himself to whistle a popular Winterfest tune as he wandered down the hall toward her. The house seemed empty except for Diona.

For a moment he stood in the kitchen doorway and watched her. She was rolling out and kneading bread dough. "The girls?" he asked. "They're not here yet?"

"Not yet, but soon." She stopped what she was doing, her eyes still troubled as she studied him. "What's wrong, Clave? Something is definitely wrong."

He straightened the stoop in his shoulders and resumed his usual good posture. "I'm fine."

"Your skin is gray."

"It's the lighting." He laughed, a natural laugh this time. "And you, my dear, have flour all over your face and hair." He touched her cheek. "And smudges of clay from your sculpting studio. Why do you take up such dirty hobbies?"

She refused to be distracted. "Are you ill, Clave? Your lecture didn't go well. You kept searching for words."

"And you weren't centering in and meditating." His words silenced her.

Casually, he poured himself a cup of coffee, grabbed a cookie from the plate, and smiled at her. "Diona, let's not quarrel. It's Winterfest Eve. The girls are coming home."

She kneaded the bread with a vengeance. He hopped up on the counter near her. "I don't understand why you refuse to use all of the latest gadgets and kitchen robots we get for you. They would do this work for you, and yet you still insist on doing it all by yourself."

She flopped the dough down hard on the counter, then relented with a smile. "I don't mind, really."

"You don't have to do any of this, you know. We could get pre-processed bread like everyone else in the galaxy."

Diona made all the household bread herself, and had done so ever since they were married. She enjoyed it, she said. Clave spooned some powdered cream and sugar into his coffee and stirred it.

"Well, consider yourself fortunate," she said. "You have the only homemade bread in the galaxy. And how dignified you look right now," she flicked a bit of dough at him, "sitting up there on the counter with red and green sprinkles in your beard. Wouldn't all your clients love to see the Man of the Year now! Maybe I should call up *InterPlanetary News* magazine."

He chuckled and wiped his beard with the sleeve of his robe.

"Take a break, how 'bout?" he said and poured a second cup of coffee and scooted it across the counter at her. "If you refuse to use one of those kneading machines, which, I might add, have been around for centuries, the least you could do is get the kitchen robots to do the kneading. They don't mind getting their hands dirty."

"I don't mind getting my hands dirty either, or hadn't you noticed?"

Diona scowled at the small lump of dough in her hand. "It's dry," she said. "It's not rising the way it's supposed to."

He nodded absently.

"I'll have to check my ingredients. Maybe they're old."

"Or perhaps it's time to let the robot do the work, Diona."

"No, the girls like my recipes." She frowned again as she wiped her hands dry. "What's wrong, Clave? Is it another headache?"

"A miserable one," he admitted.

"But you keep refusing to see a doctor. You won't even go to one of those macro-physio analyzer booths at the shopping mall."

"Too much money," he said.

She was exasperated now. "It only costs fifteen debits."

"I won't sit there in that special chair like some common customer and let some computer analyze all of my body systems."

"Then how can I help you, Clave? Should I make you some broth with those synthetic healing herbs Kara brought over?"

"Please. Not that again. It didn't work the last time. I'll be all right."

"How can I help when you won't even tell me what's wrong?"

"I'm not trying to shut you out, Diona. It's just something I have to work out by myself."

They talked about Winterfest then, the girls coming home, the presents they bought. "Clave, do you think your sister will like the dressing gown we chose for her?"

"Katron?" He shook his head sadly. "She never pays attention to her appearance. We'll be lucky if she wears it."

"And the miniature kitchen robot we bought for your parents?"

"They'll be pleased," he assured her.

For a moment he considered opening the box of candy and sharing it with her, but the bell rang. They both brightened and raced for the front door. Clave swung the door back and smiled broadly at his daughters. Nori waved cheerfully as Dierdron barreled into her mother's arms.

✦ ✦ ✦

The tree lights were too bright, and their incessant flickering nauseated Clave. He leaned his head against the back of the fabric chair and rubbed his eyes. An hour earlier he had downed a painkiller with a full glass of wine. It was doing little to relieve the pounding between his temples.

Across the room on the couch, Nori lay full out staring at the holovision. She'd found a station which was featuring a Nova Music concert, that new music which incorporated live, screeching animal sounds. Clave studied her. She'd put on weight, he decided, or maybe it was just her new haircut that made her look different. Her thick, black hair had been blunt cut straight to her cheekbones. She wore a short black skirt and underneath, silver leggings. Her feet were bare, her toenails painted bright blue. Clave wondered why she had shunned the royal purple robes of academia for this odd looking outfit.

"Volume lower," Clave spoke to the screen when he thought he could stand the shrieking no longer. It sounded to him like a tomcat being tortured in a back alley by a group of sadistic ax murderers.

"You're so old-fashioned, Daddy," Nori grunted and shifted on the sofa.

Dierdron, wearing her loose fitting purple teacher's robe, sat cross-legged on the floor, Dos's massive orange head in her lap. Absently, she stroked his ears. She had spoken very little since arriving home less than two hours ago. The contrast between his two daughters couldn't have been more pronounced. Dierdron, the elder, was taller and thinner than Nori, her hair a faded brown instead of a glossy black like Nori's—like Diona's. Dierdron, always the quieter one, was especially quiet tonight. She'd barely said two words all evening.

Diona sat on the floor by the tree adjusting figurines which didn't need adjusting, arranging tinsel and gifts which didn't need arranging, and chattering and smiling and offering them all more food and cups of tea and eggnog.

On the coffee table in the center of the room her best china teapot sat beside a plate of neatly arranged fruitcake, Winterfest cookies, and slices of oranges. Clave's little square box of chocolates (minus the cross which he had popped into his mouth before the others saw it) lay next to it. No one, except Nori, seemed interested in eating anything.

A couple of times Clave tried to bring up the subject of Mars, but he always faltered. Wait until after Winterfest, he told himself. Tomorrow evening, wait until then. Maybe this headache will be gone by then.

"Well, you know what I think we should all do," said Diona, rising from the floor. "I think we should all shut off the HV and do something like a real family, play a game."

Nori rolled her eyes.

"You guys, you're such sober sides," Diona continued, "all three of you. I'm going to turn off the HV and get out the Scrabble and all four of us are going to sit down at the dining room table."

When no one rose from their places, she put her hands on her hips. "Nori, ever since you came home you've done nothing but lie there in that ridiculous looking get-up staring at those gyrating Nova people. And Dierdron, all you've done is sit there with that dog in your lap and your mind off in outer space somewhere. And Clave." Clave looked up at her. "I know you have a headache, but you look as if your entire world is falling apart. I'm going down the hall right now and I'm going to get out the Scrabble game and all of us are going to laugh and tell jokes and eat popcorn and chips and be nice and be happy." With that, she turned and strutted down the hall.

Clave roused himself; the drug was beginning to make him feel sluggish.

"Well, you girls heard your mother, let's get going."

"I'll get out the chips, but can't we leave the HV on, Dad?" Nori whined.

"Fine, but keep it low." Pouring himself another drink, stronger this time, he settled down at the table across from

Diona. She kept busy sorting out game pieces and setting up the board and talking brightly.

Halfway through the second round, Dierdron dumped her letter squares on the table and said, "I can't do this! I just can't do this!"

Diona leaned forward. "What's the matter, honey?"

Dierdron looked down at her hands and said quietly, "I . . . I . . . had an abortion."

No one said anything. From the HV came laughter.

Finally Nori said, "So?"

Dierdron stared at the table as if trying to memorize the pattern of letter shapes, as if they would give her the words she was looking for.

Diona said, "Why, dear? That was so . . . so unnecessary. You could have taken a pill anytime during the first two-and-a-half months. You don't even need a prescription anymore. Why, Dierdron, why did you wait?"

Small tears formed in the corners of Dierdron's eyes and trickled down her cheeks. She made no effort to wipe them away.

"It wasn't for the money, was it?" asked her mother. "You know if you girls ever need money, all you have to do is ask. There was no need—"

"No, Mother, I didn't do it for the money," Dierdron said. "I . . . I thought I wanted a baby."

"I still don't see what the problem is," said Nori, helping herself to a handful of peanuts. "So, you had an abortion, so, big deal."

"It was twins," said Dierdron quietly.

"What of the father? Or was there a father?" asked Diona.

"Yes, there was a real father. I didn't buy sperm. And he left. After the abortion, when I couldn't get myself together, he took off. That was about five months ago."

"Oh, Dierdron, you should have called me. Why didn't you call me? I would have flown out. Your father would have wanted me to."

Clave said nothing.

"I thought I would feel okay," Dierdron continued. "I mean women have abortions all the time. Lots do it three or four times a year just for the money they get from the cosmetic people. And twins," she was becoming more agitated now, her eyes bright, "I got double the money. Double the money, Nori! Imagine. But right now they're scraping the skins off my babies so some rich old lady with a baggy face can get a chin or a nose replacement. And if they haven't already done so, they're grinding down their insides to make face cream, nail polish, lipstick, or whatever."

Diona rose now and went to put her arm around her daughter. "Honey, please, you're talking so foolishly. They weren't real babies. It was only fetal material, embryonic tissue. You're getting worked up over nothing. Nori, get the tranquilizers from the medicine cabinet. Run now, please!"

"I don't want any pills, Mother! Is that everyone's answer to everything around here? More pills?"

Nori rose, shaking her head, and Clave stared at his oldest daughter. The words that Diona spoke were words that he had heard hundreds of times before. He truly believed them. And yet, and yet—were there tears in his eyes, too?

"Mom, you were pregnant. Didn't you feel, didn't you know it was a human person you were carrying?"

"Of course. But that was entirely different."

"How so?"

"You were wanted. Both you and Nori were wanted very much."

"And that makes it different?"

"Yes, of course it does. When you were born, loved and wanted, a wandering soul came to inhabit the body that I, that your father and I produced."

"I know all that. But somehow it felt different for me, like these were real babies already. I felt them move. I really did. And I just can't bear that their bodies are being torn into shreds in some beauty lab."

"Dierdron," Diona soothed, "think of the medicinal purposes of the fetus. How it benefits society."

Nori returned with the pills. Dierdron knocked the bottle over. Scrabble letters and little white pills clattered to the floor.

"Oh, yes, the benefits, the wonderful benefits, the wonderful medicinal benefits; only if you're not too sick, and only if you're rich." Dierdron glared at her parents. "And once you get to be sixty-five you can't buy any more medicine anyway. You're of no value to society then so you're supposed to slowly fade away and not complain. It's an honor to die quietly. Isn't that right, Daddy? It's called 'dying with dignity,' I think. If you do, you have a good chance of moving up in this thing called 'The Universal Mind of God,' whatever that is." She paused as if collecting her thoughts. "I killed my babies. I know I did. It was wrong. Not just wrong for me, from my own frame of reference, but wrong, just plain wrong." And then she looked up at her father, "Dad, aren't there some times when something is just plain wrong, just because it is?"

Clave stood up and mumbled something about "listening to your mother's good advice," and padded heavily into the kitchen.

Lying in bed later that night, he could not bring the talk around to Mars. He wanted to tell Diona, he longed to tell her everything—Jason's demand, his feelings about Elevation, his tears now about two lost grandbabies.

Diona expressed concern for Dierdron, saying over and over, "It was such a routine procedure. Why would her mind, her soul be in such turmoil?"

Clave soothed her somewhat by offering to take Dierdron to Sister Morag. Finally, he fell into an alcohol-hazed sleep.

His dreams were dark and shadowy, filled with fearful images. Cloudy gray men pounded his forehead with hammers and laughed. Always laughter.

Suddenly Clave found himself kneeling inside a small metal rowboat in the middle of a raging ocean. Torrential needles of rain made it nearly impossible for him to see. There were no chairs, no seats of any kind in the boat, and no oars. Clave grabbed hold of the oarlocks on both sides.

The small craft crested one foamy wave only to tumble down to the other side. At the top Clave could see that the tempest seethed in every direction. No land. No boats. He was all alone.

He became aware then that he was not entirely alone in the boat. Lying on a ratty and drenched mattress half under the bow were two small identical bundles wrapped in white receiving blankets. He knew they were babies even though he couldn't see their faces. Above the din of the storm, he heard their soft, plaintive wails.

He tried several times to reach them, but could not. Abruptly, as the boat slid down the back side of one frothy white wave, it capsized, spilling all three occupants out into the unrelenting sea.

Frantic, screaming, Clave was pulled under by his heavy robe. He hung on to the side of the boat with one hand and grabbed for the white bundles with the other. The babies were just beyond his reach. They seemed to float, cresting and falling, cresting and falling.

Then they began to sink. Over the din of the storm he heard laughter. Wildly, he paddled with his hands, but they remained just out of reach. Their blankets floated aside. With perfect clarity, he saw them now—little round pink faces, eyes pleading for him to help, mouths open in silent screams. He was powerless to save them.

4

Late the following evening after the turkey had been cooked and eaten, after his parents and sister, laden with gifts, had gone back to their own sector, after all the pleasant conversation had been said and re-said, Clave found himself alone with Diona in the kitchen.

He sat at the kitchen table reading last week's copy of *Earth Today* while Diona pulled bits of meat off the carcass for soup. She had said little to him that entire day. He looked up and said, "Diona, we have to talk."

"Yes, Clave." It was a statement, not a question.

For several moments he didn't say anything. She ventured, "Clave, are you all right? I've been so worried about you. I think you might be totally burned out. I really wish you'd see a doctor. Even your mother noticed. And Katron, too."

"Diona," he said, interrupting her, "they want me to go to Mars, Sector 7. It's all arranged."

She dropped the knife she was using on the turkey, wiped her hands on her apron, and looked at him.

"They're building a new church there. They want me to go and be the director. Winterfest Eve, I got this letter from them saying that because I'm doing such a wonderful job here, they think I'd be perfect for the job there."

"They?"

"Edward, the WOC, the High Priestess."

"So, we're moving."

"I'm sorry, Diona." He looked helplessly at her but her face was blank. He knew how much Diona loved her living quarters. The kitchen was roomy and airy and decorated with dozens of floral paintings and pottery, Diona's own. Attached to the kitchen was her spacious atmospherically controlled herbarium where she babied rows of flowering plants and vegetables. Most of Earth's atmosphere was too polluted to grow much of anything anymore except in these enclosed greenhouses. And in Diona's, greenery flourished.

But it was her studio, her south-facing glassed-in studio that she would probably miss the most. For the better part of every day, Diona retreated there and sculpted bowls, figurines, and god and goddess shapes out of wet, brown clay. How could he ask her to leave this house, this sector, this planet?

Diona began to clear away the turkey pieces. "I'd better fix us some tea," she said dully, running water into the kettle. Clave noticed that her hands shook.

By the time the girls had wandered down into the kitchen two cups of tea later, Diona had come to terms with Mars as long as it wasn't permanent, and as long as they could find a nice house with a room with good light which would be suitable as a studio.

"And I think we should keep this house, not sell it," she said.

"Sell it? This house? What are you talking about?" said Nori walking in, a handful of popcorn in her hand. Tonight she was wearing a tight fitting gold top over orange tights. Dierdron, who followed close behind, was wearing her lavender robe.

When Diona told them that the WOC had assigned their father to Mars, Dierdron spoke up, "Dad, you can't go there. Mars is a political hotbed. Don't you read the papers?"

Nori added, "Sector 7, I can't believe they want you to go there!"

When the girls were small the Hammills had taken a trip to Mars. Clave was scheduled to speak at a conference on Intergalactic Mind Travel and had decided to take the whole family. Mars was by then fully terraformed.

A hundred and fifty years before that, the surface of Mars had been dotted with small nuclear reactors which pumped greenhouse gasses into the thin atmosphere. The polar ice caps had been sprayed black to absorb what heat there was. Gradually, Mars had warmed. The polar caps melted. Water condensed in the atmosphere and began to fill up the low places forming lakes and ponds and rivers. The skies turned blue. Seventy-five years later the first settlers had gone to Mars, built homes, planted crops, set up schools and communities. Much of Mars still remained under glass sanctuaries and partial greenhouses, but outside wheat, barley, oats, corn, and vegetables flourished.

"We went to Mars once—when you were younger."

"Yes," Nori agreed. "I remember you called our tour guide a 'Martian.' And she said, 'Martians are little green men in science fiction books. *We* are called 'Marsians.' "

Diona smiled. The four of them had donned rebreathers and toured the surface of the planet. It was strange to see fields of grain and blue skies, but to hear no birds singing, no insects buzzing. The atmosphere was still too thin, explained their guide. Because of the lower gravity, wheat grew taller, much taller than it had once grown on Earth, and the good news was that wheat could grow without pesticides, because there were no pests. The rampant use of pesticides, herbicides, and chemicals had virtually leached the Earth's soil of nutrients. Earth was a heavily populated industrial site now. It was Mars that had the farms and supplied the planets and settlements with food.

"Diona," he reminded her, "we were impressed with the landscape; the mountains were higher than any we could have imagined. Don't you remember riding in the aerocar and flying over Olympus Mons? At 90,000 feet, it was the highest mountain in the Solar System. It made Mount Everest look like a sand dune."

"Yes, Clave," she said sadly. "The canyons were deep, spectacular, *and frightening*. The cliffs were the highest we'd ever seen."

They had toured the Mars Historical Monument and Museum constructed to honor the first human landing on Mars in 2020. They studied displays depicting the history of space travel, beginning in 1957 when the first satellite, Sputnik, was launched. They were amused by the curious-looking rockets and space shuttles with their bulbous shapes and rough lines, so unlike the streamlined craft they had traveled in.

Night was stranger still with two moons. The moon Phobos was so close to the surface of Mars and its orbit so fast that it looked like a little misshapen potato skittering across the sky. It was an interesting place to visit, but to live there?

Yes, Clave decided, it would be a good idea to keep the house. Maybe rent it on a short-term basis.

That night, Clave fell into another exhausted sleep only to be awakened a few hours later by laughter, the same dream-laughter he had heard the previous night. Only this time it was real. He reached for the panel above his head, automatically turning on his personal bedside lighting unit. He looked over at his wife. She lay curled up and contented beside him. Her long dark hair, streaked with gray, fanned over the pillow. By day she usually wore it in one long braid which hung to her waist. Every evening she brushed it till it shone. How he loved her. Why was it he couldn't tell her of his deepest fears? He had never kept anything from her before. Why was now so different?

Tonight he had intended to tell her all about the pressure he was feeling to reinstate Elevation and about his disturbing sessions with Jason the Seer. Diona with her gentle insight would have an answer, he was sure. She always did. Why didn't he just wake her up and talk to her? Everything inside him felt so stopped up.

He got up and walked into the bathroom and fished around for the bottle of painkillers in the medicine cabinet. He didn't have a headache, but sometimes they helped him sleep. He took two.

Outside of the bathroom door he paused. A flickering glow from down the stairs caught his attention. He started down the hall. If a light was on that meant that the automatic lighting unit was on the fritz. He'd have to get into the main housing computer terminal and find out what was wrong.

Halfway down the carpeted stairs he stopped. He could hear the low mumble of conversation. He descended noiselessly. At the bottom he peered into the living room. The Winterfest tree lights were on and Dierdron and Nori were sitting on the floor. Nori was leaning against the wall, her legs extended, while Dierdron hugged her knees to her chest. Nori was talking, gesticulating with her hands.

"It's just this family, Dierdron," she said. "I mean how many families do you know with a male, a female, and two children, all living together? That's why you're so consumed by guilt over this stupid abortion."

Dierdron looked up and then Nori continued. "Of all the personal living arrangement choices you can make, this one is the most unhealthy—this marrying someone from the opposite gender, and then having children with that person and living with that person for the rest of your life. That has got to be the most unhealthy, guilt-producing family pattern there is. Me, I'm trying to escape it."

"It seems to work for Mom and Dad, Nori."

Nori broke in quickly. "They don't know anything else. They're too dependent on each other, too *devoted* to each other. It's not healthy. It's not normal to have only one sexual partner for your whole life. I mean, just look at the animals."

Clave leaned against the wall to steady himself. Is that what Nori really thought? And worse, could it be true? Did all of his problems stem from an unhealthy family lifestyle? Clave crept back up the stairs and climbed into his side of the bed, taking care not to wake Diona.

A few moments later Clave had the strong impression that something or someone was pulling him out of bed, that if he let go of the covers, even for a second, he would go tumbling to the floor. With one hand clutching his pillow and the other clinging to the headboard, he hung on, certain that if he fell, the floor would open up and he would keep on going down, down to some abyss out of which there was no escape. He held on. His teeth chattered. With one last effort he reached for the sleeping form of his wife. She sat up, hazy with sleep. Immediately, the foreboding left him.

"What is it, Clave? Clave, you're soaking wet. You're sick. Here, let me get you some—"

"No! No, don't get up. Please. Don't leave. Just stay and hold me. Don't let me go."

She curled her arms around him as she would a child who had come in crying from a bad dream. They slept that way until morning.

5 ✝

A long time ago when he was a young
divinity student, it was Clave's job
following the ceremony to wheel the caskets
out of the Elevation Suite and into crematorium slots along
the back wall. There had been five altogether who had been
elevated early that afternoon, four adults and one child. All
five caskets were made of an extremely flammable plastic-like
substance and were draped with gold brocade cloths, not
unlike the fabric of his own robe now. Easily he pushed the
four larger caskets out, slipping them quickly into the
crematorium slots.

When he got the fifth one, he ran into trouble. The small
casket was placed atop an adult-sized cart. And when Clave
grabbed the handle of the cart and pulled, the little coffin
careened to the back, hit a bracket, and settled back down on
the cart with a thump, dangerously close to the edge. He
reached out to steady it, and then tried more gently to pull it
through the doorway. It was stuck. Clave checked the cart's
glider wheels. One of them was misshapen. He pulled once
more but the cart would not budge. The gold drape fell to the
floor and Clave kicked it aside. He wondered then if he should
try to find someone to help him. Two people could manually
lift the plastic box and place it into its receiving slot. Standing
there with one hand on the cart and another on the side of the
coffin trying to decide what to do next, the lid popped up.

A little girl with blonde curls lay on her side facing Clave, her sightless eyes gazing at him, mouth wrenched, hands clenched into tiny fists by her face. Someone had tied a white ribbon to her hair. It had come undone in her thrashings and lay limp beside her right cheek. Her thin white flannel robe was rumpled and twisted up around her waist, like a baby's nightshirt after a restless sleep. What he saw was not a peaceful soul transmigration, but fear. He imagined her screams as she lay, just a few hours before, in her silent, soundproof casket while outside and all around her, pious prayers were going on.

Carefully he closed the lid, then charged through the hallways like a madman, his long lavender robe flapping behind him. He buffaloed his way into the General Director's office without knocking.

"Clave." The General Director looked up from behind his oblong glass desk over a pair of half-moon spectacles. "Do you not know how to knock?"

"A child! She was just a child," Clave sputtered, out of breath in the doorway.

The General Director removed his glasses, carefully folded them, and laid them down on the desk next to his computer screen. He began to smile then, a broad smile which filled his tanned, unlined face. He was a handsome man, a commanding man, with bright eyes and thick gray hair brushed up into a perfect pompadour under his towering headpiece. Clave wondered how many face-lifts he had had.

"Come in, my son. Take a seat," he said indicating one of several high-backed fabric loungers. "Now tell me what's troubling you."

Clave sat down and took a deep breath. "A child, one of the ones who was elevated today, was not given any drugs. I could tell by her face."

The General Director still smiled, but to Clave it looked as if a cardboard cutout of smiling lips had been pasted underneath his nose. His eyes were stern. He placed his elbows on the desk, his fingertips together. "Why, my son, why would you open up the casket of someone deep within a spiritual journey?"

"It fell open. It was on the wrong sized cart, a broken cart. I'd never do it on purpose. I was just about to get someone to help me move it, and the lid fell open. And I saw, I saw . . . That was no spiritual journey." Clave's voice broke. He steeled himself. He would not break down, not in front of the General Director.

"Why was she not given drugs?" Clave asked.

The General Director looked across at Clave and gave his best rendition of a thoughtful pose. "Do you have any idea, Clave, how expensive these drugs really are?"

"No, sir."

"And how scarce these drugs really are?"

Clave shook his head.

"Highly diluted quantities of these same drugs are sold at the Safe Drug houses. And they're expensive enough there. In the strengths that we need to fulfill the Elevation Sacrament requirements, the cost is prohibitive." He unfolded his glasses, placed them on the end of his nose, and called up the Elevation statistics on the computer. After peering at them for a few minutes he said, "Ah, yes. This child, this poor one who was so mentally unprepared for life in this world—her parents could not afford the needed dosages."

The General Director leaned back in his chair. "My son, the Church is not a charity organization. We're just like every other business. Ours just happens to be the refining of souls. Now you just put this incident behind you."

Clave thanked the General Director and backed out of the office. There was nothing more to say. Brushing tears away from his face, he hurried out into the misty dusk of a late afternoon. He didn't stop until he had reached the privacy and safety of his own dorm cubicle.

It wasn't until several hours later that he remembered that the coffin was still wedged crookedly in the doorway. He stole out through the deep night to the church and back into the

Suite where he finally managed to heave the small casket into its crematorium slot.

Why should he think of that now? He stood at the window of his third story bedroom and looked out on a gray and windy morning. In the distance he could make out the brown industrial towers of Sector 44, hundreds of them jutting out of the landscape like a jagged cutout along the fabric of the sky.

In the kitchen Diona was pouring herself a cup of coffee at the counter. Her back was to Clave when he entered.

She turned and faced him. "I've been thinking about something," she said. "I think we need to get away. Just you and me. I'm really worried about you, about us."

"I'm fine, really," said Clave forcing a laugh. "Let me explain about last night. That was just a little indigestion, too much of your good Winterfest cake."

"And the night before?"

"I thought you were sleeping."

"I know what's going on, Clave. You're burned out," said Diona. "Tell me, when's the last time you had a vacation?"

"Well, I can't take one now, if that's what you mean." He looked past her out the window. The clouds were getting darker. "I've got to finish that book. There's going to be a mountain of work over the next six months."

"Like what?"

"Like leaving this WOC in really good shape for the next director."

Diona looked at Clave for a few moments. "Is that what you *really* want to do in the next six months?"

"What do you mean?"

"You have six months left here, right? Six months might be enough time to do something really important here, something you've always wanted to do. Like write your memoirs, Earth memoirs, or something, a history of this WOC, I don't know. Is there anything, anything you want to do before you leave?"

"No," he said. "Nothing."

6

Later that morning, as Clave sat in his office, he looked out at the old stone church. Something niggled at the back of his mind. He would get into that old building, clean it up, wash it down, hang appropriate artwork, commission a brand new sculpture of the Universal Trinity, maybe even get Diona to do it. Perhaps that old building with its repressive "aura," too close to his WOC, was causing his problems. Maybe he was "haunted," like Risa said, by the ghosts of a misguided religious past. Like Nori, maybe he needed to "escape it." If he ripped down that old cross his night terrors might stop.

He would get in there, he decided, and turn the building into a place where people could go and meditate for a few minutes. "Drop-in Meditation Center," he would call it. No, that sounded too corny. "Hammill Shrine for Meditation and Communication." There, that was much better. It would be a monument to himself—the last contribution of Dr. Clave Hammill to this planet. And in doing so, he would purge his own soul of guilt and fear.

Giving his wheeled chair a push, he moved over to his messaging unit to contact Edward about getting into the building. He noticed that he had received a code-purple image message from the High Priestess, a non-imaged directive to all WOC directors. He could tell by the counter along the top of the screen that it was a long one. Another of her missives, he thought. Before he had a chance to think about it and rationalize it away, he began composing a letter to Edward. Clave decided to be fairly candid, explaining that, in his opinion, the aura of that old building needed purging; it was, he was sure, affecting his own work. He spent several minutes working out what he wanted to say. He finished the letter, saying, yes, he was prepared to go to Mars, but that he and Diona would like to make the customary house-hunting trip.

He switched on the message from the High Priestess, turned up the volume, and scooted himself back to his desk. The High Priestess started proclaiming the wonders, the privilege of Elevation, how it guarantees the recipient a higher plane than death by natural causes and that to willingly go to Elevation was considered supreme. Clave shuffled papers and computer demichips around on his desk while the voice droned on.

Looking at the agenda on his daybook screen, he realized that the next three chapters of his book were due to his publisher's on the first of the year. This book, his thirteenth, had already received advance rave reviews. He realized with chagrin that it wasn't even half-written! His publishers would soon be screaming for the next demichip. The book content, on wishing your way to physical and mental health and the use of crystals and other devices (title hadn't been decided upon yet), was giving him trouble. He was bogging down. No wonder. The foremost authority on physical self-health was suffering from uncontrollable migraines and insomnia.

While the voice of the High Priestess murmured on, Clave glanced over at his secretary robot and realized that he should activate it. Maybe he should get busy and dictate a few more pages for that book. See what he could come up with. And of course he should formulate plans for his new Meditation Center.

He rubbed his brow. Another headache. He leaned against the cool screen of the terminal as the High Priestess finished speaking, ". . . Severe measures will be taken, and have been taken, against those WOC directors who refuse to comply with this directive."

7

Edward and the High Priestess were seated in the first class section of the Galaxy Shuttle. Their dinner plates had just been cleared from the last meal they would eat on the tail end of their trip back to Earth from Mars.

Most of the seven day flight had been spent on the IPV, the Interplanetary Vehicle. It had landed at Earth's orbiting space station just a few hours ago. From there they had transferred to this smaller shuttle that would land in a few hours.

In spite of his immense, bulky frame, for Edward the long IPV flight had been most comfortable. Chairs on the IPV fully reclined, and during the artificially effected night, passengers retired to spacious, private sleeping quarters. Sometimes the IPV was called the "Pleasure House of the Sky" because of its numerous lounges, vast libraries, casinos, top-notch entertainment, fabulous meals, and, of course, all the free drinks and drugs one wanted.

Edward gazed out his window at the stars, distant galaxies, and planets, sights which never failed to enthrall him. Will humankind ever travel beyond the few worlds it had explored? he asked himself. Would we ever get to distant galaxies and set foot on planets which are not part of our own small solar system? What was out there? In the far distance to his right a meteor shower filled the heavens with glittering lights, to him a sight more dazzling than the most lavish fireworks display at a Summer Solstice Celebration.

He was startled by the voice of the High Priestess saying, "I should never have let you dissuade me."

This week's issue of *Interplanetary News* magazine was programmed on her hand-held computer screen, and the grave face of New World Order president Morley Kyzer stared up from the front. Edward ran his hand through his short, light hair; he didn't feel like talking to her.

"More coffee?" a flight attendant leaned down toward them, a pot of coffee in her hand.

"Depends," said Edward. "Pure Mars coffee?"

"Of course, nothing but the best."

He held out his cup. The High Priestess asked instead for a glass of clear raspberry wine, from Mars, of course.

As soon as the flight attendant was out of earshot, the High Priestess tapped a finger on Kyzer's picture and went on. "I should never have listened to you, you know. Our plans were almost coming together, Edward, almost coming together."

"Keep your voice down," he warned.

"Why? No one is listening," but she did lower her voice before she continued. "He wasn't my first choice, you know, Edward."

Edward knew.

"But instead I listened to you and so we tried Clave, and spent a lot of time and money the last six years grooming him."

"Hypnotizing him, you mean."

"Call it what you wish, but for six years he has been made ready. And now, and now that things are just beginning to come together, he's turning against me—against us."

"You don't know that."

"I know it very well. Spirit guides do not lie. Numerology readings are always right. Astrological readings are never wrong."

"Never?"

"Well, seldom anyway. I've had so many readings, so many channeled messages. I spent an entire week with Sister Morag. Did you know that? Everything, everything points to one thing, one thing, Edward. There is an old man somewhere—an old man who should have been elevated a long time ago, and this old man is influencing Clave against me—against us."

"Clave doesn't know any old men. I've asked him."

"Knowing that Elevation is preferred, do you think he would admit it if he did? And what about his father? Doesn't Clave have a father? And shouldn't he have been elevated by now?"

"That's one of your problems. You think you can force Elevation on people, but you can't. It's religiously preferred, but it's not law, you know."

"It will be soon, Edward. We may have to start over from scratch, but our plans will work out eventually. We'll just have to find a replacement for Clave and start all over again."

"Clave is very popular, you know. Banishing him to Mars won't change that. People will still read his books."

"Oh, they will for a time, but then he'll gradually lose that following. He won't last long on Mars, especially Sector 7. No one does." She tapped her fingers on the tray table in front of her and looked past Edward out to the darkness of space. "I thought it went well on Mars, all things considered. Didn't you?"

"No."

"Don't be so negative, Edward. I admit, things could have gone a little smoother, but considering that half the Marsians still want Earth rule and the other half are a bunch of disorganized fanatics, I think it went about as well as could be expected. I mean, the construction company has been hired and the building is already going up. That part went well."

"They had no choice. After all, you are the High Priestess of the World Order Church. The Governor of Mars had to give in."

"You have to admit, they were impressed that Dr. Clave Hammill will be their new director."

"A stroke of genius, my dear. I believe it's called 'killing two birds with one stone,' ensuring devotion from the Mars sector and getting Clave out of your hair, all at the same time."

The High Priestess switched off her computer. The face of Morley Kyzer disappeared. "Clave—the future WOC High Priest," she intoned, "the one who would work under me—under us, and help us defeat that sniveling little wretch, Morley Kyzer. It was all working out so well, Edward. Why is it going wrong now?"

Edward leaned toward her. "You know, this little forced change of plans might just work for the best. Hear me out for a minute. You wanted Clave to head up the Earth WOC while you took over its political leadership; but look at it this way: Mars, which was going to be a trouble spot, will now have Clave, one of the most popular WOC directors. He may just be the key to winning Mars over to our side. We just need to persuade the Mars leadership, both political and religious, that sending Clave has been an intentional move of goodwill."

The High Priestess brightened. "That could work, Edward. That could work to our advantage. It may solve one of our problems, anyway,"

"Of course it will. The whole thing might just require a little more planning, that's all."

Their conversation momentarily stopped while the attendant returned with the glass of wine.

"There you are." She placed the glass of wine on a napkin on the tray in front of the High Priestess. "If you require anything else, just speak into the screen in front of you."

The High Priestess picked up the glass in her thin, translucent fingers, her nails long and crimson. She took a long sip and brushed back a strand of black hair from her thin face. She looked all bones and sharp angles, thought Edward.

She continued, "All these spiritualists ever say is an old man. None of them can give me a name or even a description no matter how I press. That old man must be gotten rid of before he influences every WOC director in the universe."

The pilot's voice came over the loud speaker. They would be landing soon. She ignored the loud speaker and went on. "Still, Edward. A better choice would have been Vaney. I knew it then and I'm sure of it now. Perhaps the whole Earth thing can be solved now with Vaney Stodge."

Edward sighed. "I'd be cautious about Stodge."

Edward's large, square hands always looked as if they didn't belong to him. He never seemed to know what to do with them. Now, his hands lay folded in his lap. He had been the WOC's General Director for Quadrant 3 for a little more than six years, coming to the High Priestess seemingly out of nowhere to apply for the job. His references, however, were impeccable. Little by little, she had let him in on her "plan." He went along without question. More and more, she had deferred to his judgment on many issues, the first being his choice of Clave Hammill over her choice of Vaney Stodge. Stodge was a self-styled Satanist who had developed his own form of black arts. Like Clave, he was a popular and prolific author with a large following.

But Edward had been insistent that Clave, a quiet "nobody," was the best candidate. The High Priestess had groaned. "But he's so peachy and pretentious with his cute little family."

Edward had disagreed. There were many, many monogamous, heterosexual marriages with physically produced children. He pointed to the last poll which had suggested that about 38 percent of adults were opting for heterosexual marriages. The High Priestess, however, felt that Stodge with his "succession of young things," as she put it, would appeal to the majority.

They had gone back and forth. Finally, the High Priestess had succumbed to Edward.

"I've issued a directive, Edward," she said, placing her wine glass on her tray. "Just last week I issued another directive."

"The one on Elevation." It was more a statement than a question.

"Yes, the one on Elevation. If we are to get rid of that old man, whoever he is, I can't think of a better way than ordering every WOC on Earth to reinstate Elevation. And, of course, I'm starting with Clave."

"And have that 'old man' come back as an Ascended Master to 'influence' Clave even more."

"Don't be sarcastic. More likely he'll come back as a snake."

Edward leaned against the high seat back and turned to face his window. He didn't feel like going around this one again. The fact that he had to miss Winterfest with his family and friends was bad enough, but to have to hear her go on endlessly about Clave and her Master Plan was almost too much. He was becoming tired of the role he had to play. He wondered how long he could continue.

In the distance he could see the familiar globe of the Earth and the brown haze which surrounded it. Occasionally, a bit of blue and a swirl of white was visible, but mostly brown, the brown of too much carbon dioxide, too much industry, too little ozone. Home. Mars, with its clean air, its unspoiled lakes and rivers, its fields of pestless wheat, was certainly a contrast. Mars could not be allowed to hold the Earth economically hostage. The Earth needed Mars, he knew. That was why, almost 200 years ago, scientists and researchers from all nations had combined their skills and spent billions on Mars's terraformation. And it had worked—they had a new clean place to grow crops. And now Mars wanted to sell its crops to Earth. That couldn't be allowed. Kyzer wanted peaceful negotiations and trade agreements. The High Priestess wanted a complete military takeover. The former was proving to be ineffective. The latter would cost so many lives, and might leave the entire planetary worlds in disarray.

The High Priestess leaned over to Edward. "Edward, Kiki will be all right, won't she? I mean, I've never left my hamster alone for this long."

Edward heard the childlike pleading and put one of his square hands on her small ones. They were cold.

"She'll be all right. We'll be home in less than an hour." He thought of the nurturing robot. "I'm sure Nina's taken good care of her," he said.

8

The following morning the ground was covered with a thick layer of white. By late evening, yesterday's somber sky had finally unburdened itself of all the snow it had been hoarding. The first real snowfall of the year drifted up against the sides of the Hammills' living quarters and blurred the distinction between walkway and concrete yard. Clave added a couple of extra layers of thermal linings under his heavy cloak before he set out for his WOC early that morning. Outside, he activated the yard maintenance robots to clear the walkways, then he whistled for Dos. He could use some company in his office on this bitter morning.

Dos had been a gift from his sister, Katron, some ten Winterfests ago. The Hammills could scarcely remember a time when the lumbering golden retriever hadn't been a part of every family holiday, every family outing. Sometimes he followed Diona to her studio and sat all day underneath one of her large sculptures. Other days he wagged eagerly to go along with Clave.

A gust of cold hit Clave square in the face as the front gate closed behind him. Perhaps he should have taken the hovercar today, he thought. But his daily walks were important to him. It was his time to order his mind. He paused as he always did beside the warehouse where he had seen the Winterfest lights a few weeks ago. He bent down. The lights were gone. He had only seen them once. I must have been hallucinating, he thought, another dream.

He had barely stepped out of his boots and hung his cloak up on the hook in his office when the familiar beep-beep at his door informed him that a package was being delivered by robot courier.

"Receive," he said aloud. A slot midway up the door opened and in slid a white envelope on a tray.

Clave pulled out a small flat object; a demichip was attached to it by a string. The object was made of some kind of metal alloy no longer used today. He knew it was a key. He had seen plenty of them in museums. Now a lot of people wore them around their necks as charms.

He inserted the demichip into his small computer handreader and skimmed the note. His idea of transforming the old building into a Meditation Shrine was a laudable one, read the memo from Edward. Edward had also included a diagram on how to position the key for use. "The lock is old and may be very rusty. You'd be advised to use some spray oil to loosen it."

"Spray oil!" said Clave aloud. "What in the galaxy is spray oil?"

Dos lumbered over, thinking that Clave was calling to him. Scruffing him under the neck, Clave activated his secretary robot with a voice command and asked it to find something called spray oil in Sector 44.

Activating another control chip in his secretary, he opened his bookfile. As he fingered the little key, he thought about writing a chapter or two on the healing power of charms such as antique tools like keys, primitive screwdrivers, and staplers. Lately, more and more of his clients were holding on to the implements of an earlier age, as if the power of a bygone era could somehow impart itself to the present. One of his clients never went anywhere without a small wooden pencil encased in a clear crystal tube around her neck. She claimed that the energy and peace of that centuries old tree remained in the pencil and imparted itself to her.

From another part of the cathedral Clave could hear muffled conversation, laughter, and the shuffling of feet; his assistants were arriving for work. There were thirty-two on staff at Sector 44's WOC: fifteen men and seventeen women. They generally took a coffee break together, followed by a daily mid-morning planning session. Clave used to enjoy the office camaraderie, but in recent weeks, he kept more and more to himself. He was the director, after all, their boss. They were his assistants. He was the one who was supposed to have all the answers. But he had none.

He had no answers for Dierdron who had asked, "Is there ever a time when something is wrong just because it is?" He had no answer for Nori, who wanted to escape her "repressive" upbringing. He had no answer for Diona who asked him again and again what was troubling him. He ran his hand through his hair. A flashing light on his secretary indicated that spray oil had been located in a hardware store that specialized in refinishing antique furniture. Clave keyed in his PDN and ordered a can of the stuff.

The mid-morning staff meeting was unusually quiet. Men and women sat around the long glass table, all alike in their purple cloaks, conversing with the same nuances of speech, smiling the same smile, all drinking coffee out of identical silver mugs. When Clave entered the room with his impressive gold cloak and high headpiece, the conversation ceased. A few of them suppressed smiles and two men in their early thirties at the far end of the table snickered at each other behind their hands. The staff at Sector 44 knew of his impending move to Mars. Clave could sense that they, like himself, thought it to be some kind of punishment.

Clave sat down and listened as his financial advisor talked about an idea he had for raising money by offering small glass figurines of Gaia, the Earth goddess. He had a friend who could manufacture them for a song. They could then turn around and sell them for an inflated price to clients with the promise that the figurines would guarantee riches to those who meditate with them in hand. The whole idea sickened Clave.

Next, his media producers reported that the weekly HV transmission to the Moon and Mars would be increased to twice weekly. One of his technical assistants was working on accompanying the regular transmission with "scent-vision." Scent-vision, or the transmission of not only audio and video, but of aromas, was currently used with much success across the surface of the Earth. Only recently had the technology been perfected to allow aromas to be transmitted interplanetarily.

Clave purposely did not tell his staff about his Meditation Shrine. Instead, he divided up the lecture duties among them for the next four months, citing "personal reasons." They exchanged glances, but said nothing.

Just after lunch, the can of spray oil arrived by courier. Clave held up the odd little canister to the light and read the directions which were imprinted around it.

He donned his outer cloak, dropped the key and the can into its deep pockets, grabbed an oversize flashlight, and headed out. Dos sensed adventure and scampered ahead. Clave exited by the back stairs and trudged through the deep snow to the stone church, leaving boot tracks which were blown clear almost as soon as they were made.

The massive front door of the old building was constructed of heavy wood which looked about a foot thick. Wood was very expensive now and seldom used except in jewelry and fine sculptures. Clave wondered that someone hadn't come along earlier and chopped the door up for ankle bracelets and toe rings. But that, too, was a part of the mystique of this place—no one had touched it.

He fumbled in his pocket for the key and it fell into the snow.

"Drat," he said, bending down. It took several minutes of digging around in the white powder to locate it. He tried to imagine a time when people used keys for all sorts of things: buildings, transporter vehicles, offices, safes. He imagined everybody walking around with hundreds of loose keys jangling around in their pockets, forever dropping and losing them. How complicated life must have been then, he thought.

Clave inserted the end of the spray oil can into the lock and pressed the top. He waited a few minutes and then inserted the key and again it fell into the snow. After several tries and turns he got the key to fit into the lock. Finally, something deep inside the door clicked. He stood there waiting for the door to automatically open. Nothing happened. He realized with chagrin that he didn't even know how to open a door. Did one push or pull? He pushed, but pushing didn't seem to work. Pulling maybe? That's one of the first things I'll have to do, get a sensor lock installed, he thought.

He grabbed the rusty black handle and pulled with both hands. With a great creak and a thundering which Clave was sure would bring all his assistants running out into the snow, the door opened just enough to let Clave and Dos inside.

The air inside was at once cold and very still; motionless, unbreathed for centuries. Dos whimpered and leaned against his master. Clave switched on his flashlight and discovered he was in a wide anteroom; it covered the entire width of the building. There were various racks and shelves attached to the walls, devoid of whatever it was that they used to hold. To his left, Clave noticed a staircase descending to a lower level. Straight ahead were two ornate, wooden doors, almost as large as the ones to the outside.

He walked forward and gently pushed. The door creaked loudly and opened into a cavernous auditorium. As he stepped inside, Clave was struck with a feeling of immense, enormous calm. It was as if he had been escorted to a place and time of solace. The snow and wind outside had nothing to do with this place. He would not have been the least surprised to see the director of the church come striding out from somewhere in the back, smiling and warmly welcoming him here and apologizing for not popping over to the new building yet. The room was like a still painting which had hung for a hundred years in the same musty hallway. Clave stood still for a moment. Maybe this place is sacred, he thought. That would bode well. People would come for miles around to the shrine just to experience the aura of the walls alone.

He was standing at the back of a long aisle. Bench chairs winged out on either side of him. Directly in front of him at the far end of the aisle was a raised platform; on it sat a wooden structure which looked like an archaic lectern. Behind it, attached to the wall, was a tall, wooden cross. Clave gazed up at it and shivered. He wondered if he should turn around and walk out and forget this place existed. But no, this building needed purging. He needed purging. This place was somehow connected with his own deep torment. He had vowed to see it through, and he would.

A high-vaulted ceiling rose steeply in the center. All along the sides of the room stained-glass windows were darkened by the outside boards. He tried to imagine what it would look like with sunlight streaming through the colored panels. He would keep these windows, he decided, but he would change the images. Depicted in one picture were a lot of strangely dressed people and a white bird in flight above two men standing waist-deep in stream water. In another, children in tunics clustered around a bearded man, and in another, a couple and their baby were surrounded by animals in a structure made of rough wood. He would have to see if he could replace these images with ones more familiar: crescent moons, rainbows, pentagrams, the astrological signs, the Mother Gaia and her children.

Clave walked down the aisle with Dos close at his heels. The wooden benches were covered with tattered, rotted fabric. When Clave pressed his hand down on one of them, tufts of gray fluff came away and mingled with the dust in the air. He wondered that people actually sat on these during an entire lecture. He contrasted these with the seats in his own sanctuary which automatically molded to a person's individual body proportions. How uncomfortable these must have been, he mused.

He stepped up onto the raised platform and stood behind the U-shaped lectern. He wondered if this was where the director stood. How close he would be to his clients! He tried to imagine what his own church clients would think were he to suddenly descend the loft and stand here. He ran his hand over the top of the lectern and clouds of dust sifted into the air. This will need a good clean up before a shrine can be built, he thought. I'll have to get a few assistants to program some robots for the job.

The lectern had two shelves. With Dos nosing up next to his hand, he bent down and reached inside. Nothing. Just dust, layers and layers of it. He knelt on the dusty platform and carefully felt along the bottom shelf. Was there something there? A sheet of paper, was it? Carefully, very carefully, he drew out a small brittle piece of paper and shone his light on the scribblings it contained.

> Welcome
> Opening hymn #43, Great Is Thy Faithfulness
> Hymn #206, There Is a Redeemer
> Responsive reading #649
> Announcements
> Offering
> Choruses: Great Is the Lord
>   Awesome God
>   His Name Is Wonderful
>   Majesty
> Prayer and requests
> Special music: Ladies Trio
> Message
> Closing hymn #452 Make Me a Ble . . .

The last word was indecipherable. Clave looked long at the strange little note. What did it mean? This was a church, so presumably it would have something to do with God. But what? He wished that old church director really would come walking out of the shadows and explain the meaning of this note. Clave was angry at his own scanty knowledge of history. He had graduated with honors from divinity school, yet he seemed to know so little about ancient religious practices. His study of church history began in the early 2000s. Students were told over and over again that it wasn't until after the Age of Aquarius, or the Age of Enlightenment as it was sometimes called, that anything of any real importance occurred in the church. Before that, people were in bondage to repressive, moralistic beliefs, and they were not free to pursue their own realities. The *Second Dark Ages* it was called. The symbology of the cross, an ancient instrument of torture and death, was said to be at the center of that unenlightened time. It was best not to know anything about it. With the Age of Aquarius came the freedom to be, the freedom to do whatever one wanted as long as it didn't infringe on another's reality.

He looked at the note again. The only word which was familiar was *God*; "Awesome God," the note read. He felt himself frowning, his thick brows knitting together. How could he purge what he did not understand? How could he understand the thoughts of the church director who had lectured here? Clave knew—he had taught his own clients, week after week—that God was the universal mind, the highest Nirvana. Had he not said, over and over, "We all, as parts of God, fit into a whole"? No, God is not a personality, or a "thing" even, that can be given the adjective *awesome*. God is the universe. The universe is God. It just is. The man was wrong. What is this "Redeemer" in this other notation? And who is this "Lord" they are writing about?

Clave left the lectern and began to pace. Spirit guides were sometimes called "lords." Perhaps that is what the writer of this note was trying to convey, he thought. But why the list? And these numbers? What could they refer to?

Behind the platform were doors on both sides. The one to his right (he was getting pretty good at this door opening now!) opened onto a descending staircase. He tested the planks for safety, but Dos bounded down onto them. If they could hold Dos, perhaps they were okay, he thought. Carefully he descended. The lower room was divided into various smaller rooms, all with doors. He opened the double door to his left and walked into what looked like a primitive kitchen. A strange stove or cooking chamber leaned up against one wall; a sink was beside it. He placed his hands in the sink under what looked like water taps. Water did not automatically spurt forth. Perhaps the main water switch is turned off, he thought. Or maybe one had to manually rotate these knobs somehow. The cooking chamber had all sorts of knobs, too. "You'd spend half your life fiddling with knobs and buttons and doors," he said aloud. "Diona would enjoy seeing all this old-fashioned stuff." Dos whined in agreement.

As Clave wandered around the kitchen, he began formulating plans. The kitchen could be stripped and new appliances installed for brewing synthetic herbs, vegetables, and thought-altering drugs. He walked through the musty basement, opening doors, leaning his head in, and closing them again. The various small rooms could be used for meditation, massage, or small-group therapy. He ascended the stairs, suddenly anxious to get on with his plans for the Center.

He walked across the platform, careful not to touch or even look at the cross, and opened the door on the opposite side. It was small and lined on three walls with floor to ceiling shelves. In the center was a large desk and behind it a chair. The window was boarded up. He decided at once that this room had been the church director's office. One by one, he pulled out the desk drawers. All empty. Someone must have come in here like a whirlwind, he thought to himself. Hardly a scrap of paper anywhere in the entire building.

Dos wiggled his long nose between the bottom shelves and sniffed. Clave wondered why a person, any person, would need so many shelves to display artwork and sculptures. Even a vast array of crystals and other meditative aids would be dwarfed on these vast shelves. Dos began to whine.

"What is it, boy? A mouse? You find a mouse or something?"

Clave bent closer. Dos was now pawing at a spot on the back wall. Clave reached in and touched the wall between the shelves. Dos had broken loose the plaster.

"Careful, boy. This is antiquity stuff. Don't go wrecking the walls of my new Study Center, now."

Clave picked up the piece of plaster that Dos had knocked loose and attempted to fit it back onto the wall. His fingers touched something that felt like a latch. With his key he began to scrape off more plaster. It came away in chunks. Finally, Clave grasped the latch and pulled. The remaining plaster broke away from the wall and Clave dragged out a small drawer until it rested on the bottom shelf.

"What the . . . ?"

Inside of the drawer was a heavy, gray metal box. Clave lifted it out. The latch was rusted, but he sprayed it with the oil and chipped away at the rust with his key. He lifted the lid. At the bottom lay two bound books. The one on top was square and thick with a soft cover, frayed and browned around the edges. On the front in long-faded gold lettering were the words, *Holy Bible*. Underneath was a larger book, not as thick. He picked them up with care wondering how old they were. He wiped the desk chair with his handkerchief and sat down. He had never handled a bound book before. He'd seen plenty of them in museums, but had never actually touched one. It was then that he realized that all of these wall shelves were meant to house books such as these. Clave's own vast library fit easily into a glass box in his desk. Modern books were on micro demichip now and were read via small electronic handreaders. With his own handreader and his personal code he could access any book in his personal library from anywhere in Quadrant 3. To access a public library book, a different code was needed. Book stores each had their own access codes and they required one's PDN as well.

Clave scanned through the pages of the Holy Bible. The print was uniform; it had been printed on some sort of machine. He marveled at the heaviness of it. How awkward bound books must have been to read, he mused, especially if one was curled up in bed or lounging on a couch. By contrast, handreaders were light and usually backed with some soft, comfortable fabric. Print size could be adjusted to suit one's individual reading needs. He realized that old, bound books like this one would require an external light source. Modern handreaders came with their own internal, adjustable light. He wondered that anyone read anything at all back then. They still used paper now, but anything beyond a dozen sheets was transferred to demichip.

He put the smaller book down and picked up the flat, thinner one. It was handwritten, not machine-printed like the other. The letters were small and easy to read. Some of the pages were written in black, others in blue. Centered on the first page were the words in neat script:

The Personal Journals of Pastor Jim Swanson
1995–1996

Just prior to the Age of Enlightenment, Clave noted. He felt chilled as if the wind had found a crack in the old stones just behind the desk. He pulled down his headpiece until it covered his ears and wrapped his scarf around his neck. Ignoring the beginnings of a headache, he began to read:

March 5, 1995

To Whom It May Concern,
Is this the correct way to begin a journal? I'm not sure. This is a new experience for me. I've never kept one before. I really don't know why I'm starting one now other than I feel the Lord compelling me to. I'm not much of a writer, yet I feel as though Jesus Christ Himself is urging me to write down my concerns, my fears, my prayers for this little church–Northridge Community Church.

So the other day in the mall, I bought this book of empty pages.

"Are you doing archival work?" the girl in the office supply store asked me as she rang up my order.

"Archival work?"

She lifted the bottom of the cash register and placed my check underneath the tray of bills. "This is archival quality paper, the kind they use in museums—acid free."

"Oh?"

"That's why I asked if you were doing archival work."

"No, I'm not really doing archival work," I said. "It just looked like good quality paper in a blank book."

"It's that all right. This book will probably outlast you!" She handed me the bag and smiled. "Have a nice day."

How could I tell her that the Lord God Himself was asking me to keep a journal and that's why I was buying this little blank book?

The Lord God? Clave pondered. Was this Jim Swanson demented? Clave read on.

I've been a pastor for nearly fifteen years, here at Northridge for six now. For the first time I understand how Paul felt when he wrote that he grieved over his churches. He saw them becoming more concerned about their own personal status than with a lost world, more concerned with material gain than with gaining the kingdom.

Clave's headache pounded. Kingdom. Kingdom. He toyed with the word. Did Jim Swanson mean Mars or one of the other planets?

Why do we in the twentieth century fall so far short in so many areas of our lives? Why are there such glaring gaps between what we know to be God's truth and how we really act, between what we affirm on a Sunday morning and how we live our lives during the rest of the week?

Our Christianity has become merely a "religion," something we practice, something we have to "do." The rest of our life is devoid of the life of Christ.

Maybe all God wants me to do is to pour out my heart for Northridge Community Church on these pages. If that is it, then that will be enough.

For a moment, he felt a strange kinship to the man, a lonely man as he was now. Clave turned the journal page, sneezing as he did so.

March 12, 1995

This church used to be called Northridge Bible Church. That was years ago, long before I came. The church voted to change the name "in keeping with the times," as the old annual report put it. According to the report, it was felt that the word "community" would be more embracing, more "inviting" to the people of Northridge than the word "Bible." That word tends to conjure up images of Bible thumpers and hell fire and brimstone.

Perhaps that decision was a good one. Perhaps the name change was more inviting to the community of Northridge. Maybe more people have been drawn in and have turned to Christ because of it. Perhaps the word "Bible" did turn some people off.

But I'm wondering that if in losing that name we have lost far more.

His gaze strayed to the words on the thick book: Bible. Holy Bible, he read again.

March 19, 1995

"What have you done with My Son, Jesus?" That is the only question that will be asked us by God the Father. Not, how many choir cantatas you sang in, or how much you donated to the food bank, or how many cookies you baked for DVBS; but what have you done with My Son, Jesus?

There are those who say that Jesus was a "good man," a good teacher, somewhat of a prophet; maybe, and if we're stretching it, on a par with the angels, but never, never God.

Then there are those who would bring man up to the level of God. They say, sure Jesus is God, but there are lots of gods. I'm a god. You're a god. That tree is a god, or if I'm not a god or goddess now, I can become one with a lot of hard work. After all, Jesus was once a man, just like me, and look where He is now. The potential for Godhood is within all of us.

Both views reduce Jesus Christ, the Creator and second member of the Godhead, to the level of man. That is the basis, the beginning of all sin in the world. That was the downfall of Lucifer, thrown out of heaven for wanting to be God. That was the sin of Adam and Eve. They saw a chance to "know good and evil and become like God." They weren't satisfied with their created state. They weren't satisfied with merely worshiping God, they wanted to be God. They wanted to worship themselves.

Jesus Christ was all God, took the body of man and lived among us, died on the cross to redeem us, and rose from the dead to guarantee our final bodily resurrection from the dead.

Then the only question God will ask us is, "What have you done with My Son, Jesus?"

Odd names, he thought. *Lucifer. Adam. Eve.* Aloud, he repeated the words *My Son Jesus.* The words seemed strange and familiar, both convicting and convincing.

Clave slammed the journal closed. He felt uneasy. The back of his neck ached. He reached up and massaged it. The room felt cold. Dos began to whine. There was still much to read, pages and pages of entries, but Dos was whimpering to be let out.

Clave rose, placed the books back in the container, pushed it back into the wall, and walked out into the main sanctuary. It was colder and more dismal than he remembered. Dos was galloping to the front door. Who was Jim Swanson? Clave had never heard anyone talk about God the way he had. It was all so foreign to Clave.

And then Clave heard laughter. As he raced down the aisle after Dos, the laughter grew louder. When he finally shut the door behind him and was again in the blustery, white world, the laughter ceased. He shivered. Where was that peace he felt upon entering the old building, the peace he felt when he was reading those first few entries, before Dos became impatient? Was it all a mirage, like Winterfest candles on the window of an abandoned warehouse? Like a broken chocolate cross?

9

The man in the wheelchair sat alone. A multicolored knitted blanket was draped across his frail knees, and only a table lamp beside him cast any light into the room.

Outside the warehouse, he heard someone's boots crunching through the snow. He peered through the crack in the wallboards. A tall, bearded man picked his way carefully, his thick cloak wrapped snugly around him, his bright scarf flapping in the wind. His body was bent forward, his expression pensive, his hands thrust deep into his pockets. The old man watched Clave Hammill cut across the street.

Slowly, the man in the wheelchair picked up the well-worn, leather-backed handreader from his lap, the one he reserved only for the Bible. On the screen in front of him in large print were the words, "Your hand lay hold on all Your enemies; Your right hand will seize Your foes."

He read it, then closed his eyes. His lips moved, silently, reverently.

10

As the wet clay fell apart on the wheel, Diona Hammill lost her concentration. For one minute she had lost it and the wine goblet spun wildly off center, lengthening into grotesque shapes, frightening shapes, before it collapsed in on itself. Diona stopped the wheel, bowed her head into her wet clayey fingers, and began to weep; tears for the dark day, the snow, for a heaviness that pervaded her mind, her body. Winterfest was over. Her family was gone. Nori had gone back to university. Dierdron was back on the Moon, and Clave was high up in his office surrounded and protected by crystal and chrome. And nothing had changed. Nothing. Clave had even failed to keep his promise; he hadn't taken Dierdron to see Sister Morag.

With her cutting wire, Diona cleared the mess of clay off her wheel. She was alone in her studio that morning. Even Dos had scampered out into the snow after Clave. Winterfest was always her favorite time of year—the lights, the decorations, the gifts. Holidays past when Diona was a little girl, she would climb the stairs to her bedroom at the end of Winterfest Day and cry. Her mother would join her on the bed and ask, "What's wrong?" Diona would only sob, "It's all over and I don't want it to end."

This year she had worked doubly hard to make Winterfest a time the family would remember forever. She had baked special breads, decorated cookies, and had spent hours decorating the house. Somehow it hadn't been enough this year. Dierdron was sullen, Nori was self-centered, and Clave—Clave was still tormented by nightmares and private fears.

Upstairs in the Hammill living quarters sprigs of artificial fir boughs were still strung along her hallways. Tiny bells and stars, gingerbread men, and sparkling Earth children and red felt elves smiled from their perches. Diona knew that once there was a time when people used real fir and pine branches to decorate their living quarters, and had real trees for Winterfest. That time was long past. Crops for the whole of the planet were grown in large, domed, and carefully regulated greenhouses. There was no room to grow Winterfest trees. The only vegetation on Earth outside of the greenhouses was the occasional prickly weed that sprouted up between the cracks in the concrete. She knew that there were trees, forests of them, on Mars. On their trip to that planet they were shown acres and acres of small saplings. They were told by their tour guide that because of Mars's reduced gravity, these trees would grow into giants very quickly. Apparently, they were giants now. A few months ago she had watched a documentary on Mars's agriculture. It was the kind with "scent vision." The pines had smelled so good. Perhaps Mars wouldn't be so bad after all.

In the large sitting room sat the Hammill Winterfest tree, still decorated. This evening she'd have to lug the boxes out of the attic and put all the decorations away for another year. She dreaded that task. She was sure it would only add to her feeling of "blueness."

She should get some of the household robots to help in the de-decorating. But many of the crystal balls were so fragile she didn't trust them in the metal arms of the robots, no matter how carefully she programmed them. She'd do it herself.

Sighing, Diona picked up the ruined clay and carried it over to a table on the opposite wall. She would try again. The clay was full of air bubbles so she wedged it on the flat plaster surface. She pushed hard with the heels of her hands, then she pulled it forward with her fingers.

Tears coursed down her cheeks and she ignored them. If Clave would only talk to her. She hardly knew him anymore. Many nights she lay in bed pretending to sleep while he rummaged around downstairs. So many nights she woke up and held him while he sobbed, and then in the morning he would pretend everything was okay. "A little bit of indigestion," he would tell her. Right.

Diona sliced the lump of clay in half with her thin cutting wire to check for air bubbles, then slammed it down hard on the plaster once more. She started the wheel again and rammed the clay as close to the center of the wheel head as she could. She drenched her hands with water from a bowl she kept on a table beside her. Water splashed in all directions, but she kept both hands firm and steady on the clay. Running the wheel at full speed, Diona leaned slightly forward. Concentrate, she told herself. Her hands around the clay ball, she pushed toward the center. The clay rose up into a cone shape. Her left hand around the cone, she pushed down on the top with her right palm. The cone flattened out. The clay still wobbled slightly, so she did it again. She closed her eyes. The lump felt centered. It was smooth. It didn't fight her.

She slowed the wheel and pushed both thumbs firmly into the middle of the clay. She pushed hard. Then she wet her hands again and began pulling up the walls. Steady. Steady.

As the wheel turned and her goblet took shape, Diona's thoughts returned to the time when she and Clave had met—a month before college graduation.

She was in her final year at the university as a fine arts major. The week-long art exhibit was her first public showing, her "final exam." Her portfolio included sculptures and pottery as well as watercolors and some oils.

Late on a Friday afternoon she was carting the last of her boxes from the students' studio to the gallery a few blocks away. She was tired and sweaty, and still had much to do.

Another two trips at least, and then shower and change with only an hour before the wine and cheese reception.

On her last excursion into the studio, she picked up her largest piece, her best work. It was a freehand sculpture of a spotted fawn standing in a bed of leaves and flowers and looking sideways, almost a surprised expression on its face. An "idyllic scene," remarked her art teacher who gave her an *A*, "one reminiscent of a bygone era when the planet Earth was still unspoiled."

The piece was heavy, heavier than she remembered. Still, she decided she could make it to the gallery without going for robot help. Mistake.

Not more than a block from the studio her foot hit a loose pebble in the road; as if in slow motion, Diona watched her fawn go tumbling end over end down to the cement walkway.

She grabbed for it in one last desperate attempt. Crash! The sculpture hit the pavement head first. Pieces of fawn and flowers flew in all directions. There was nothing she could do. In the gathering dusk she knelt down beside her fractured fawn and cried.

"Is there anything I can do?"

She turned around and looked up into the face of a young man. She could tell he was a divinity student by the gold sash he wore. Hers, from the fine arts department, was red. Diona wiped her cheeks with the backs of her hands and looked up. His eyes were gentle.

"Not unless you can work miracles and put this all back together again. I'm an art student and I'm showing tonight and this was supposed to be my best piece."

He knelt beside her and examined the remains. After a while he turned to her. "It's beautiful," he said.

"Was, maybe."

"No, is."

She watched as he picked up one broken piece after another and fitted them back onto the base of the sculpture, holding them in place with his fingers. "I think it can be fixed."

"It would take a miracle."

"Well," he smiled. "I *am* a divinity student."

She smiled for the first time.

"Will you let me take it to my dorm and see if I can put it together for you?"

"Be my guest."

He scooped the broken fawn into the folds of his purple robe and walked down the pathway toward the dorms.

At the reception later that evening, her fawn stood mended and whole in its stand in the center of the room. Each piece had been carefully glued, and only faint lines were visible.

They were married the following year and the little mended fawn still stood on a pedestal in their entryway. Whenever Diona passed it, she was reminded of how much she loved him.

He was so different from her. An artist, she was the one who was supposed to have that solitary, artistic temperament. But she loved people and parties and socializing. She often said it was because she spent so much time alone in her studio that when she emerged the first thing she longed for was conversation. Clave wasn't like that. He craved study and solitude and long, meditative walks. And he always questioned and never accepted the pat answers of others.

Clave told her that he was a seeker and wouldn't stop seeking until he had found the highest God. By searching and meditating and calling up the spirits, he intended one day to be a god, he told her. He didn't know it, but he was already a god to her.

After graduation he applied for and was accepted by the World Order Church. His first posting was a very small WOC in Sector 35. The manse had only two rooms, but the young couple filled them with what little they had, and of course Diona's pottery and paintings took up almost all available wall and shelf space. He used to walk in and say, "Is this an art gallery or our living quarters?"

Half a year later, Diona became pregnant. It was quite unplanned and unexpected. They hadn't even bothered to get tested and genetically approved. She considered an abortion, knowing that if the baby was deformed in any way it would be terminated. But she kept putting it off. They could certainly use the money they could get for fetal tissue, struggling as they were.

One morning Clave came to her with one long-stemmed red rose, real, not artificial. He had been meditating, and he said that since the baby was conceived during his own astrological season, it must be a sign, therefore, to keep it. The baby would be born healthy, he assured her. His prophecy was correct. They kept her and named her Dierdron. Three years later Nori was born. Two children was the maximum number allowed each family by law, and the Hammills settled into the life of a WOC family.

They moved quite a few times during those early years, and each manse was just a bit bigger than the one before. When the girls were still in high school Clave accepted the posting in Sector 44. The church was small and struggling, but as soon as Clave arrived things started happening. The church expanded; a large Worship and Meditation wing was added, as well as an increased sanctuary size. The Hammills purchased a huge, twenty room mansion on the top of the hill with robot service in every room. Half the time Diona didn't even use the robots to their full capacity.

She wanted for nothing. Nothing but Clave, the way he used to be. The man who at one time accepted no pat answers was now inventing them. That night when Dierdron had cried for someone to grieve with her, Clave just sat there. Diona was forced to give out the "pat" answers, to say things she really didn't mean, things she knew nothing about. She had never had an abortion. All she had to go by was what other people said and wrote about—that it meant nothing, that women could go through repeated abortions with no ill effects physically or emotionally. That's what all the experts said. And the experts were always right. Weren't they?

Later, when she confronted Clave, he had said, "Well, you were handling it so well, I thought I'd stay out of it."

She looked down at the goblet on her wheel. She would make it in two parts, first the cup and then the base. She had managed to form the bowl. She was planning to make a large chalice and two smaller goblets for the Humanity Celebration Service. She wondered if she would leave the display here at this WOC or take the pieces to Mars. Maybe she should donate them to Clave's new Meditation Shrine or whatever it was he was working on. She really didn't know what to think about Mars. Clave was sure it was some kind of punishment. She was certain that he was being put in that difficult place because he had done such a good job here. This was just another manifestation of his paranoia, she thought, that he felt he was being punished.

At the end of the week they would be leaving for Mars to find appropriate living quarters. Despite herself, Diona looked forward to the seven-day luxury cruise on the IPV. There would be movies to watch and lots of conversation in the lounges. She wasn't too keen on the casinos even though she knew plenty of people who took the IPV ride just for the chance to gamble. It would be a nice change, anyway. Maybe she and Clave would even get a chance to renew themselves. Maybe.

Following the trip she was thinking of spending a week or two at Sister Morag's Retreat for Inner Healing. Maybe Morag could help her. Maybe she could even help Clave.

Diona set the completed cup on the shelf behind her, wiped her hands on a red rag she wore around her waist, and picked up another piece of clay from the bin, smaller this time, for the stem.

11

The receptionist at the Mars Plaza Hotel, a beefy, red-cheeked woman with stark red hair, stared up at the Hammills. "Don't walk in the streets at night," she warned. "No one ever walks after dark. Half a dozen murders happen here every night. No one even keeps track anymore."

The Mars Plaza Hotel was the one "nice" hotel in Sector 7. Business people, unfortunate enough to find themselves doing business in that Sector, stayed at the Plaza Hotel. The building, like most of the downtown section, was under a dome. The gravity in the dome, although somewhat weaker than that of Earth's, was not as weak as the gravity out on the surface of the planet. It wasn't necessary to strap on the rebreathers to take a walk under the dome.

The hotel had the usual array of shops, beauty salons, swimming pools, a weight room, and two Jacuzzis. In addition, each room had its own virtual reality booth where one could literally take a trip without leaving home.

Vacationers, or "trippers," as they were sometimes called, sat back in the lounge chairs, strapped on the head gear, and gazed at the screen which encircled them. They could choose the location for their fantasy trip. Trips included the sights, sounds, and aromas of a "real" trip to that destination. Virtual reality vacations ranged from family vacations to lakes and ski resorts to erotic X-rated fantasies, the kind Safe Drugs and Pleasure Parlors were known for.

"It's best to just stay inside. That's what I always tell our guests," the receptionist continued. "Stay inside and you'll live to tell about it. We've got enough in here to keep everybody happy. And you're from Earth?" Her gaze strayed to Diona. "Never mind, I can tell by your accents. We get a lot of tourists from Earth here. Let me say it's best not to broadcast that fact, if you catch my meaning."

The flat, rectangular bellhop robot led them to their room and left after depositing their suitcases on the bed. Clave and Diona declined its invitation to iron and hang up their clothing.

Complaining of a headache, Diona begged off going for a walk. She told Clave she wanted to watch the HV and see how its programming differed from Earth. He left her on the bed, a cup of raspberry tea on the bedside table. Being cooped up on the IPV for a week had made him itching to get outside, despite the receptionist's dire warning. It was early evening as he left the hotel by the main lobby. He found the street the WOC was on by using the map Edward had drawn for him.

The twilight was odd, he thought as he walked down the deserted roadway; it lasted longer than on Earth. At the beginning of the IPV cruise, they had changed their watches to the twenty-five-hour Mars day. With seven days to get used to the lengthier day, it was hoped that "IPV-lag" could be kept to a minimum. It was always surprising to Clave how that one hour could throw off a body's schedule for weeks.

In the shadows of the long twilight, Clave stood in front of the partially constructed WOC. The massive structure spread out before him, its chest-high partitioned rooms looking like some sort of maze game for giant rats. Even though it was only five feet high, he knew what it would look like when finished. All WOCs were constructed along the same lines. It would be high and imposing, made of gleaming chrome with a single spire reaching to the sky. Two intertwined goat heads would stare down from the very top of the spire.

This WOC was different in color from any Clave had seen. Made largely of Mars ground metals rather than the chrome alloy used on Earth, it was rust-red.

The street in front of the half-finished edifice was empty. Builder robots were neatly lined up and parked beside the construction vehicles, computerized shovels, and hovercranes. He thought for a moment about this future church. What kind of people will come here? he asked himself. What will they seek? What do I have to offer them? He realized that he hadn't meditated or called on his spirit guide for a long time. Perhaps that's why I feel so alone, he thought. Perhaps that emptiness needs to be filled, as the human species is meant to be filled, with the spirits of another age. I will visit Morag as soon as I get back to Earth, he decided.

And then he thought of Pastor Jim Swanson. Swanson was from another age. What had he looked like? Had he worn a long, gold robe? Or was there another type of garment then? Why had he urged his people to worship the Ascended Master, Christ?

"What will you do with My Son, Jesus?" The words came back to him, like an audible sound. He looked around, perplexed. Was someone speaking, calling to him through a Mars twilight? *"What will you do with My Son, Jesus?"* Was the spirit of Jim Swanson calling him through the dimensions? Was Jim Swanson a Master? He looked at the quiet building. Why did he feel so confused?

As he stood looking at the maze of red metal that was to be his church, he was barely conscious of the fact that the twilight was fading into night.

He turned back toward the hotel. Something had happened. In the few moments it took to look at the building, the neighborhood had come alive. Multicolored laser lights were ripping pathways up and down the shabby walkways. The streets teemed with people: walking, standing, leaning against buildings, or sitting cross-legged in the center of the walkways playing card games. Clave wondered when all these people had descended to street level. Had they swarmed out of their living quarters and apartments all at the same time? He shook his head and started back toward the hotel. What an odd planet, he thought. Apparently not everyone heeded the advice of his receptionist.

One thing he would have to get used to here on Mars was the constant temperature under the dome. No cold, no wind. No movement of air at all except the exhaust fans of restaurants which spewed forth all kinds of strange and exotic aromas. What did these people up here eat, anyway?

High above him, through the clear roof, he could see the stars: the Big Dipper, Orion—funny that he would see the same constellations as he did on his home planet. As he continued down the street he heard howls and screams and thumps. He felt a sudden panic until he realized that it was Nova Music. It was said that live animals were tortured on stage. As the cacophony grew louder, he wondered if he should have heeded the advice of the receptionist.

On the corner two prostitutes leaned lazily against a bright yellow wall that was covered with graffiti. The young women wore short, shimmery neon jackets, the kind that glow in the dark, over striped tights. How different from the Earth, thought Clave, where prostitutes worked out of licensed Pleasure Houses. They called out to him, but he ignored them as he walked by the anti-Earth slogan scrawled on the wall in black chalk—"We don't orbit the Earth." Underneath this were the three intertwined circles, the symbol for Mars freedom fighters called the Triple-O league and standing for, "Our Own Orbit." "Freedom for the Marsians" and "Whose grain is it anyway?" were spray-painted on another wall, plus a number of other slogans which were much cruder and more foul.

The sidewalk was a checkerboard of various hues, purple and black and pink and yellow, lit with rotating laser lights. He felt as if he were walking on a continually changing game of chess. Just a few hours ago it had been the metallic-red color of Mars concrete, dark and ordinary. The buildings facing him had been dull shades of red-brown, and he hadn't noticed any graffiti.

Two black-robed witches, deep in conversation, crossed the street in front of him, their silver ankle bracelets clanking noisily against their black boots. Under the pink street lights, he could see that they belonged to the Damaen-Marsian order of Satanists. On their foreheads were tattooed two intertwined crescent moons, symbolizing the two moons of Mars.

Clave felt conspicuous in his flowing robe and silver sandals. Would he and Diona ever get used to this alien land, where strangely clad people noisily roamed the streets at night? Where the citizens had no regard for the occupational status of clothing colors? He passed a series of Pleasure Houses and heard more of the thumping, grating sound of Nova Music. He wondered if they were torturing animals. A picture of Dos, shackled and poked with lighted cigarettes came to his mind; he shuddered and closed his eyes. He knew that musicians had recently won the right to torture animals for art's sake. The WOC's only concession was that the necessary incantations be made—guaranteeing the removal of their souls prior to the concert. It was reasoned that without the soul the body could barely feel discomfort. Nova musicians insisted that animal howls of pain were just instinctive reactions, much like a chicken running around after its head is cut off.

For people as well as animals, Clave knew that the body was of little worth; the soul was chief. To reach the state of eternal, body-less soulhood was supreme. *"The bodily resurrection of the dead."* Why should that phrase leap into his mind so suddenly? Where was it from? And then, again he remembered the journals of Jim Swanson. I must read them all, he said to himself. I must go back and read the rest, at least to understand the prevailing thought during the Second Dark Ages.

On the streets drug dealers in glowing tights and fiery jackets urged passersby to try their special drugs and drug combinations, each one trying to out-shout the other. Clave ignored them, also. Somewhere in the distance he heard the sound of a cat howling or a baby crying. He couldn't tell which.

A dozen orange-wigged teenagers emerged in front of him from a lavender alleyway, arguing loudly. Some of them wore pentagram-shaped eyeglasses with colored lenses. One dark-haired, sinewy boy in a Hard Rock Cafe-Mars T-shirt grabbed the shoulders of a short, chubby boy in a fuzzy blue suit and shook him. A tall boy in a thick jacket made of synthetic pink feathers scowled and flicked his wrist. Others yelled and jumped back. Clave saw something glint—a knife! He shrank back against the building.

The feathered boy swiveled on his heels, knife in hand, and grabbed the short, chubby one.

"I said I didn't do it," the boy cried. "I swear it. I swear I didn't."

Clave watched, shocked, as the taller boy pierced the long knife through the layers of blue fuzz until just the handle was visible. Clave lifted his hand in an effort to stop them, but he couldn't speak. His mouth was dry; his stomach lurched. The feathered boy and his friends laughed and danced a macabre jig, mimicking the injured lad as he staggered and fell on his knees, screaming obscenities and clutching the end of the knife that protruded from his chest. Moments later the simpering subsided; the boy in blue lay prone and still on the flickering checkerboard sidewalk.

The tall feathered one sauntered over, kicked the body a few times, and then pulled out the blade, wiped it on the blue fuzz, and slipped it back into his inside pocket. The group walked on jostling and laughing. Clave recognized that laugh. He had heard that laugh many times before, on his bed at night, in the old church. Clave trembled and leaned against the building, unable to move. He vomited against the flickering neon wall.

Then he heard a soothing female voice intoning over and over again, "Your power is low, please recharge. Your power is low, please recharge. Your power . . ." It took Clave a few minutes to realize that the voice was coming from inside a hovercar parked across the street. Someone had left its door ajar.

Clave was dimly aware that he was being pushed along the tiled walkway, in the middle of a press of people, with no way out. Everyone nonchalantly stepped over the dead boy as they would a discarded candy wrapper. They seemed to be rushing toward the gaudy restaurant just ahead, the showy Mars Coffee Shop.

A man in a green-feathered jacket with a thick Marsian accent turned toward Clave. "Are you coming in with us then? You're welcome, you know."

"I'm heading back, actually," said Clave, muffled and confused. He wiped his mouth with his handkerchief.

The man in green feathers didn't seem to hear him, but took Clave's arm and firmly guided him into a large, bright orange-walled room. Huge artificial butterflies, scarlet parrots, and humongous feathered eyes in triangles hung from the ceiling and twirled in the breeze of ceiling fans. Antique implements spray-painted in hues of bronze and silver were attached to the walls: personal computers, fax machines, answering machines, photocopiers, and touch tone telephones. Quaint, thought Clave.

On each table thick black candles burned in pyramid-shaped stands. The man in green feathers seemed grouped with four other Marsians who led Clave to a back booth where they shoved in and sat down. A young barefoot waitress, wearing layers and layers of diaphanous material tied at the waist with a braided rope, sauntered over. She patted the green-feathered man's cheek.

"Coffees all around," he ordered.

Just at that moment one of their group, a large man with fluorescent tattoos on his bare chest, pulled out a curved flute-like instrument and began to play. The melody was haunting, in a minor key. Everyone listened politely and Clave wondered how he could excuse himself from this unusual little group.

Coffees arrived and Clave sipped his. It was surprisingly good. It even settled his stomach somewhat. Mars grew exceptional coffee beans. That much was certain.

The musician finished, placed his instrument inside a cloth bag slung on his back, and took a long drink of coffee.

A man with a black, waxed mustache banged his cup down on the table. "I tell you, we will not stand for that Kyzer character trying any more of his tricks." He looked at Clave. "We're glad you could make it," he said. "We should get started now. Yes, is there a problem, Maeva?"

He had turned to the person across from him. Maeva was an angular woman with short cropped brown hair. She held a flaming yellow cigarette holder in her slender fingers; her fingernails were so long they curled inward toward her palms.

"Did any of you see the news last night?" she asked. "Kyzer has the audacity to call us a 'colony.' Did you hear that?" She mimicked Morley Kyzer's drawl, "'I'm sure that a peaceful trade agreement can be made with our colony on Mars. Just as we have with our other colonies—the Moon and the small Io settlement.' Those other 'colonies' he talks about have nothing, nothing compared to us. The Moon is dead except for a few mines and Io is too far away to be of much practical use. We're supposed to grow crops so Earth-fat-cats can live high and mighty."

Another smaller woman spoke up. "It's time we did something. How many groups are there on Mars now?" As she talked Clave noticed that the intricate minuscule daisies on her fingernails exactly matched the minuscule daisies painted on each of her teeth. She looked over expectantly at Clave, her eyes boring through his. He winced.

The green-feathered man looked at Clave too. "By the way, I like your disguise," he said.

Clave slumped down in his chair and slowly stirred his coffee with a red metal spoon, trying to appear calm. What was going on here? Who were these people?

The words of the receptionist came to him: *Let me say it's best not to broadcast that fact, if you catch my meaning.*

He looked around for the men's room. Perhaps, if he excused himself, he could make a mad dash for the front door. But he was crunched in at the very back of the booth. He kept quiet. He knew that if he spoke, they would realize immediately that he was from Earth.

The mustached man turned to him. "That's a good disguise—a WOC leader. I like it. Tell us more about what's happening in some of the other sectors."

Clave nervously cleared his throat. He couldn't think quickly enough. "I—if you will excuse me, please," he stammered in his best imitation of a Mars accent.

The group members put down their coffee cups and stared curiously at him. "You are the one who's supposed to help us get organized, right?" asked Ms. Daisy Teeth.

"We were told to look for a man dressed as a WOC leader," said the tattooed man.

"That you were going to help us," said Daisy Teeth again.

Clave tried to rise, "There must be some mistake."

"Who are you?" Maeva asked as she tapped her nails on the table.

Clave tried to push past the knees in the booth. "Anthon," Maeva demanded, "what's going on here?"

Mr. Green Feathers shrugged. "Sit down. Now!"

Clave sat.

"Now, tell us who you are," Anthon said evenly. "I take it you're not the Triple-O Director."

"Well, no. I'm a director, but not a Triple-O Director. I'm a WOC director, here to direct the new WOC in Sector 7."

The tattooed man slapped his chest. "Well, how do you like that? A real WOC director!"

The group laughed. Clave didn't. Then they all began speaking at once.

"We thought you were—"

"Fancy that!"

"This is unbelievable."

"You're here for the new church? I saw them building that."

"You have an Earth accent. Are you from Earth?"

A sudden inspiration came to Clave, a half-truth, sort of. He said, "I'm from Earth, yes, but I've been exiled, politically exiled. The WOC wants to get rid of me, so they are sending me here."

"Why don't they just kill you?" said Tattoo Man.

Clave groped for his next words. "It's not that simple. I have certain—how shall I say it?—connections." He was beginning to sweat profusely under his cloak.

"A holy man, a real holy man," said Maeva. She turned to the man in the green feathers. "You have a real holy book, don't you, Anthon?"

"Darn right. A real genuine one, too. Hold it. We've yet to properly introduce ourselves to this good exiled man of the cloth," said Anthon.

Introductions were made all around.

"Well, want to join us?" asked Maeva, her cigarette holder still in her hand.

"Perhaps, perhaps." Something else had caught his attention. "Holy book? What kind of a holy book do you have?" he asked.

"An ancient one. An outlawed one, too." And then he laughed, a deep, guttural sound.

"But that's never stopped you," said Maeva.

Anthon pounded his fist on the table. A waitress quickly appeared and filled his coffee mug.

"Have you read it? What does it say?" asked Clave.

"Never read it. Keep it locked up. Why the questions?"

Clave started to say something, then hesitated.

Ms. Daisy Teeth, staring at her fingernails, said quietly, "I just hope they clean up that body out there. I hate it when they leave them for days and days."

"Nikke's the clean freak," explained Latz, the one with the tattoos and the flute.

"Won't they try to catch the gang that did that to him?" asked Clave. "I witnessed the entire thing. I could testify if needed."

Five bewildered faces looked up at him.

"Why?" they asked.

"It was murder."

"He's better off. You, of all people should know that," said Roderick, the man with the waxed mustache. "He's on to a better life. He's been released."

"He's that much closer to becoming an Ascended Master," said Latz.

"An avatar," said Nikke.

"He's actually very lucky. What kind of life did he have here anyway?" asked Latz.

"It's the best thing that could have happened to him. It's the best thing that could happen to anyone," said Anthon.

"Death is unreal, anyway," added Latz.

Before Clave left the coffeehouse Anthon wrote something down on a paper napkin and handed it to him. Clave regarded it before pocketing it in his robe. On it was a phone number. Across the top Anthon had written, "Join us" and then the three intertwined circles.

Clave nodded. Something inside him began to feel oddly dulled. He saw the faces around the table, heard the noise of people at the other tables eating and drinking, some talking, some laughing and playing musical instruments, some dancing. Certain other faces raced across his mind: a little girl screaming in a silk-lined casket, two grandbabies, their tiny forming bodies being shredded into cosmetic jars, and a fuzzy blue, chubby boy, someone's son, eyes open, mouth pouring obscenities, blood pooling beneath him on the ever changing colored walkway. The boy's face—first pink, then yellow, then green, then blue.

And someone named Pastor Jim Swanson calling out across the worlds, *"What have you done with My Son, Jesus?"*

12

The real estate agent's thick dark eyelashes fluttered behind rhinestone-studded glasses. "I'm sorry that I am unable to find anything remotely suited to your current living accommodation needs," she said.

The agent was odd or odder than the apartments she had shown them. She was very tall and spindly, wore rose-colored pantaloons and a tight fitting top made of red spun-metal. On her feet were the highest spiked heels that Clave had ever seen anyone walk on. Yet she seemed to have no trouble trotting the Hammills from one inappropriate living space to another, and chattering continuously.

After a morning of looking at one squalid apartment after another, she said amiably, "Perhaps some place other than Sector 7 would be better. There are some larger houses I could show you. Most of them are well away from the Sector 7 downtown core.

"It's winter outside of the dome now," she continued. "The houses are all atmospherically self-contained, but you'd need rebreathers to go outside. But that's not really a problem. All the farmers use them." She paused. "Well, I could show you a farm house. Some of the living quarters are magnificent, like Earth homes, I'm told, but I've never been to Earth, so I don't know."

Uneasy at Clave's silence, she said, "What's it like on Earth? I have a cousin on Earth, well, actually it's a second cousin.

She's my mother's cousin. Her name's Lucinda, but I can't remember her married name. I think it's Day or Gray, something like that. Have you ever come across her? If you met her, you'd never forget her. If you want, I could show you a couple of farm houses. You could lease out the land, or program robots to farm it for you."

Clave said, "Thank you, no. We'd rather live in Sector 7. I prefer being close to my WOC."

"He likes to walk to work," explained Diona.

It was late afternoon. They were now standing on the street outside of yet another duplex. This one at least looked a bit cleaner, thought Clave. The front door opened in response to the agent's handprint; she led them inside. It wasn't spacious. It wasn't luxurious. But it was clean and it was within walking distance of the WOC. Inside, the narrow, long building had three floors with two small triangular rooms on each floor. It would do.

The agent pointed with pride to the second floor. The walls and ceiling were painted with large, gaudy gold sunflowers with yawning feathery eyes in the center of each one.

Clave whispered to Diona, "Maybe I'll buy you a pair of pantaloons in the same pattern as this wall!"

Diona smiled. It was the first time he had seen her smile in a long time.

Downstairs they walked out of the back door into a small, walled back garden. Diona exclaimed and ran over to where shrubs and grass and flowers grew in tangled abundance.

"It's in a bit of disrepair," apologized the agent. "It might take a bit of work."

Diona stroked the long grass and tree saplings and smiled. "Oh, Clave, look! Yes, we must live here. We must!"

13

Two days after they arrived back on Earth, Clave decided to finish reading Jim Swanson's journal. This time he was prepared: a large thermos of hot coffee, a couple of sandwiches, a blanket to wrap himself in, a bright overhead light, and his reading glasses. Before he moved to Mars, Clave was determined to discover the secret of the Second Dark Ages.

He was so intent that he didn't notice two gray-robed men who stood across the street and watched him make his way through the snow and into the old church.

Inside the building he began to feel that silence again, that centuries-old calm. He easily found the wall-drawer, unlatched it, and set up the bright light over the desk, confident that the boards on the window would prevent anyone outside from peering in.

Clave took out the journal and, adjusting his glasses, started reading from where he left off.

March 21, 1995

When I first took the pastorate here, I was told that this was a church with enormous capability. Now, six years later, it's still a church with enormous potential. Having potential is like having a treasure all locked up. It doesn't mean anything. It doesn't do anyone any good unless it can be accessed.

Potential is a term reserved for the very young, for babes. You never point to a fully mature man and say, "He is capable of accomplishing much." He has either used the gifts that he had as a child and is now successful, or else he has squandered them and is a failure.

There are a lot of talented people here at Northridge: musicians, teachers, communicators, administrators, but when Sunday comes a lot of them just sit back and say, "I work hard all week, let someone else do it." The potential is there, but it has a time limit. There comes a time when it runs out. I'm wondering if Northridge Community Church has passed that point.

March 22, 1995

Something I notice about churches in general and Northridge in particular is that growth seems to occur from the inside out and not from the outside in. New members and new church families are not brought in from the surrounding non-Christian community, but this church seems to grow only when Christian families move into Northridge, or when church-hoppers decide to give Northridge Community Church a try. I'm sitting here at my desk racking my brains to come up with even one name of someone who has been brought into our fellowship from the "outside."

The early Christian church grew by thousands daily, and I can't even come up with one name in an entire year. What does that say about us?

April 5, 1995

Sally Martin (not her real name—I've decided to change all the names in this journal) came into my office about three months ago with a request. She felt the need for prayer in her life, she said. What did I think of a group of women meeting once a week for an hour of prayer? She had been talking with other women who felt the same way, that one hour of prayer once a week would benefit them and the church. "Wednesdays at noon might be a good time," she said, "because working women might be able to make it there for half an hour." She asked if the nursery could be used. She talked fast. Sally always talks fast.

I was thrilled. Perhaps some of this "potential" would now be realized. "Of course," I said. She reached into her coat pocket and handed me a crumpled up announcement for the bulletin.

My secretary put it in the bulletin for several consecutive weeks, but I sort of lost track of it, I am ashamed to say. Last week Sally came into the office in the middle of the day to use the photocopier. I asked her how the noon hour prayer meeting was working out.

"It's not," she said, looking down at her papers.

I could sense that she didn't want to talk. She kept straightening her little stacks of paper on top of the copier. But I persisted. Finally, she told me that the first week nobody came. "So I went in and prayed anyway," she said. "Then I phoned a few people during the week. They all said they were still interested, but a lot of them had been busy that week. But the second week still nobody came again, so I prayed by myself again. The third week still nobody came, so I just left. I can pray by myself at home; I don't need to drive five miles just to pray in the nursery." She ran a hand through her hair and pushed her glasses back up onto her nose. "I decided I don't want to push it. Everyone thinks I'm a fanatic as it is."

Prayer—our direct line to Heaven itself, our only weapon against the enemy, and we are too busy. Wednesday night prayer meeting in this church attracts a mere handful of senior citizens. And even then it's just mostly a Bible study: Bible study for half an hour, request-listing for fifteen minutes, and real prayer for ten minutes. I read somewhere that the average Christian spends only four or five minutes in prayer per day. No wonder churches have so much "potential" and so little "power." Satan is at the very doorstep of this church, and we are not praying.

Clave felt a dampness against his ankles, a chilling breeze that didn't exist. Satan, he mused. Who was this one, this enemy, that had camped on the doorstep of the old church and robbed Jim Swanson of his hope?

A few weeks ago I got a call from a pro-life group in neighboring Mountainview wanting to know if anyone in Northridge would like to take part in a nonviolent forty-eight-hour prayer vigil outside a local abortion clinic. I made the announcement from the pulpit the following Sunday morning. After the scheduled vigil I was in Mountainview on an errand and happened to bump into the prayer vigil organizer in front of the drug store.

"How'd it go?" I asked him.

"Fine," he said.

I stood there looking at him oddly. He certainly didn't look fine. Finally he opened up, "Not fine, really. We'd hoped for a group of two to three hundred people all raising their voices in a concert of prayer. Instead, we had seventeen. You remember, it stormed that weekend. We didn't even go the full forty-eight hours. The abortion clinic staff just laughed at us."

That evening when I mentioned it at the board meeting, I got a mixed response.

"We thought it was a good idea, but we couldn't make it. Our daughter had figure skating."

Another said, "These kinds of things are important, there's no doubt; but in our case, Gloria had to work and I had to babysit."

Still another said, "You know, we have to live in this town. It's difficult enough without getting branded as a radical."

A few heads nodded in agreement. Finally our chairman said, "Well, gentlemen, let's get on with the business of the church. Shall we open in prayer?"

I came home after that board meeting feeling so very, very tired.

April 15, 1995

Starting this week and throughout the summer there will be no more evening service. It was just a matter of time, I suppose, before we dropped it. Right now it's just an experiment for the spring and summer, but I think I know what will happen. People will get so used to having their Sunday evenings "off" that come September there will be even fewer in attendance. The service will be scrapped entirely.

We've tried all sorts of special programs to boost attendance—a film series, a string of musical performers, and panel discussions followed by coffee fellowships. But attendance has continued to dwindle. We moved the time of the service to 6:00 p.m. in deference to all those who said the service was too late for their young school-age children. It made not one bit of difference. Now those same people have come up with other reasons as to why they can't come out.

While the church is watching television on Sunday evening another child is being sexually assaulted, another teenager is dying from a drug overdose, another AIDS victim is perishing without Christ, a woman is being raped, a man is robbed and brutally murdered, and another "law" is passed quietly and without fanfare, this one allowing clinic abortions at thirty-two weeks, another one endorsing Eastern meditation practices in the grade-school curriculum. And all of this while Christians lean back on their couches laughing at "Funniest Home Videos" and eating popcorn.

The journal pages stuck together, fragile with age. Clave fingered them gently, working them free, his pity for Jim Swanson mounting as he did so. It was obvious to Clave that Swanson had no Sister Morag to turn to, no power of meditation that could bring him back from despair. And, yet, Clave had to admit that the man had tried, that he had not quit. A tiny piece of the page broke free, but Clave managed to separate the pages.

April 22, 1995

A group of school children, my own two sons among them, planted a tree this morning in front of city hall. It's Earth Day. The entire ministerial staff was invited to attend the ceremony. I went. After the planting, the children stood in rows in front of city hall and sang songs about the beauty of nature while the newspaper photographer furiously snapped pictures from all angles. I even noticed a TV camera. A little girl with curly blonde hair recited a poem about mother earth. Then a group of second graders, complete with flowers in their hair, held hands and did a little dance to a guitar accompaniment. Their teacher said it was an ancient Celtic folk dance.

As I stood there in the grass, an overwhelming sense of darkness suddenly filled me. It was a warm day, but a chill went through me. I was rooted to that spot on the grass. I felt I could not have moved even if I had wanted to. My arms and legs felt like lead. Something is wrong here, I thought. Something is so dreadfully wrong. But I couldn't name it. It was too elusive to put my finger on. Even now, I can't find the words to describe what happened to me this morning.

After the little ceremony ended, I tried to articulate my concerns to another local pastor as we walked toward our cars.

"It's harmless," he said laughing, "completely harmless, and as Christians we should be concerned about the environment, don't you think?" he said, getting into his car.

"Yes, but. . . ." I sputtered at his retreating car.

I looked up at my two boys running toward me across the grass.

"Were we good, Dad?" It was my eldest son.

"We're gonna be on TV!" yelled my youngest.

I bent down and hugged them, barely able to keep the tears in check. "Keep them from the Evil One," I prayed.

That was this morning. This afternoon as I sit at my desk, looking out the window at the new spring grass, the tulips and daffodils beginning to bloom, I wonder–what came over me this morning? Why such a feeling of fear as I watched the children dancing on the lawn?

Do I have a clearer understanding of it now? I don't know. It's like–it's almost like the Earth was somehow seeking praise for itself this day, taking credit for its own beauty rather than giving that credit back to God. Does that make any sense at all? It was as though the children were worshiping the creation rather than the Creator.

*A fellow, I'll call him Bob, took me out golfing the other day.
The morning was warm and the course was practically empty. (I
wonder if arriving there at 7:30 a.m. had anything to do with
that.)*

*Despite Bob's patience with me, my game was atrocious (my
game usually is atrocious). Bob and his wife, Joan, are
newcomers to Northridge. Bob has taken over the Boys Club and
done a great job. He took them all to a pro hockey game this
past season. They had a great time, I heard. As we sat at a table
in the deserted clubhouse following the game I looked across at
Bob.*

*"You and Joan seem to be fitting in here at Northridge," I
ventured.*

*Bob put down his coffee cup and looked at me. "We're not
fitting in at all," he said. "There's about five or six cliques in that
church and we don't fit into any of them." He broke his doughnut
in two and dunked half of it into his coffee. "We don't feel like we
belong anywhere."*

*All Bob did was reinforce something which has been turning
over in my own mind—that the Christians here at Northridge are
living as islands. Bob and Joan are not alone. I see others hurting
here at Northridge, other lonely people who don't realize that it
doesn't have to be this way; this is not the way God intended for
Christians to live. God's Word has a lot to say about "one
anothering." We are to pray for one another, love one another,
teach one another, lift up one another, exhort one another. We are
not to live in isolation, carefully separated and protected from each
other by the defenses we set up. Bob's right. There are a lot of
cliques here at Northridge. The new Christian brother is not made
to feel especially welcome. His new ideas are shunned. His
enthusiasm for the Lord is quietly sneered at. We sing, "I'm so
glad I'm a part of the family of God," but ours is a broken and
dysfunctional family. God help us.*

In his mind's eye, Clave saw Diona pointing her finger at him. He heard her say, "You're shutting me out, Clave. We're not communicating." *A broken and dysfunctional family.* The Northridge family? Or my own?

May 27, 1995

It's raining today, that steady kind of late spring drizzle which serves no purpose but to depress. I've a mound of papers on my desk, letters from all over the world. "Will you help us in these last days?" one reads. On another a painfully starved child, stomach distended, stares from the front of a glossy trifolded brochure. A local pro-life organization is asking for donations. In another, a tattered man is sitting on a filthy bed, his face showing despair as he looks up through the bars of his prison. The caption reads, "I was sick and in prison. . . ." The demands are real. The Christian church is not.

We have rafts and rafts of those artificial silk flowers lining the front of the preaching platform. I don't know where they keep coming from, they just keep appearing, week after week. On Easter Sunday last month I walked into the church and at the front were these oblong wooden boxes filled with bright, multicolored tulips. This is Resurrection Sunday, I thought to myself, a morning for real life, not fakery. I walked to the platform and ran a blossom through my fingers. Silk.

And then I thought, these flowers are a lot like Christians, full of color and show, but non-living. They do not breathe, they do not bend toward the light, they do not grow. They are the same showy flowers, week after week, just accumulating more dust.

It's May already and those tulips are still "blooming" at the front of the church. Everyone knows that tulips don't bloom at the end of May, yet they remain in their coffin boxes blooming and unreal.

The needs in this world are very real. And the Christians are made of silk.

Clave wanted to flee, to forget the purging of this building. How could he, in the little time left, remove the ashes and failures of a century? He tried to picture his own WOC auditorium filled to capacity, but the faces blurred to flimsy silk.

June 4, 1995

This has been a most difficult week for me and I'm not sure where to turn. I am so tired. Last week in the "Pastor's Column" in the Religion section of our local paper I came out against homosexuality. Not viciously, but gently, or so I thought. I know I'm not the world's best writer, but I had sweated and prayed over that article. My words were chosen with such care. Yet I received phone calls, threatening ones, even, from gay rights groups in our city. It wasn't three days later that the paper wrote about me, "typical homophobic beliefs put forward by evangelical religious leaders." I've even been called a "racist," as if homosexuals are a race unto themselves. All I wanted to do was to present the other side, bring in a little balance to all that media hype we are getting on gays. I notice today's paper is announcing their Saturday "Living" section will be devoted to "gays and lesbians trying to live normally in a world which still regards them as queer."

In my timidity, Lord, I stepped out for You, I thought. I got my hands severely slapped. And now I feel like retreating. This thing has been hard on my family, too. My wife, Cindy, is more stoic than I, always out there inviting the neighbors in for coffee, but I know she shares my frustration and some of the backlash.

September 11, 1995

The summer has been especially hard on me. I haven't even written in this journal since June. I'm still receiving backlash from my homosexual stand. A few people have left this church as a result of it. One man told me, "My family needs a place where we can worship God quietly without getting involved in political issues." Since when is sin a "political issue"? As I struggle in my soul concerning this, my church also struggles.

There are a number of programs we are going to have to drop this fall. Boys Club for one. Bob, the one I golfed with, has been virtually carrying that alone during the past year. He told me he just can't continue without any help. I don't blame him in a way. I understand his frustration.

The teen program has all but folded. Oh, they still meet Friday nights for pizza or burgers, but there isn't one couple in this entire church of two hundred who are willing to be youth sponsors. So, they meet, but there is no devotional time, no Bible study, no prayer. This is our next generation.

The evening service has gone. My predictions were correct. The next to go will be the Sunday school. Already we have many combined classes because we can't find enough teachers.

Where is the commitment? Where is the worship? Where is true religion? Oh, God, what is happening? Last evening I called an old friend of mine from seminary days. We must have talked and shared, and prayed and cried together for almost two hours. He told me that he is experiencing similar difficulties in his church out East. What is happening across this country?

September 13, 1996

More than a year has passed since I wrote in this journal. Many times I glimpsed this gray volume lying at the bottom of my wall file drawer, but I haven't been able to bring myself to write in it. Today with the Lord's help I will write. 1996 has been a year of endings and a year of beginnings. Endings because so many of our programs have come under the chopping block. Endings because so many people have just drifted away from the church.

But it has been a year of beginnings for me. As I wept and struggled with the lack of commitment, the lack of family, the lack of support from my own church family over "political" issues, the Lord in His gentleness began to point certain things out to me. Where was my commitment? Where was my worship? Do I pray? Or am I a silk flower? Where was I when Sally was praying by herself in the nursery? Home eating lunch with Cindy, my wife. Why didn't I urge us both to go back and fast and pray with her?

Where were we, Cindy and I, when Bob and Joan were feeling so alone? How often did we have them over? How often did I even pray for them? Where was I when seventeen people were standing and praying in the rain for unborn children? Sure, I wrote one article about homosexuality, but then what did I do? I cried and blamed God for the threats against me and my family.

The Lord began to reveal to me that I was nothing but a silk flower myself, selfish and private, an island protected by the waters of my own position in this church. I have begun now to pray, to really pray, probably for the first time in my life. I have covenanted before God to pray for each member of my congregation once a week. I've taken our church directory and divided up the names and each day I pray for approximately twenty individuals. If I can do nothing else, I will pray.

I've also begun to pray for the church worldwide. I began to pray for homosexuals, and God in His mercy led me to Harlan, a young man who is dying of AIDS in our local hospital. (I happened to meet him by chance. On a pastoral call to an elderly church lady, the nurse's station gave me the wrong room number.) I visit Harlan at least once a week, sharing God's love with him, reading the Bible to him, and praying with him.

About two months ago our area denominational coordinator called to tell me that a bright new church in Fairview Heights needs a pastor. "It's a growing, dynamic work," he said. "They have a youth group with fifty kids and a real program with the seniors. Souls are being saved all the time," he told me. "Their current pastor is on his way to the mission field. Here's your chance to get out of Northridge. You don't want to stay at Northridge. That church is dead."

"If it's dead," I answered, "isn't that all the more reason to stay?"

Jim Swanson's words played themselves over in Clave's thinking. *That church is dead.* If the church in Mars is dead, isn't that all the more reason for me to go there? But if I go, he reasoned, what will I tell the people?

This will be my last journal entry. I've really nothing more to add. Even though I see only small changes in my flock, I will pray and continue to pray. It's my responsibility to pray, not to question.

Harlan died two weeks ago. I've been criticized by my board for holding his funeral service here. I've no doubt that Harlan is in the presence of his Savior now. Very few of our own church people attended the funeral. The sanctuary, instead, was filled with many of his former friends. I was able to present Christ's love to them, the way Harlan would have wanted.

It's funny. Despite Harlan, I'm still being criticized for my stand on homosexuality. The newspaper never fails to label me "that evangelical homophobic." One small victory followed by so many defeats. Satan will not let go.

I am also beginning to understand what happened to me a year ago on the lawn in front of city hall. It was the Spirit of God witnessing within my own spirit that something was not right. I now see demonic forces behind some of the Earth Day events. The earth is Satan's home. He rules it. It would make him jump with joy to have people worship his home, his dwelling place. To have people worship the creation rather than the Creator would be his ultimate victory. This year I declined involvement in Earth Day. We kept our boys out of school that day. Continued prayer is the only answer.

Lately when I pray, however, I feel as though I am wrestling against the powers of hell itself. I almost feel that Northridge is at the center of some very great demonic attack, that Satan's talons lie just inches above the rooftop of this old stone building.

Yesterday my young son brought in a handful of wildflowers to me. They grow in abundance in the vacant lot beside this building. I looked at them for a moment and smiled, and hugged him. It seemed as if God was telling me at that moment that I am beginning to become a live flower. I have shunned the silk and phony in my life for a real life of prayer and communion with Christ. I don't know what God has for this church, but I do know one thing. He is more powerful than the legion of demons we would wrestle against.

Give me the courage, God, to walk, like Shadrach, Meshach, and Abednego, right into the fire.

> *And tho' this world, with devils filled,*
> *Should threaten to undo us;*
> *We will not fear, for God hath willed*
> *His truth to triumph through us.*
> *The prince of darkness grim—*
> *We tremble not for him;*
> *His rage we can endure,*
> *For lo! His doom is sure,*
> *One little word shall fell him. (Martin Luther)*

The rest of the pages were empty. Clave leafed through them slowly. Toward the back he felt a slight bulge. He opened to it and a little bunch of dried flowers fell to dust before him on the desk. But remaining on the thick cream pages were their perfect imprints, every petal, every leaf, even the colors—red, yellow, green, orange, flawlessly preserved, a centuries-old mosaic of exquisite beauty.

Clave closed the book. He rose then and walked toward the boarded office window. Through a pinhole crack he could see to the outside. It was snowing again, large white flakes gently wafting downward.

"Who are You, God?" he asked aloud into the snow world of white.

He sat down again and opened the second book. It was heavier and dense with print. He adjusted the light, lifted the book toward him, and turned to the first page. He looked at the title page—"Holy Bible, The New King James Version containing the Old and New Testaments." Who was this King James, he wondered, the author of this volume? He read the table of contents, the copyright information page, and began reading something called the "Preface."

He learned that King James was not the writer of the book, but that it was some sort of very ancient volume, a compilation of manuscripts and translations and versions in Hebrew, Greek, and Latin languages long dead. A lot of it he didn't understand, but he carefully went through it nonetheless. He sensed, somehow, that this book he held in his hands was very special. Was this the only copy?

If the author of this is truly God, he thought, then why have I never seen it before? Why have I never heard of this Holy Book? Clave lived in an age when there were many, many words of gods. Because everyone was a part of God, anyone, it seemed, could write a book and declare it holy. And yet these people and Jim Swanson wrote as if God were a separate entity, not a soul-mind—a person. If that were true, what did that make Clave? If he was not a part of the Universal Mind of God, then who was he? What was he?

He read paragraph after paragraph of how and why the translators used certain words and not others. It was fascinating.

Clave wrapped a plaid wool blanket around his shoulders. The overhead lamp illuminated the book, but cast eerie shadows on the shelves beside him. Slowly, he turned the page and began reading,

"In the beginning God created. . . ."

He bent over the book, page after page he read, his coffee cold in the cup beside him, his sandwich still in its wrapper.

Inside the boarded office he could not know that the early morning snowfall had been replaced by a radiant sun which was making the landscape below look as if it had been sprinkled with diamonds. He did not know that while all over Quadrant 3 of the Northern Hemisphere a fierce blizzard was raging darkly, the sun was shining on the little stone church in Sector 44.

Halfway through the book of Exodus, Clave lay with his head on the desk and wept.

14

There was only one thing on Clave's mind as he ran out of the office, raced down the aisle, and out into the cold, his robe billowing out behind him. I've got to tell Diona. Diona has to know about this. I have to get Diona, he thought. So intent was he on this one purpose that he failed to notice the two gray-robed figures who slipped through the large doors and into the church behind him.

"Diona," he yelled as he tore through the house. The kitchen was empty. He bounded down the stairs two at a time. Her studio was empty.

"Diona! You've got to come with me. I've found it! I've found it!"

He finally found her in the bedroom calmly folding clothes into a large suitcase.

He stood in the doorway out of breath. "What did you find, Clave?" she said looking up.

"I found God!" was all he said. And then he grabbed her hands and danced around the room. She shrugged away.

"Clave, are you on drugs?"

He frowned and dropped his arms to his side.

"I'm not on drugs. This is real," he said. "I just came to get you, to show you something."

"Well, what is it, Clave?"

"A holy book."

"A holy book?"

"It's called the Holy Bible. I only read a couple of chapters, just the first part, really, but it makes sense. It really does. It says that God is the Creator, and we are His creations. He created us. But that wasn't good enough for people. Those two people He created wanted to be like God and that was their downfall. That separated them from God."

"Wait a minute, Clave. Hold it. How can we be separated from God when we are God?"

"But we're not God. That's a lie."

Diona shook her head. "I don't understand a thing you're saying. How can you be so sure of this?"

"I talked to this God, Diona. I actually spoke with Him."

Diona sighed and sat down on the bed. Clave continued, "The person in the Book talked to God, so I figured that maybe I could, too. So I tried it. I was sitting there reading and I said out loud, 'If there really is a God like this, then let me know somehow.' And that's when it happened."

"What?"

"It's hard to explain."

"Try me."

Clave gestured with his hands. "It was like this peace came over me."

Diona stared hard at him.

"I started crying and laughing all at the same time," he said.

"So you had a spiritual experience. That's not so unusual."

"But this one was different. It was like no other. I feel like I've found the thing I've been searching for a long time—a treasure. And I feel cleansed, somehow. That sounds strange, I know. But Diona, will you come back with me and see the books?"

She went back to her folding and didn't look at him. "Why didn't you bring them here? If they were so wonderful, why didn't you bring them with you?"

Why not, indeed? "I don't know," he said. "I guess I should have. I didn't think of it. I just put them back in their secret compartment."

"Secret compartment, Clave? Aren't we getting just a bit melodramatic? What is this—a B-grade movie?" Diona walked over to her closet and began gathering robes and cloaks and sweaters. Clave noticed this activity for the first time, as well as her irritated tone of voice.

"What are you doing?" he asked.

"Packing."

"What for?"

"Clave, even in your drugged stupor you should have remembered that I'm going to Morag's retreat for a soul-cleansing. I'm going with Kara after the service tonight. Do you remember now?"

"Oh."

"And, Clave, I wish you'd come, too. You should come. You really need to come."

A sudden panic came over him, the same fear he felt when back in the office of the old stone church he had considered telling this new revelation to Jason the Seer. It was almost as if he heard an audible voice saying, "No."

"No," he said. "I'm going back to the stone church to finish reading the Holy Bible. I wish you'd come to see the books with me, just come before you go to Morag's."

"Clave," she said, brushing out her long hair to re-braid it. "These new ideas you have about God are really crazy. You know that, don't you? Saying that God is separate from us, and that God is a person and not the Universal Mind. Well, it just doesn't make any sense," she said, gesturing with her hairbrush. "How could God be a person like you or me? Is everything and everybody all in little pieces and separate from the Universal?"

Clave didn't know. All he knew was that an hour ago it had made sense, and now he couldn't seem to find the right words. Everything he said was coming out wrong, sticking on his tongue.

15

Diona sat by herself in the vast auditorium. Clave had not come with her. He had, instead, gone back to that old stone church to read more of that holy Book or whatever it was he had found there. She had never known him to miss the lecture. Even when it wasn't his turn to speak, he always came and they sat together. She missed him now.

The lecturer was droning on and on. Little she had to say was innovative or new; Diona had heard it all before. It wasn't like listening to Clave, she thought, whose lectures were always stimulating and interesting.

She looked around her. The place was full tonight, fuller even than Winterfest Eve, the last service at which Clave had presided. The fact that he had missed every service since Winterfest Eve had not gone unnoticed in the Sector. People stood two rows deep at the back and looked away when she glanced in their direction. Perhaps she shouldn't have come here either. The rumor mills were running overtime already. The same brush which was tainting Clave would taint her as well. That Clave had suffered a nervous breakdown was the most common theory going around. Another one had him manifesting two different personalities. Still another one had his mind and body being taken over by aliens from another galaxy.

The speaker said, "And this is how we have inner power, by expressing our being, by manifesting our inner self one to another, by not suppressing our reality, by not distressing the cosmic balance." The lecturer was a small, animated woman, who spoke with great flourishes of arm and upper body. Variegated colored lights glinted off her robe and face. Diona knew that high above the loft in a hidden booth a team of technicians varied the lighting to the intensity of her emotional display. But tonight, thought Diona, the shadows just made the little red-haired woman look ghoulish and grotesque.

In her mind Diona could see Clave standing proud and handsome in the loft, the way he used to. Tears came and she reached into her satchel for a handkerchief. He needed help. That much was for certain. I'll tell Sister Morag about him, thought Diona. Maybe she'll know what to do.

The red-haired lady was becoming more exuberant. "Our souls must be purged. All repressive, non-essential belief systems must be eliminated if we are to truly make use of the god-power within us."

What is she talking about? wondered Diona. She was having trouble keeping her mind focused on the lecture. She was glad that after the lecture she and Kara were taking the night shuttle to the soul-cleansing retreat at Sister Morag's Hostel. She needed to get away. She had been there many times before and knew the routine well. In the morning they would eat silent ritualistic breakfasts consisting only of clear vegetable fluids and teas. No meat. Never any meat at Sister Morag's. Even though Diona was not a vegetarian, she enjoyed the body-cleansing foods.

The mornings would be spent in collective meditational dialogue where as a group they would attempt to reach altered states of consciousness. Afternoons would include small group hypno-therapy and mind cleansing. In some sessions they would be aided in contacting their higher selves through visualization of the chakra. In still other rooms, under the guidance of counselors, they would reach backward into their former lives. In the evening and far into the night they would participate in incantations and candlelight rituals where drugs and herb treatments would be freely distributed.

"And that, my friends, is truly where living begins." The red-haired lady raised both hands and the audience rose and began to clap, hesitantly at first, until loud, thunderous applause and cheering filled the auditorium.

Diona sat there confused. They never did that for Clave. What was going on? When the applause died down the lights were slowly dimmed and a quiet, repetitive pan flute was heard throughout. Usually this music enveloped her with peace, but tonight she was troubled. What was happening to her? What was happening to her family? All of her life she had lived in a protective shell. First, her wealthy parents had provided her with everything she wanted. Her ensuing marriage to Clave was an extension of this protection. Clave was not only her husband, but also her best friend. Even her friend Kara lived with several men. What did Diona know about that kind of lifestyle? What did Diona know about poverty, suffering, want? Sure, things had been tough for her and Clave at the beginning, but they always had a roof over their heads. She never had to sell fetal tissue, or prostitute herself like so many young wives did today. She lived on an estate with dozens of robots and lacked for nothing.

And now Clave seemed to be changing, drifting away from all that had been their life together. Was this some kind of mid-life crisis? And what if Clave suddenly wanted to leave her or take another wife? What was all this prattle about a separate God? She closed her eyes and bowed her head. It was becoming more difficult to keep the tears from squeezing past her eyelids. She quietly blew her nose. She was conscious of bodies brushing past her as she sat there, dozens of people, Clave's clients, who used to be her friends walking past without speaking, looking away from her.

"Diona." It was Kara's gentle voice and arm on her shoulder. Kara had the softest, most soothing voice Diona had ever heard from a human person. Merely listening to her talk about anything was spirit-soothing.

"Diona, are you about ready?"

"I'm sorry. Yes. I'm all packed."

"Our shuttle doesn't leave for another two hours. If you wish to meditate further, we've plenty of time."

"No, I'm fine really." Diona stood up and slung her satchel over her shoulder.

"You know," said Kara, "this will do us both good." Then Kara embraced her. "Friend, friend," she said.

Kara drove an older model hovercar, but it, like Kara, was scrubbed and country-rustic. Kara had replaced the standard metallic computer readout panel across the front with a wooden one. Kara was very fond of wood. She picked up bits and pieces of it here and there at garage sales and auctions. Then she would carve them into jewelry and hair ornaments, and now, a dashboard. She drove the hovercar up to the Hammills' front door, causing snow to fly high in all directions. Neither Clave nor Diona had remembered to activate the robots to clear the walkway again. Diona felt slightly embarrassed thinking about how spotless Kara's walkway probably was.

"My bags are right by the front door. I'll just be a minute."

The house was dark. Clave wasn't back from the stone church yet. He hadn't even shown up to say good-bye! She keyed in a quick note for him on the kitchen message screen and left.

16

Clave knew something was wrong as soon as he reached the front door of the old church. There were an awful lot of footprints about. He didn't think he and Dos had made so many. Maybe the neighbor dogs had scuffled around, but these looked like bootprints. Lots of them.

And the door was unlocked. Hadn't he locked it? He couldn't remember. He was usually so careful about things like that. His eagerness to get back into the office and read the rest of the Bible outweighed any anxiousness he felt. He made his way quickly down the aisle and into the now familiar room. It looked okay. Or did it? He easily found the handle between the two bottom shelves and pulled out the drawer. There was that feeling of uneasiness again. The books were still there. He lifted them out. Just as he sat down behind the wooden desk he saw a fluttering of gray out of the corner of one eye. He felt a sharp whack on his head and then he lost consciousness.

He woke up with an excruciating headache, a numbness in his arms, and a sore back. As he made his way out of the layers of unconsciousness, he discovered that he was slumped forward in the chair, his cheek pressed against the cold and dirty desk, his arms hanging loosely at his sides. And then it came back to him in bits and pieces—the box, the books, a blow on the head.

Clave lifted his head. It felt like it weighed fifty pounds. He joggled the feeling back into his arms and then with one hand firmly on the edge of the desk, he stood up on shaky legs and placed a tentative hand on the top of his head. No blood, but he'd have a whopper of a headache for a while. He retrieved his flashlight from the floor and directed it above his head. Had a loose board come crashing down on him? But everything looked in order. Then he shone his light on the desk, the box, the shelves. Gone! The books were gone. Frantically, he searched underneath the desk, the metal box, the floor. And then he remembered—a bit of gray cloth, that feeling of uneasiness. Whoever had struck him on the head had probably taken the books as well.

He walked as quickly as he dared out through the office and down the aisle; his flashlight cast eerie shadows on the walls. He was conscious that he was praying, not to the higher powers within himself, but to a real God, a God who heard real prayers. He stumbled home in the night, his head still aching.

It was late. Diona and Kara were already jetting to a retreat in a warmer place. He had wanted to say good-bye, at least. He read the note she left on the screen: "Clave, don't try to call me. I love you, Diona."

Then he called the police.

About a quarter of an hour later a single officer landed a silver and blue hovercar in his drive. He wore the silver and white spun-metal uniform which also served as a full suit of body armor. He appeared to Clave to be a rookie, about the same age as Dierdron or Nori.

"Ancient books, you say?" he asked as the two of them stood in Clave's foyer. Clave nodded. The young officer keyed all of Clave's answers into his pocket handreader.

"And now these ancient books are gone?" he asked.

"Yes."

The two of them climbed into the police hovercar and sped to the church. Oddly, Clave's front door key didn't seem to work. He pushed it this way and that, turned it upside down, and still it refused to fit into the lock.

"Are you sure that's the right key, sir?" asked the officer.

"It's the only key I own. Yes, I'm sure."

The officer aimed his gun at the lock and with two quick bursts was able to blast it open.

When they walked into the office, Clave was stupefied. The drawer and box were not on the desk. He had left them there just moments ago.

"They were right here," he said, over and over.

When Clave tried to locate the opening between the two shelves, all he touched was an ordinary wall, no hidden compartments, no loose plaster.

"I don't understand. They were right here."

"Right here, you say?" The officer bent down, his knee-high, soft metal boots creaking slightly. He aimed his laser light underneath the book shelf where Clave groped around the wall. The plaster was wet, Clave was sure of it.

"Feel, this plaster is wet. Someone just plastered up this wall," said Clave.

"It doesn't feel wet to me, sir."

Clave was insistent now, talking rapidly about finding books and reading them and then getting pounded on the head. He was desperate to make the officer not think him certifiable.

"Here, here, feel this," Clave said. "This is real, feel this bump on my head. You can't deny that!"

"You got a bump on your head, sir?"

"Yes, you can't hide a thing like a bump on the head. Someone attacked me."

"You got a bump on your head, and now you think there were ancient books in this building, ancient, paperbound books?"

On the trip home they said nothing. A few times the young officer looked over at Clave, his face a mixture of pity and scorn. Clave tried to make sense of the day and especially of the past few minutes.

Sitting at the table in a darkened kitchen, Clave wondered if maybe he really were going crazy. Maybe this whole Mars thing had finally gotten to him, making him dream up fantastic personal gods. Was that feeling of peace and cleansing just another drug-induced hallucination? Was Diona right? But no, this time it had been so different. He got up, and for want of something to keep him occupied, made a pot of tea. How he wished Diona were here. He would call her first thing in the morning even though she had asked him not to.

He sipped the tea. It tasted acrid. He dumped it down the sink. In the silence and darkness of the middle of the night, Clave decided he would find out. If there was a Bible, he would find it, somehow. He sat down in front of his computer terminal.

He spoke the voice command, added his Personal Access Code, and said, "The Holy Bible, The New King James Version."

"No record," came the canned computer voice.

He tried another tack. "The Holy Bible, The New King James Version, try archives."

"No record."

Finally, he said, "Try all—Bible."

"No record."

"Try all—Bible, archives."

"No record."

Clave was stumped. He sat there for a few minutes rubbing his forehead, silently praying. And then he thought of something. A few months ago while going over some WOC records, he had stumbled on the Personal Access Codes (PACs) of both the High Priestess and Edward. For some reason he had memorized them. He decided to try them now.

Using the High Priestess's PAC he had no more success than with his own. Then he ran Edward's through the system.

"One record," came the reply.

"Name, please."

"The Holy Bible, Authorized Version."

Could this be the same one? he wondered. He decided he would find out. "Access, please," he said.

"Access on this system is impossible. This is a personal archival bound book and is available for loan by charge only.

Please enter your Personal Debit Number, purpose for loan, and the book will be sent by robot courier."

Clave thought it odd that Edward had access to the Holy Bible. What archives could it possibly be a part of? Obviously the WOC had secret archives that he knew nothing about.

Clave told the faceless voice his PDN and paused for a moment on "purpose." He finally said "research" and hoped that would satisfy the library, although he knew that records such as these were computer catalogued. It would be many months before an actual human person would check them. He would have a few months, maybe, before Edward realized that someone had borrowed a book using his PAC.

He shut off the terminal, let out a whining Dos, rinsed out the teapot, and walked upstairs to bed. Even though he was alone, even though he felt uncertain about almost everything in his life, he fell into the first peaceful sleep he'd had in many, many months.

17

Edward adjusted the light source, spoke the voice command, and the recorded message began. While the face of the High Priestess lit up the screen, he busied himself at his desk organizing a stack of demichips into two piles: *urgent* and *done*.

"Edward," she began, "this is a message for your ears only. It has been scrambled to all other points. We have made a profound discovery. As you know, I have been having Clave followed. I am determined to locate that old man I've been warned about before he disrupts all our plans. But my men have found out something else. Clave has uncovered some rare old books in the building next to his WOC. I hear, Edward, that it was you who gave him the key to that old church. I'm not sure of the wisdom of that move, in light of what has been discovered there."

Edward fingered a demichip and looked up at the High Priestess—red lips working, dark eyes unblinking.

"Our men found him reading a book called the Holy Bible. That book runs counter to everything we have been preserving here in the WOC. As you know, all Holy Bibles were supposedly destroyed in the Purge. It contains numerous falsehoods and is a very detrimental book to our cause." She paused and looked down as if she were referring to notes. "In addition, Clave has also read handwritten journals circa 1996. We must stop any rumors of the old Josiah Files surfacing now when we are so close to accomplishing all we have set out to do."

Edward dropped the demichip he was holding; it clattered noisily to the floor. He stared at the screen, his mouth agape. No, it couldn't be, he thought. Is it?

"We have found the books and removed them," the message continued. "Unfortunately, we ran into a little bit of a problem." On her grim face was the merest hint of a smile. "One of my men became a little overanxious, shall we say, but the problem has been rectified, the books have been removed, and we are attempting to discredit Clave in the eyes of the world, and of himself, I might add. We began by initiating a certain clapping spree for his lecture replacement. Edward, you could help in that regard."

"End," he spoke sharply to the screen. He rose and paced his office floor. He knew about the Josiah Files and the story surrounding them, even though the furor had died down long before he was born. The legend centered around the events of 150 years ago when one Bible and a personal diary somehow escaped the Purge during the Age of Aquarius. During that Purge, all repressive religious paraphernalia was gathered up and destroyed to make way for a wonderful new age of freedom and choice.

The seeds for this new age had been sown decades prior to the Purge. As barriers of war were battered down and the world made ready for a global New Order, people began demanding not only freedom from war, but freedom from oppressive religious mores as well.

Citizens of this New Order gladly gathered up their religious materials and books and gave them as a symbolic offering to the Earth during a July Summer Solstice Celebration. A dozen years previously, the new holiday, called Summer Solstice or Sun Solstice, had replaced any festivities of a "national" kind. There were no more nations, no more patriots, just one massive, free, global village.

A few months after this symbolic "offering," a rumor arose, from what quarter no one could be sure, that two books had escaped the Purge. Legend had them hidden in an old church. No one could remember who first coined the term Josiah Files, but it caught on.

As the months passed, the tale took on mythic proportions. Soon, everyone was rummaging through attics, old buildings, searching even through graveyards for these elusive books. Two full-length feature films were produced on the theme, the first one called simply *The Josiah Files,* and its sequel, *The Search Continues.* Edward remembered that the latter received numerous Academy Awards; among them, best actor, best supporting actress, best special effects, and best soundtrack.

Years passed and interest in the Josiah Files gradually waned. Few people even knew about the story now. But Edward knew. He sat down. It couldn't be, he told himself. But if it was truly happening, was it happening too soon? Would they be truly ready for this?

He immediately made five message calls in quick succession.

18

The sound of the wind and rain gushing and whirling and endangering the very seams of his living quarters woke Clave. He pulled the rose colored quilt up to his chin and snuggled deeper under the covers. He heard the wind lashing at the walls of his house. The mid-winter westerlies indigenous to this part of the Earth had arrived in full armor to do battle with every bit of snow or ice. If they continued, by the end of the week the entire Sector would dissolve into a soggy, wet slickness.

Clave got up, still wrapped in the quilt, and looked out of the bedroom window. Wind-borne snow rose and swelled and whipped across his grounds, threatening to topple his collection of statues and marble works. Directly underneath the window, Dos was curled up against the front entryway. He was probably whimpering, but his sound was lost to the gale. To the far right Clave could see the corner of Diona's summer greenhouse. During the winter it was dormant except for the few plants she wintered over. In the spring it would come to life once more when she filled it with hundreds of colorful annuals.

It was odd. Despite the gloom, Clave remembered those flowers. The promise of spring. As he looked out into the swirling snow and rain, he felt a strange excitement well within him, as if he were at the beginning of a grand adventure. "Thank You, God," he said aloud. The words even surprised him. What had happened to him?

Downstairs, he hummed as he turned on the kettle and poured cereal into a bowl. He even sliced himself a piece of real cheese, one of the few extravagances the Hammills allowed themselves.

He decided not to go into the office today; it seemed a good day to stay at home. And he knew what would be waiting for him there, frantic code red messages from his publishers. They could wait. It looked as if his next book might be quite different. He keyed in a message to his assistants.

After breakfast Clave called Morag's retreat. He was able to charm the number to Diona's and Kara's private suite from Morag's dozy receptionist. Clave was glad that Morag still used real people at her front desk. A robot would never have given him the number!

He spoke the number. "Access not available. Try again later," the canned computer voice told him. Carrying his cup of coffee and breaking off a second piece of cheese, he headed out to his front room and sat on the couch to compose a long letter to Diona on his handreader. Paragraph after paragraph, he described the events of yesterday, how he had found the Holy Bible and what the revelation had meant to him. He seemed to be finding the words today which were so elusive yesterday.

It was a strange story, he wrote, of a Creator God's love for His people despite their continual self-worship. He described his attack, and told Diona that the books that had made him see everything in a new light were now gone. He added that he had made a blundering fool of himself in front of the police. He ended by saying that he was sorry for months of shutting her out of his life. He told her of the fears he had, how he hated and feared the sacrament of Elevation, and how his nightmares seemed to be all tied into it somehow. He still had questions, he wrote, but the answers didn't seem so distant anymore. He told her that he loved her, had always loved her, even though, at times, it may not have seemed so. Because his letter to Diona was so private, so much of his own heart, he did not want to risk sending it along the message lines, even with a scrambled code. Instead, he printed it on paper, folded it, sealed it, and sent it off by confidential robot courier.

Around 11:30 the beep-beep at the door and Dos's barking informed him that the book from the archives had arrived. He took the stairs two at a time to the front door and grabbed the package even before the robot had a chance to place it on the receiving tray. Clave held the brown paper-wrapped parcel in both hands and chuckled as he watched Dos chase the lumbering robot down the walkway as it headed to its next destination.

He turned the parcel over and read the black formidable letters: Archival Library Loan/Government Property. He unwrapped the package and lifted out a large, black, soft-cover book. He skimmed through the pages. It seemed similar to the book he had started yesterday, though the preface was different. This one talked about it being commissioned for King James of England in 1611, to be written in the language of the people.

Clave re-read Genesis and Exodus; they were essentially the same as the other Bible. He made copious notes on his handreader. By lunch he had finished 2 Chronicles, and by nightfall he was in the middle of Isaiah. Every hour or so, he tried Diona's number. Always the computer voice mocked him, "Access not available. Try again later."

The next few days passed in much the same way. While the wind whirled outside, Clave studied the Bible, taking notes and scanning large sections onto his handreader. The disappearance of the other Bible was never far from his mind. He didn't want to lose this one too.

By the end of the fourth day Clave finally came to the part about the cross. He knew it had to be in there somewhere. Matthew 10:38 said, "And he who does not take his cross and follow after Me is not worthy of Me." At first he didn't understand, but then as he moved further through the book he discovered that Jesus was executed on a cross. He began to understand that this Jesus was a kind of sacrifice. Earlier in the week he had spent hours listing the sacrifices and blood offerings that were required by the nation of Israel. Now he understood why Jim Swanson had written, *"What will you do with My Son, Jesus?"* He began to see that the hated instrument of death was really a symbol of life.

Excited, he read further, until by late afternoon of the fifth day he had read through the entire Bible. And then he remembered a tiny string of Winterfest lights strung in the shape of a cross. A cross! The lights in the warehouse were gone now (he always checked when he walked past), but he decided to investigate.

He got out the leash for Dos. Like himself, thought Clave, the dog could use some exercise. Although the temperature registered a few degrees above freezing, the damp wind made it seem much colder. Clave threw an old blue rain slicker over his tattered wool sweater and pulled on a pair of lined rubber boots. He automatically picked up his gold headpiece, and then laid it down again. The headpiece, although it did provide protection from the elements, was a symbol of godhood. Only WOC directors who were authorized to perform the prescribed sacraments were allowed to wear them. It suddenly seemed odious to him.

He groped around the top shelf in the hall closet and came up with a striped knitted hat that used to belong to one of the girls. He stretched it down over his ears and set out.

Five minutes later Clave stood in front of the door at the bottom of the stairwell. It was dark. Should he knock? He had just about made up his mind to turn around and go back home when the door opened. Standing directly in front of him was Edward!

Edward—the WOC General Director of Quadrant 3.

19

For a long moment, they stared at each other. Clave trembled, thinking, this is a trap. They continued to stare, openmouthed, until from somewhere inside the room came, "Praise the Lord! Praise the Lord!" Clave looked past a stunned Edward to a small group of people sitting on chairs in a circle. Another "Praise the Lord!" came from an elderly man in a wheelchair whose gnarled hands were raised.

"We've prayed about this for a year," Clave heard him say. "Is it so amazing, Edward, that God has answered our prayers? We act like that group of Christians in Peter's day. They prayed and prayed and prayed and then when God finally answered their prayer and Peter was standing at their door, they didn't quite believe it. Come in, come in, Dr. Clave Hammill. We've been expecting you, or rather, God has been expecting you. No, don't tie your dog up outside; it will be too noticeable to passersby. Bring him in, bring him in. Come in quickly. Close the door."

Edward ushered Clave and Dos inside and the door shut behind them. Clave was surprised that such a bright and modern interior was hidden behind so drab and dark an exterior. Every wall in the cheery room was covered with paintings and banners. There were sculptures on several shelves. With a pang, he thought of Diona. He remembered their first apartment, the walls crowded with paintings, the tables crammed with bright colored pottery.

"Come in, sit down," said the old man, indicating an empty chair beside him, "and tell us why you're here."

Edward looked shocked.

Clave looked from Edward to the old man to the wide-eyed faces watching him. Nervously, Clave said, "I saw a cross of lights on Winterfest Eve; I wanted to see what was down here."

The circle of faces looked skeptical. Edward said, "I know about the old Bible, Clave. Is that why you really came?"

Clave was startled. So Edward already knew that Clave had used his PAC to get a copy of the Holy Bible. For a few moments he said nothing, then, "I don't know what to say. I'm sorry, Edward. It was a bit of bad judgment on my part, but I was eager to finish reading the Holy Bible before I left for Mars. I tried every access code I'd ever come across, including yours. Yours happened to work."

Edward's eyes narrowed. Clave thought about turning on his heel and running out the door and up the stairs. What fool notion had made him come wandering down here in the first place? Who were these people? And what was the WOC's connection with them? Help me, Creator God, he prayed.

Finally, Edward spoke, "Personal Access Code? Clave, what are you talking about?"

"You said you knew about the Holy Bible."

Edward rubbed his large hands together. "I do. I was told that it was stolen, along with another book you found, a journal of some kind."

I am trapped, thought Clave. "Yes, I found a Holy Bible in the stone church, the one beside my WOC, but it is gone now. Do you know something about that?"

Those in the circle began whispering among themselves.

Edward turned to the group, "That's why I flew in here tonight, to alert you to what is happening. Yesterday the High Priestess sent me a message. The Josiah Files have been found! I came in to find Clave, but now he's here. He's the one who found them!"

The entire scenario made no sense to Clave at all. "Josiah Files? What are the Josiah Files, Edward?"

The members of the circle seemed to be just as puzzled about the files as Clave was; once again, they began whispering to each other.

The man in the wheelchair put up his hand to silence the group. "Edward. Dr. Hammill. Perhaps we had better start from the beginning. What Bible are you talking about? There are many of us here who know nothing about the Josiah Files."

Clave listened intently as Edward told the group about the Josiah Files legend. "And now Clave has found what we think might be the Josiah Files, right here in our own Sector!"

A thin woman with light, wispy hair asked, "The name? Is it from King Josiah in Second Kings who found those old scrolls, and then began worshiping God?"

Edward nodded.

"I've heard about that old story," said a stout man in blue work clothes. "They made a couple of movies on it, I think." Others nodded and muttered.

Edward continued. "I think something may be happening, something big. I've put in calls to five Christian Communities across the Northern Hemisphere. I'm worried that our Christian Communities may not be ready for an all-out attack by Satan. We have been underground for so long, I don't know if we're prepared mentally, physically, or spiritually to come out in the open. We may need more time."

"Well, hallelujah!" cried the old man, his hands again in the air. "We've been too long sitting here like bumps on logs. I've been praying for something like this to happen my entire life! Now, tell us what you found." He smiled at Clave.

Clave was still confused. "I don't understand, Edward. Who are you, really?" he asked.

Edward nodded. "It's only fair that we tell you who we are. We're Christians. Underground Christians. I am a Christian too, a Christian spy. I work for the High Priestess to try to undermine her power and the power of the WOC."

"You're working *against* the WOC?"

"Is this wise?" asked a female voice from the back. "After all, this man is WOC."

"He's here now. God brought him here," said the old man. "Perhaps for a purpose. We've been praying for him. Remember?"

"Wait a minute," said Clave putting his hand to his forehead. "What is a Christian? And why have you been praying for me?"

Edward put his hand on Clave's shoulder. "A Christian is someone whose God is Jesus Christ, not self, not the WOC, and not Satan. And we've been praying for you because we felt the Lord urging us to."

"Now tell us your story," said the old man leaning forward in his wheelchair.

Clave still stared at Edward, stunned that a group like this had been meeting for years right in his own backyard. He thought about his headaches and all the confusion he had felt during the past year. Was that because they were praying for him? Or something else? What about his new experience with God? Had they prayed about that, too? Clave picked at a loose piece of yarn in the striped hat in his lap, and decided to trust them. To trust Edward. Haltingly, he began. He told them about his experience with God. They smiled and nodded for him to continue. Encouraged, he told them about the attack, and then about the missing books, and his encounter with the police.

"Did you say the journals were written by a Pastor Jim Swanson?" asked the old man, who suddenly strained forward in his chair, his eyes bright. "Do you know what my name is? It's Swanson. My name is Hirsch Swanson. My father's grandfather was Jim! It could be his journal."

He sat back in his chair. "My grandfather used to tell me stories about his father, how he was a real man of God, one who prayed continually. Did you know he prayed for every member of his congregation by name? It was because of his influence, the influence of a man I never met, that I came to know the Lord."

"That's him! He wrote about that in his journal!"

"And now they are gone—the journals?" asked Hirsch.

"I'm going to see if I can find them using my channels," Edward interrupted.

"Do you know who took them?" asked Clave turning to him.

"The High Priestess probably has them. She had two of her minions follow you. She told me that today."

"Were they the ones who bashed me over the head?"

"Right."

"But why? Why is she having me followed?"

"You were her golden boy and now you pose a threat to her. And she knows that you are having difficulty accepting some aspects of WOC doctrine, particularly Elevation. She also believes that an old man is unduly influencing you and may be threatening to undermine her power in the WOC. She's hoping you can lead her to that old man."

"An old man?"

"Introducing," and Edward put his hand on Hirsch's shoulder, "the one who has been praying for you faithfully for six years. I would call that influencing, wouldn't you?"

"But how does the High Priestess know that Mr. Swanson is praying for me?"

"She doesn't. All she knows is what the demon-spirits have told her. And they are not omniscient. They don't know everything. They feel the presence of an elderly, wise man, but we feel they know nothing of our community. We're hidden. We're safe."

"Bully for us," said Hirsch.

From across the room a young woman stood. She wore a purple academic robe tied in at the waist with a white sash indicating that she was a part of the medical establishment. Blonde hair fell straight to her waist and her smile was wide and friendly. She looked about Dierdron's age, thought Clave. "We haven't introduced ourselves," she said. "My name is Star.

I'm a physician, a doctor of computer medicine. It is my job to continually update the body analyzing booths with new information. My specialty is the endocrine system."

"And she's saved lots of babies from termination, too," said an intense-looking, dark-haired young man named Simon. He was an artist. "I was the one who put up the Winterfest lights, and constructed the banners and fashioned the holograph of the three crosses."

"It's beautiful, isn't it?" said Star pointing to the holograph.

Next to Hirsch sat Tommi, a little boy, who Star explained had Down's syndrome.

"When he was born, they were going to terminate him," she said quietly so that only Clave could hear her. "But I hid him in a laundry basket and brought him here to the Safehouse."

"Safehouse?" asked Clave.

Simon continued, "This is a Christian Safehouse. No one knows about it, not the WOC, not the NWO, nobody. Some of us live here, like Hirsch and Tommi, but most of us have other jobs. We come here in the evenings to pray and study the Bible and carry out the underground ministry."

Clave met the other members of the group. He learned that Sam, the fellow in the blue worker's uniform, drove the garbage shuttle to the space station which orbited Venus. Compacted trash was rocketed into that planet's extremely hot atmosphere where it disintegrated. Sam wore a baseball cap imprinted along the front with *Venus Reclamators.*

He met the musicians Sharan and her husband, Rawn, and a young man named Zig.

"Zig used to be in a Nova Music band," said Sharan, "but now he plays the praises of God."

There were more couples and families with small children, teenagers, single adults, elderly, and handicapped, about forty in all. Suddenly, Clave realized that they were risking everything by trusting him. The sensation of being trusted thrilled him. He turned back to Edward, a strangely different man tonight, and smiled.

Next, Edward gave him a tour of their facilities. Below street level, it consisted of twisting and turning corridors, all surprisingly well lit. The "catacombs," Edward called them, had numerous entrances. Many were below ground level, like the one Clave had entered, but some were on main streets many blocks away. There was one hidden entrance which led into a shopping mall's men's washroom, and another that led into a restaurant. Still others led from office buildings, hospital broom closets, and secret supply rooms.

He was shown a modern kitchen with two robots, a large dining area, another sitting room in the back, a corridor of living quarters for the residents and guests, and a few small prayer rooms. Each of the prayer rooms had copies of the Bible on handreaders.

"You mean the Holy Bible is on handreader?" asked Clave, looking over to a demichip marked Bible on a nearby table. "I couldn't access it."

"That's what Star's doing for us," explained Edward as they walked back into the large, front room. "During the Purge, Bibles were relegated to archives or destroyed. But not only Bibles. There were hundreds, thousands of books written by Christians—books of sermons, books on how to live the Christian life, books explaining hard passages of the Bible, books of personal experience, novels, poetry, music. And they were all destroyed or hidden. Star is trying to locate some of them in obscure archives all over the Earth. Then she scans them into our library system using a secret, scrambled access code she's developed. We want to make them available to Christians worldwide."

Star opened her computer files with a voice command and showed Clave a long list of books already accessed onto their library system.

"I have them cross-referenced by author, title, and subject—here, you appreciate a good lecture, you may enjoy the sermons of Charles Haddon Spurgeon." She flipped further down the screen, "or the writings of C. S. Lewis. Hirsch is reading a series of Lewis's books to Tommi every night, and Simon is working on some illustrations for the handreader."

Later that night most of the families left, one by one from separate exits, but Hirsch and Edward and Clave stayed. They talked far into the night. Edward told Clave about the High Priestess's secret agenda and Clave's supposed part in it. Clave was totally mystified. He learned that there were thousands of secret communities all over the Earth, the Moon, and Mars.

After taking Dos for a walk around a hidden, covered courtyard, Clave was shown to a comfortable guest room where he spent the night. When he finally retired, it was with peace and a newfound sense of understanding of his Savior.

20

The High Priestess paced the floor, cradling her hamster Kiki and shouting at the two men who stood sheepishly side by side in front of her.

"A simple thing like keep an eye on Clave—like follow him until he leads you to that old man, whoever he is, then terminate the old geezer, and you bungle it. You almost kill Clave, and then you lose him. Did I tell you to kill Clave? No. Did I tell you to bash him over the head? No. Will you kindly explain yourselves to me?"

"Well," said the pudgy man with greasy dark ringlets all over his head, "we did get those books for you, didn't we?"

"Books, shmooks. I want to know where Clave is now. Why did you not follow him? Tell me that much."

"We been telling you, over and over. It was this other guy we saw leave. It wasn't Clave." This was spoken by the other man, a diminutive fellow, clean-shaven, whose totally bald head reflected the light from the overhead chandelier like a billiard ball.

"Yeah," said his partner. "It didn't look nothing like Clave. I mean we thought it was some kind of servant or something, like one of his clients, maybe."

"Or maybe like somebody delivering a pizza," the bald man said.

"Or Chinese take-out. That's what we thought."

The High Priestess groaned.

The large man gestured with his hands. "And anyways, what are we to think? Here's this guy come out with this dog and this guy's wearing this blue raincoat and this stupid looking stripy hat with tassels."

"They was pompons, not tassels," said his partner correcting him.

"No, they wasn't. I know what tassels look like. My kid's got tassels on her hat. Pompons are round things, tassels are these long yarny things," he said indicating with his hands.

"I am completely losing patience," said the High Priestess. "I don't care if they were pompons, tassels, or miniature human skulls. Why, pray tell, did you not follow him?"

"We was looking for a guy in a headpiece, not pompons."

"Tassels," corrected his partner.

"And a gold robe."

Without speaking the High Priestess placed Kiki back into the cage and said evenly, "And his living quarters are now empty, you say?"

"Yes. That's right, ma'am."

"Well, it doesn't take a rocket engineer to figure out that the 'guy' in the blue raincoat and striped hat must have been Clave in disguise!"

The two men looked down at their feet.

"Now get out of my sight, both of you! Don't come back until you find him!"

The two men shuffled miserably out of the room.

"Total incompetents!" said the High Priestess as she poked a bit of lettuce through the cage bars. "I am surrounded by total incompetents. No wonder my plans have been so slow to come together. The only person I can trust around here is Edward."

She stomped over to the message screen where she voice commanded the number for Vaney Stodge. "It's time I did business with people who have plans, people who can really get things done."

21

Two thousand miles away in Sector 3 of Quadrant 2 of the Northern Hemisphere, a black-robed Dr. Vaney Stodge stood before his group of frenzied, chanting dancers and held the silver chalice high in both hands. The cave-like room was dim, shadowy, lit only with candles which glowed out from the inside of hundreds of leering, smirking skulls, animal and human, which rested in crevices all along the walls. They cast darting, macabre shadows on the walls and ceiling as the dancers whirled past them.

Nestled in a large crevice in the wall behind Stodge was a statue painted in brilliant neon hues. The creature had a squat body and wild, savage eyes which seemed to look in all directions at once. Its stubby arms and legs reached ahead, making it look off balance, as if it would topple forward; but it was securely fastened to the wall. In front of the statue black wax candles glowed.

At the very center of the room stood a large, rough-hewn wooden table with candles on each of its four corners. It was an ancient table that bore the knife marks and gouges of the hundreds of sacrifices which had been made across its pitted surface.

Stodge stood near the table. The others swayed around him, their eyes glazed and unfocused. They had been dancing for a long time and within the closed confines of the underground room the hot, sweaty smell of their bodies mixed with the thick odor of fresh blood. They chanted one name, over and over again in their frantic worship.

The silver chalice was filled to overflowing. As Stodge lifted it high, blood dripped down its sides, spilling onto his hands and robe. He brought it to his lips and drank deeply. He did not wipe away the blood that trickled from the sides of his mouth. Then he passed the chalice around and each of the dancers sipped of its contents.

When it was passed back to him, he placed it on the table, raised both hands, and uttered two words to the frenetic group in front of him.

"It's time," was all he said.

"It's time," they chanted back.

He turned around then and ascended the long stairway, pressed his hand on the sensor lock, and slipped through the heavy, metal door into his ordinary looking office. From the inside, the door to the cave was cleverly disguised behind an intricate wall mural of astrological signs. He knew he could count on his followers to dispose of the body which lay bloodied and limp on the table, and exit one by one out of the back doors. They would be careful. He knew they would. Even in this new age of freedom and choice, the NWO had its laws against the sacrificial killing of healthy young people, young people with many years of good work ahead of them.

The taste of warm blood lingered on his tongue. He wiped his mouth with his sleeve.

Suddenly, an obese jowly woman draped in layers of pale silk glided through the door and placed both of her ringed hands squarely on his desk. She looked up into his piercing dark eyes. "I know all about your little coven," she told him. "It's time we did business."

He sighed and looked down at his desk. "I haven't the faintest idea what you're talking about, Morag."

"Don't even think about trying to get rid of me. I've got dozens of my people outside."

He sighed. "That's nice. I really haven't time for this."

"We go back a long way, Vaney, you and me, and this time I think you had better listen. I've got pictures, my friend, hundreds of them. I've been collecting them for years. Photos and videos of the activity which goes on downstairs." She eyed the poster of astrological signs on the wall. "You know and I know that people will tolerate Satanism and witchcraft as long as the witches are 'white' witches and go around promoting goodwill and peace for all, and love of Mother Earth."

"All that WOC garbage," he said dryly.

"What they won't tolerate is the murder and sacrifice of lovely, young, nubile virgins."

"In that regard, you have nothing to worry about, my lady."

"You know I'm right."

"First of all, I don't believe you have pictures and second, the WOC has its own brand of sacrifice. It's called Elevation, I believe. And the NWO also has its own brand of sacrifice. It's called euthanasia. Now will you leave me alone? I've got things to do."

"I have the ability to let everybody know about your little coven. The tabloids would love to see your picture in connection with all of this, Vaney boy."

Stodge moved to the front of his little desk and sat down on the edge. "So what do you want me to do?"

Her gown swished as she walked around the desk to him. She looked straight into his eyes and smiled. "I know the High Priestess has great plans for you. She's in the process of building her dynasty. She thinks you have the charm, the charisma to become the next High Priest."

"And that is news to me? Come now, Morag. I know all about that. She's a fool, but never mind. She called me yesterday. With golden boy Clave in the midst of some sort of breakdown, pity his poor soul, I put two and two together."

"And got five. Did you also know that Clave is involved in a secret renegade group of Christians? I have in my possession proof that there are thousands of these Christians all over the Earth and that their headquarters seems to be in Sector 44."

Stodge rose and paced his office, clenching and unclenching his fists. "You are making this up to taunt me! Clave is a WOC director; he has nothing to do with those people!"

"Why would I lie to you, Vaney? What purpose would be served by making you angry? Think, dear boy, think. No, I have irrefutable proof, letters from Clave to his lovely little wife." She paused. "I think you and I had better sit down and hammer out a deal, my boy. These Christians could become a force against us if we don't take steps immediately."

Stodge's voice thundered out in rage, "Please do not utter that despicable word in my presence again!" And then he uttered a string of expletives that made even Morag wince.

"By the gods, Vaney, settle down," she said. "From here on in we will call them fundamentalists if that will make you happy."

"If what you're saying is true, we must find them and kill them. At once!"

Stodge sat down at his desk.

"A bit of decorum is in order." Morag stood behind him and began massaging his shoulders. "Ah, my Vaney, you have always been like a son to me. Killing them doesn't work. You should know that. History has shown us that much. Always a few of them escape and it makes them even stronger. Come now and listen to me. I need you and you need me. Listen to me for a minute."

When she finished laying out her plan, she rustled out of the room before he had a chance to respond. On her way out the door she turned back to him, "And Vaney, wipe that blood off your chin. It doesn't become you."

22

For the better part of that week, Clave returned to the underground Community Safehouse each morning. All day he sat with Hirsch and studied various portions of the Bible, and every night he walked the few blocks back to his living quarters. With most people away at regular jobs it was quiet in the Safehouse during the day. A few were there, Hirsch of course, and Tommi, who was already becoming fast friends with Dos. There were also two live-in housekeepers and a number of others, mostly handicapped and elderly who had no place in the society of the twenty-second century. But Clave was constantly amazed at their spiritual insight and at the peace they seemed to possess. These who were shut away showed joy despite their circumstances. Tommi, especially, was so bright and cheerful and seemed to have no trouble understanding even difficult passages that baffled Clave. Each evening, before the others arrived, Clave found himself listening intently as Hirsch read to Tommi from his large child's handreader.

Every night the place would fill up as groups of people came. Star and Simon were always the first to arrive and they usually came together. Then the others would come straggling in, two by two, and about mid-evening Hirsch led them in Bible study and prayer. At Clave's request, they prayed for Diona.

As the days passed, Clave missed Diona more and more. His concern for her deepened, especially in light of Edward's pronouncement that Morag's retreat was a "hotbed of Satanism."

The Community had offered Clave a room, but after the first night he decided to go home where he could check his messages and keep an eye on the place. But now, as he trudged to his dark, cold, and lonely living quarters, he wondered if he shouldn't have taken them up on their offer. Late that night he left a message for his WOC assistants—he wouldn't be in the office for the next few weeks. He was finally taking that vacation time he had coming to him. How ironic. Diona was always after him to take time off, and now that he was, she wasn't even there.

At least twice a day he called her, but always the computer voice taunted him, "Access not available. Try again later." He wrote her at least a half a dozen more letters and had them delivered by robot. In them he told her about the Community and about the Christians he had met. He told her about the Lord and about how Jesus Christ was coming to mean so much to him. He also told her that when the group sang it was more beautiful than anything he'd ever heard. He wrote about Simon and his artwork. He also wrote letters to Dierdron and Nori and to his parents and sister.

On the sixth evening Clave told the group of his futile attempts to try to reach Diona, and of his suspicion that she had programmed her phone to refuse calls from his PDN.

"Why didn't you say so in the first place!" exclaimed Star, rising from her seat and heading toward the back hall. "Follow me," she said.

Clave could use the blue emergency audio-phone in the farthest prayer room, Star explained. She had hooked it up to a phony PDN. To a receiver it would look as if the call came from a shopping mall in Sector 53. That, too, was phony.

He voice commanded the number, which he had memorized, and it was answered on the second ring.

"Hello." He was so stunned that it was finally answered that for a moment he couldn't speak.

"Hello?" Clave recognized Kara's soft voice.

"Kara, may I speak with Diona, please?"

"I'm sorry. She's not, she's not—here now."

"Can you get her to call me when she gets in? It's important. This is Clave."

"Yes, I know, but she's—"

He heard a muffled scuffling at the other end, as if someone had covered up the receiver microphone and was talking. He thought he recognized Diona. "Please, God," he prayed.

"Just a minute," he heard Kara say. He held on.

"Clave?"

"Diona!"

"Clave, I'm sorry about all of this. I know I said not to call, but I was hoping you would. I'm glad you did now."

"I've been trying for days."

"I know, and I'm sorry. I set it up to refuse your PDN. I was just so confused, but I'm glad you got through."

"When can I see you?"

"I don't know, Clave, I'm so mixed up. I came here wanting a soul-cleansing, and all I seem to be is more confused, especially when I think about you and this new religious experience of yours. Well, it scares me. I've had a couple of deep counseling sessions with Morag, and with a new spirit guide named King Nathan V; he was a twelfth century Norse king with great insight. He speaks through her."

"Diona!" He hoped the panic in his voice wasn't too evident. "Did you get my letters?"

"Yes, I did. And Clave, I showed them to Morag."

"You let Morag read my letters?"

"Well, not all of them, just the parts about your spiritual experience, the way you explained it. Do you know what she said?"

"What did she say?"

"She said you've been brainwashed by fundamentalists."

Clave paused. "That's not true. I didn't meet these Christians until days after that experience I had with the Lord, the one I tried to tell you about."

"But, Clave, she is interested in this little group of yours. She said that people who have new religious experiences shouldn't keep them to themselves. She wants to know where your group is and how you found them and all that. So she could go, she said, and have this experience, too. You didn't mention that in your letter."

No, he hadn't. He had never told her about the Winterfest lights. He had never described the crisscrossing catacombs which wove a path underneath a good portion of Sector 44. Why not? He didn't know, but a sudden foreboding told him not to.

"Diona, please come home," he said. "I want you to meet my new friends. I want you to meet my God."

"Soon," was all she said.

23

The night was still and very dark in Sector 17, Quadrant 1 of the Northern Hemisphere, Earth. High clouds completely covered the stars and the Moon. Near-perfect weather for the task, although the crew could have wanted for a bit more wind to cover up the sounds of their movement. They would have to do without. The date and time had been preset. It couldn't be changed.

The black-panel hovervan, lights out, crept soundlessly up to the gatehouse beyond which lay the presidential palace. Inside the squat metal building, a rotund guard was reclined, feet up on his small desk, watching a Moon versus Earth all-star hockey game on his portable HV and munching on a ham sandwich. His attack-sensor belt hung on the hook behind him. As the van moved past, the guard barely had time to look up and lift his hand in alarm when the fatal blast of nerve gas hit him. Seconds later he lay dead on the floor.

The three in the van, sheathed in black from head to foot, scrambled out. Ignoring the body that lay at their feet and the cheers and play-by-play on the HV, they set about to reprogram the palace guard robots. It had taken months of hard work to crack the security codes. But they had done it. Five minutes. Ten minutes. The three worked feverishly without speaking. All seemed quiet within the grounds. No alarm had been raised. Eighteen minutes later all of the guard robots were reprogrammed.

Next, the alarm system had to be disabled. That was a bit more tricky; the codes were re-scrambled daily. They couldn't be sure that by fiddling with them they might not accidentally set off another alarm. Sweat dripped down the forehead of the tallest of the three. He wiped his face with the palm of his hand and continued. Another twelve minutes and the security alarm was crippled.

The three climbed back into the hovervan and ahead of them the iron gates opened noiselessly. The van crawled forward and settled down behind a high row of artificial hedges. The digital readout at the front of the van said 20:15. Fifteen minutes more and they could get out of here.

In front of them, the lights were on in the sitting room of the palace. Behind the drawn drapes, New World Order President Morley Kyzer sat comfortably in a large armchair sipping a glass of iced tea, the latest issue of *Interplanetary News* magazine on his handreader. His wife, Janetta, was curled up on the couch reading the latest mystery from the pen of her favorite writer.

At 20:46 P.M. the porch light flicked on.

"He's late," said the driver of the van.

The others said nothing. The gunman aimed and waited. It seemed an eternity before Kyzer, his two white poodles, and his bodyguard turned the corner. The poodles whined. Did they sense the presence of the van behind the hedgerow? The three in the van watched as Kyzer reached down and scruffed them under the ears a few times. He looked over to the guard and said something. Finally, the two men and the dogs rounded the corner. Soon, they would be out of the light of the building. The pattern never altered. Until tonight. Tonight the two men lit cigarettes, leaned against the wall, and let the dogs run loose!

"He's never done that before," said the driver.

The hit man tensed. "Shut up," he said. "Keep your eyes on those dogs so they don't come bounding straight toward the van, Kyzer and his bodyguard with them."

That is exactly what happened.

"Great," said the driver bitterly.

"We'll have to take them both out," said the hit man.

"We can't. The guard's got his sensor belt on," said the third, a woman.

Unlike the gatehouse guard who always took off the cumbersome belt when he ate, Kyzer's personal bodyguard never did. In the event that he was shot, the sensor would raise an alarm that would sound at NWO Security Headquarters.

The two miniature poodles barked and raced toward the hedgerow, their tall master ambling in pursuit. Mercifully, twenty feet away, the guard still lounged against the building, drawing deeply on his cigarette.

"Now," said the gunman. He squeezed the laser rifle and the silent blast hit Kyzer square in the chest.

He was dead before his body hit the ground. The poodles whimpered and whined and licked his face. The black van crept silently away about a foot above the ground, past the dead guard in the gatehouse, and past the reprogrammed robots who were moving about in dizzy circles and uttering gibberish. By the time the bodyguard had finished his cigarette and realized that something was amiss, the black van was already parked in its underground garage, its inhabitants laughing and slapping each other on the back.

24

Morley Kyzer was not a powerful man, nor a particularly effective leader; nevertheless, he was well-respected in many circles. He was a thoughtful man, a strong advocate of reflective, well-researched study. It was felt that his scholarly approach to politics and decision-making would offset the impetuous boldness of young President Samson Kroger. Instead, Kroger had suffered a heart attack two and a half years ago and died a month later in the hospital. Shortly thereafter, Vice-president Kyzer and his wife moved into the presidential palace and gradually began to win the trust of the people.

Kyzer was best known for his steadfast stand on the separation of church and state. He advocated an individual's right of choice during a century when religious freedom meant one either embraced the WOC, or one did not. Kyzer chose not. A confirmed atheist, he never went to church and was constantly at odds with the High Priestess and with the WOC leadership in general.

Although his achievements were not numerous, he was able to hammer out a successful trade agreement with the Moon. The Lunarites were certainly pleased that their rich mining resources, needed by the Earth, were traded practically straight across for the air and water which they so desperately needed. The Interplanetary Travel and Trade Tax, or the ITTT, an extremely unpopular tax, especially on resource-rich Mars, was deferred in the agreement between the Moon and the Earth.

The same kind of agreement was also signed with the newest small settlement on Io, one of Jupiter's moons.

Kyzer's slow, dignified manner did not go over well, however, with the fiercely independent, garish, and fast-talking Marsians. They had their own air. They had their own water. And both were cleaner, far cleaner than the Earth's. They cared little when Kyzer reminded them that it was the Earth and the now defunct NASA which had researched and financed the terraformation of Mars in the first place.

So when Morley Kyzer was assassinated, everyone naturally attributed it to the radical Triple-O league. When forensics experts verified that the blast which killed the president was from a type of laser gun manufactured on Mars, it only added fuel to the fire. Even when the governor of Mars stated that he personally was appalled by this violence and knew of no Marsians capable of such a dark act, it did little to alleviate the growing tension between the two planets.

But what it did to the High Priestess and Vaney Stodge was to thrust them very quickly into the limelight. Four days after the assassination, while the worlds were still reeling, Stodge and the High Priestess appeared together on "Morning Interview," a highly rated, hour-long HV show which featured in-depth news, views, and interviews.

They were seated at a round glass table across from their interviewer, a heavily made-up brunette with dangling, green metallic earrings. Stodge stated, "In my opinion, the crime looks very much like the work of the Triple-O league. It has their name, their trademark all over it. They're a radical and violent group of hotheads." He paused for effect. "They would be the only ones I know who would be capable of assassinating so peaceful and able a leader as Morley Kyzer."

A sedate-looking High Priestess added, "Restructuring the NWO should be everyone's highest priority now. We are concerned that the Earth and all of the worlds, especially Mars, get a fair deal. We must all work together."

"This crime is abominable," Stodge told the anchorwoman.

"There is some speculation," she said, turning to the High Priestess, "that you are now a candidate for the presidency."

"And it's just that: speculation," the Priestess answered. But the eagerness in her small, dark eyes was evident to Clave who sat at his kitchen table drinking his morning coffee and watching the HV being projected on his kitchen wall.

Stodge smiled across at her, his elbows on the transparent table, his fingertips together as she said, "The first priority of every citizen of the universe should be to find those responsible for this horrendous crime and bring them to justice."

So the High Priestess would get her wish, thought Clave as he got up and poured himself another cup of coffee. Stodge would be the WOC head, and the High Priestess would take over the government. Stodge would take the place Clave had been unwittingly primed for. Things had changed so quickly.

He heard a new voice on the HV, a voice he recognized. Sister Morag was being interviewed from her wooded retreat. Clave put down his mug and peered at her closely. "Probably the most detrimental course of action now would be the continued disunion of the New World Order and the World Order Church," Morag said. "I have nothing but admiration for the High Priestess. She of all people has the political will and ability to pull us out of this horror pit of uncertainty that the worlds have fallen into."

So Sister Morag was somehow a part of all this, too, Clave reasoned. And Diona was down there, under her direct influence. He still called and wrote to Diona every day. She took his calls, but was becoming increasingly distant, constantly pressuring him for the location of the Community. She admitted that she was in deep counseling sessions with King Nathan and that Sister Morag had prescribed a special cleansing herb and drug treatment. Diona didn't know if it was working or not, but it was making her feel sleepy, she told him. When he begged her to come home, she simply said, "I'll come when I'm ready." All he could do now was pray for her.

The screen went back to Stodge, the High Priestess, and the anchorwoman. Stodge was speaking. "In this violent world," he said, "one needs the soothing influence of religion. One needs an awareness of one's inner spirituality. We cannot separate them. I'm sure that even Morley Kyzer, whom I respected tremendously, would agree with me at this point in time."

The scene on the HV shifted again. In front of the Presidential Palace a group of about fifty people carrying signs and banners featuring the faces of the High Priestess and Stodge were marching down the wide avenue. "A good team, we need them now," they chanted in unison.

"Power off," said Clave as he put his coffee cup and bowl in the dishwasher. He grabbed his heavy coat and headed out toward the Safehouse. Each day he used a different entrance. Today he strode down the street past the warehouse, turned left into an alley, darted into a shoe store, then back out a side exit. Two doors down, he entered an office building, rode the elevator up to the fifteenth floor, got out, walked past glass-door offices with names like Doctor of Laser Surgery, Computer Networks, Dental Systems, and strode into a men's room.

A tall, somber gentleman with a long, horse-like face was leaning over one of the sinks washing his hands. He kept washing his hands right up to the elbows, adding more and more soap. Clave examined his own face in the mirror, combed his hair, adjusted his hat, and washed his hands, while the tall man washed his hands, washed his hands, and washed his hands. Must be one of the doctors, Clave decided.

On his way out, the tall man nodded at Clave. When he finally left, Clave walked into the last stall, pressed a small, hidden button, and the toilet moved away from the wall, revealing a narrow descending staircase. Carefully, Clave grabbed the handle on the opposite wall, hitched up his cloak, and stepped down. The toilet moved silently back into place just as two men entered the men's room.

Clave made his way down the steep spiraling staircase, down, down to the Safehouse and to the friends he had come to cherish.

25

Clave noticed that Hirsch Swanson's frail hands shook more than usual.

"I sense in my spirit that we will soon be undergoing testing," Hirsch said. "Persecution, like the Christian Church hasn't seen in a long time, will seek to undermine us. But I also see us coming out of it with more power than when we went into it."

The two of them were finishing their study in the book of James. They had been examining and discussing the passage all morning, their handreaders propped in comfortable reading positions in front of them. A small coffee urn and the remains of their lunch were on the table as well. On the floor in the next room, Tommi snuggled next to Dos, reading to him from the illustrated stories on his handreader. The gentle dog had become a permanent resident of the Safehouse now.

Clave took a sip of his coffee just as his small personal messager began to flash.

He unhooked the small image screen from his belt. "Receive," he spoke to the screen.

"Dr. Clave Hammill." The face of a young assistant, a university student on a divinity practicum, lit up the two-inch screen. The student's fiery red hair tufted out all along the edges of his headpiece. On his freckled face were lines of worry. How old was he anyway? Nineteen? Twenty? Clave had so many on staff, yet knew so little about any of them.

"Hammill here."

"Dr. Hammill, I know you're technically on vacation, but there's something you should know." The young man paused and blinked nervously a few times. "Your office has been broken into. There's stuff all over the place, and—and uh, strange drawings on the wall. We called the police, and they're coming, but I think you'd better come down too."

After he and Hirsch spoke a hurried prayer, Clave left by the exit closest to his WOC.

Someone had broken into his office. That's what the student said. But why? Mentally, he checked off the list of things he kept there. Aside from a few expensive crystals, there wasn't much of any value. His library? Breaking physically into steel demichips was absurd. The best thieves cracked access codes and took them from central computers. In fact, most robberies nowadays were done by computer thieves. His brow furrowed as he hurried down the roadway to the WOC.

As he rounded the corner on foot, he looked up at the familiar high spire on the top of the WOC. The sight made him shudder. The place suddenly reminded him of death. The intertwined goat heads on the top of the pinnacle seemed to be sneering, their unblinking eyes overlooking Sector 44 like evil sentinels.

Looking at the building where he had made his livelihood, his *home* for so many years, the faces of his clients came to him, as they used to gaze up at him while he stood in his lofty perch. In his mind he could see the respect and awe on their faces. Then he saw something else there, too: a sadness, a striving, a despair, and a searching. Their lives, he realized, were like his used to be, fraught with personal nightmares and dark shadows. They had come to him for some way through the maze of living and all he had given them were little glass statues and wooden carvings to hang around their necks.

A heaviness fell upon him as he got closer to the chrome and crystal building, glistening now in the morning sun. He had steered hundreds, thousands—millions of people, if you counted his books—away from the living God.

"God, forgive me," he said aloud. Someone had to get them on the right track. Someone had to tell them that the Earth Mother and the goat heads and the tarot cards and the meditation and all the crystals in the world would never make them free. Only Christ could. Why did the Christians feel they had to stay hidden? To Clave, his new life in Christ was too precious, too exciting to be locked away, buried in the subterranean tunnels of an abandoned warehouse.

Ahead, a police hovercar was parked by the entrance to his office. He walked quickly past the old stone church and up the back stairs to his office. Two of his assistants hurried down to meet him.

"We're so glad you're here, Dr. Hammill," one of them said. "Things are thrown all over the place. We don't know who it was or how they got in or why or anything."

Clave stepped through the door. His desk was overturned, his chair upside down; deep knife gouges were embedded in the brocade. His computer terminal and message screen were smashed. His secretary robot lay on the floor in a pile of printed circuits, gears, bolts, nuts, and twisted metal. On the floor a small pile of demichips smoldered like the remains of an old campfire. The faint, pungent smell of burning silicon hovered in the air. Clave's library was virtually destroyed; the glass demichip box was shattered into a thousand fragments and scattered about the floor.

One of the officers who crunched through the glass on the floor, handreader in hand, was the rookie who had taken Clave's call about the stolen books.

On the floor next to the door was a chunk of white crystal, the one Diona had given him. It was sheared in two, as if by a laser. Bending, he retrieved the two fragments and tears welled in his eyes. He remembered that Winterfest morning when they'd sat close together on the couch next to the shimmering tree. "May your life and work always shine as bright as this," she had written on the little tag in her distinctive, artsy handwriting. It was an expensive rock and for many months previously, Diona had put aside money from her artwork earnings. As a charm, it meant nothing to him now, but he grieved nonetheless. Who would do this? Who would destroy the mementos of his life? He wiped away the beginnings of the tears on the sleeve of his cloak. As he stood, he looked up at the upside-down cross inside a triangle that had been scrawled in red on the wall.

"We've examined that," said the young officer, following Clave's horrified stare. "Our analysis device suggests that the writing compound is animal blood."

"Animal blood!" said Clave. "Who did this?"

"That's what we're hoping you can tell us," said another officer, a paunchy, middle-aged man with a day's growth of beard. He looked as if he was better suited to sprawling in front of the HV, a can of beer in one hand and a dish of pretzels in the other, than being in here investigating a break-in.

"Do *you* have any idea who did this?" he asked, giving Clave an odd look.

"Do you have any enemies? Anyone who might want to do you harm?" The officer keyed Clave's answers onto his handreader.

"I don't think so." Clave righted his chair and sat down, a wave of dizziness coming over him.

"Dr. Hammill." The small, pudgy officer stood over Clave and looked down at him. "My partner here tells me you dragged him down to some old building a couple of weeks ago where you claimed you found some old books, and when he arrived the books were gone. Is that true?"

"I guess so."

"And that you protested greatly on the return trip, claiming over and over that there really were old books there."

Clave rubbed his face with his hands. He pulled off the striped hat and shoved it into his pocket along with the broken crystal.

"What does that have to do with—?"

"And according to your staff, you are on an undetermined vacation leave due to emotional breakdown?"

Clave looked up. "Now, wait a minute."

"And that you've written to your wife and daughters about some strange new religious experience?"

Clave stood up again and sent the chair wobbling back to the floor.

"Isn't that true, Dr. Hammill?"

"Leave my family out of this. They have nothing to do with someone walking into my office and smashing it to bits. Are you going to investigate this crime or not?"

Near the doorway a few of his assistants whispered behind their hands and exchanged glances.

"That's precisely what we are doing, Dr. Hammill," said the young officer.

The older officer's large, rubbery face inched closer and closer to Clave's face with every question. Clave refused to back up.

"What we have here is the ransacking of the office of a disturbed and emotionally unbalanced religious leader."

Clave stared into the rheumy eyes of the officer and said nothing.

The officer cleared his throat and continued, "Our portable crime-time analysis device has confirmed that your office was ransacked sometime early yesterday evening."

The younger man held up the black metal box with dials and readouts. "Where were you yesterday at approximately nineteen hundred hours?"

"Are you accusing me of tearing my own office apart? Why would I do that? Why would I destroy my own computers? Burn my own files?"

"Just answer the question. Where were you yesterday at nineteen hundred hours?"

"This is ridiculous. Where was I? I was with friends."

"Friends, ah," said the questioner leaning back on his heels.

"And who might these friends be?"

"I'm not at liberty to say."

"Ah, yes, not at liberty to say. What a wonderful alibi, Dr. Hammill. Take note of this, deputy. He's not at liberty to say."

"What do you want with me?"

"We'd like you to come downtown for a little while, Doctor. We have a few more questions for you. Yes, a few more questions," said the officer, chuckling.

At the police station, they ushered Clave into a musty, windowless room where he sat on a hard, old-fashioned, straight-backed chair. Across the table from him sat another officer. Easily two-hundred-fifty pounds, he bulged out of his uniform and smelled of garlic and coffee. He looked at Clave a couple of times, then grunted and keyed something into his handreader. He grunted some more and squinted at his handreader. It was clear that the man was in no hurry to begin.

Finally he said, "We have it on file that your behavior has been irrational. Your staff has verified it. Your own wife has left you. We have a letter here from the High Priestess." He opened up a letter and flattened it out with his pudgy hands. "She states here that you can no longer fulfill your duties as WOC director and that the WOC Advice Board has, on several occasions, recommended that you seek professional counseling. It also says you steadfastly refuse to do so."

"That's not true. I know nothing about that," Clave protested.

"We have contacted the High Priestess. When she heard you were detained here, she said it was probably for the best as you are a menace to yourself, to your family, and to society at large." The officer looked across into Clave's eyes.

The fight was rapidly leaving him. They would listen to nothing he had to say in his own defense. Clave said nothing when they handcuffed him and roughly led him down three flights of stairs to an airless, cellar jail.

26

The narrow underground corridor was flanked on both sides by small identical cells. The place smelled of urine, vomit, and unwashed flesh. As the guard led Clave down the hall, prisoners reached out their hands to him through the bars and called to him.

"A divinity cloak! Say, speak the magic words and get us all out of here," they taunted.

"Hey, holy man!"

Clave said nothing. He just looked down, trying not to step on dirt and spit which dotted the hallway floor. The guard opened the door to the far left cell and pushed Clave roughly inside. Clave's handcuffs were not removed; when he lifted his wrists up, the guard only laughed.

"Forget it! It's not every day we get a doctor of holy stuff in here. We'll take them off tomorrow."

"Tomorrow! How long will I be here? What wrong have I done?" Clave backed in and slumped against the far wall. His cell was just like all the others, made of rock-hard gray plastic. Molded into the cell walls were two beds, a sink, and a toilet.

Clave was not alone. On one of the beds sat a scruffy little man in rags. White wispy hair stuck out all over his head, and the deep lines on his face were embedded with dirt.

The two were silent. Clave leaned wearily against the wall and appraised his situation; the man on the bed appraised Clave.

"Welcome," the man finally cackled. "It ain't much, but we call it home."

"I don't know why I'm here," muttered Clave. "The whole thing just doesn't make any sense."

"Don't none of us know why we're here." And then the man on the bed opened his mouth in a broad, toothless grin. "But ain't that your department? As I live and breathe, ain't you the famous Doctor Clave Hammill? As a man of the cloth, the *gold* cloth, you're the one supposed to have all the cosmic answers like as to why we're here."

Despite himself, Clave smiled. At least his cellmate wasn't going to murder him. He hoped.

"You are the famous doctor, am I right?"

"You're right."

"Well, ain't it my lucky day. I never shared me a cell with a man of the gold cloth before. Wait'll I tell my buddies. You see this?" He reached under his tattered, dirty undershirt and drew out a little ring hanging on a grimy, plastic thong around his neck. Clave recognized it immediately. Two years ago his WOC had offered these crystal chip rings as good luck charms. For a "small donation" the recipient was mailed this little ring, guaranteed to have been blessed by a thirteenth century monk called Monk Sylvester, now an Ascended Master. Seeing the ring made Clave feel ill. How much wrong had he furthered on Earth? How many people were in darkness because of him? Clave looked away.

"See this? My daughter got me this. I don't go nowheres without it."

Clave turned to him. "Why not?"

"It's my good luck charm."

"Has it worked?"

"Huh?"

"Has it worked? Has it given you good luck?"

"Yeah. Why not? I ain't dead yet."

"You call being in here good luck?"

"What're you saying, Doc?" The man eyed him warily.

"What I'm trying to say is that piece of rock gives you zero protection, zero luck."

"That's not what you said on the HV."

"I know," said Clave quietly.

"What, you telling me you been lying?"

Clave swallowed and nodded, not knowing how to continue. He prayed for guidance. A few seconds later the door at the far end of the hall clanged opened and Clave picked up a new aroma, the sweet smell of sour milk. Involuntarily, he raised his shackled hands to his nose.

The man on the bed grinned. "That's just Stinky," he said. "You'll get used to him."

Clave watched Stinky, a robot laden with food trays, chug noisily down the hall. When it deposited two trays on the receiver slots in their cell, he discovered the source of its odor. The robot was splattered with decomposing bits of food and dirt. As the squat piece of machinery clattered down the hall, prisoners pitched bits of leftover food from previous meals at it, making the hallway even more grimy.

A restaurant with the same robot, Clave thought, would be shut down within minutes. Dining facilities that used robots as waiters had to abide by strict health regulations. A minimum of two times a day robots had to be completely disinfected from top to bottom. It looked like this robot hadn't been cleaned in months. Clave left his food tray untouched, but his cellmate sopped up the green gruel with a grayish hunk of bread.

"So, Doc, you been lying? That why you're here?" said the man between bites.

"That's not why I'm here, but yes, I've been lying, not intentionally. But then, a couple of weeks ago, I didn't know the truth. I really thought that those rings would work. Now I know it's all trickery, all lies. Every bit of it. All the crystals, the auras, the colors, and the meditations—garbage."

"Is that why you're here? 'Cause you don't believe none of it no more?"

"Maybe," answered Clave. Perhaps that was the reason after all.

Clave walked over and sat on the other bed. "For years and years I led everybody down the wrong path. Everything I taught was false. Who knows, maybe if you hadn't listened to me you wouldn't be here in this place. I want to start making it right. I want to start telling people the truth, the real truth."

The little fellow put his mug down on the tray and said quietly, "The real truth to what, Doc?"

"The real truth to life itself. The final answer to the question, Why am I here? It has nothing to do with some universal mind. We are not a part of God. We are not God. I know that now."

The man continued chewing and looked curiously at Clave.

"May I tell you what happened to me?" asked Clave.

"I seem to have left my calendar at home, but I don't think I got me no pressing engagements in the next while." The old man chuckled, got up, and deposited his food tray in the receiver slot. As soon as he returned to his bed, Clave began talking. Over the din of the noisy cell block, he told the little scruffy man how he, the famous Dr. Clave Hammill, the man with all the answers, the man with all the money, the man with the huge mansion, needed a Savior.

As Clave continued, he became aware that the cell block was quieting. He glanced across the hall to see the prisoners sitting on their beds, or leaning up against the bars, listening.

He went on. "He created people to worship Him, but then the people decided they didn't like that idea. They didn't want to *worship* God; they wanted to *be* God. They all wanted to be gods and goddesses. And so they chose not to worship the God who made them."

Clave waved a fly away with his manacled hands and went on, "It's just like now. I used to teach that we are God, that the whole universe is part of the God-mind. That's not true."

The door clanged open again and the robot clattered down the hall and picked up the supper trays. No one threw their remaining crusts of bread at it or cursed it. The whizzing and clanking of the machine was the only sound in the hallway.

When the door closed behind Stinky, Clave continued. "There's only one God, not many gods. Every tree isn't God. Every person isn't God. This God loves us and wants us to get to know Him. But our continual self-worship, which God calls sin, keeps us away from Him. God is all good. He can't look at sin."

"Sin?" his cellmate asked. "Them's odd words coming from you."

"But the good part is that He made a way for us to get close to Him again. And that's through Jesus Christ. Jesus is more than just a good man who worked himself up through the ranks and became a god. He is not Mitrea, the highest Ascended Master. He is God Himself. And He came as a man almost 2,200 years ago to redeem us."

"Ancient history, ain't it? You a little bit touched, Doc? You don't really believe this stuff?"

"Yes, I believe it. We should have been executed for our own sins, but Christ took them all instead. He died in our place. And He did it because He loves us and wants to be our friend. He wants us to come down from our pedestals of self-worship and bow before Him, our Creator, our Redeemer, our Friend."

The man wiped the sweat from his brow with his torn undershirt. "No wonder they tossed you in here."

As Clave spoke, he recalled a little slip of paper with the words, "There Is a Redeemer," "Awesome God," and "His Name Is Wonderful." They must be songs, he realized now, just like the songs that Rawn and Sharan taught the group in the warehouse.

"I ask your forgiveness," he said to the man on the bed, "for years and years of telling you lies." And then he was finished. He had no more to say. He bowed his head.

His ragged cellmate sat motionless. He looked at Clave intently for a few minutes, then bowed his head, too.

Seconds later the door clanged open again, shattering the quiet. Loud voices and clomping boots made their way to Clave's cell. Now I'll be let out, thought Clave. He got up and walked toward the bars.

The two guards ignored him and moved to the man on the bed.

"Time to go, Mac," they said grabbing his arm, "your daughter's waiting."

On his way out, Mac pulled the plastic thong from around his neck and flung it toward Clave.

"Hey, throw this in the garbage for me next chance you get, okay? I ain't going to need it no more." His face lit into a bright smile.

27

Despite his handcuffs, Clave slept comfortably on the plastic mattress. He hadn't expected to. After Mac left he had lain down thinking he was in for a long night of tossing and turning. He had worried about Hirsch and the others at the Safehouse. They hadn't seen him since he was called out hurriedly the previous morning. He had begun to pray and then the next sound he heard was Stinky clanging down the hall with the breakfast trays. Clave woke hungry and his mouth tasted sour, but he still didn't think he would partake of Stinky's offerings. With his hands still in cuffs, he stumbled over to the basin. He splashed icy water on his face and rinsed out his mouth.

Stinky's runny eggs and damp toast didn't appeal to him, but, oh for a cup of coffee! He eyed the stained white ceramic mug doubtfully. Brown and black particles floated on top of the mud-colored brew. They might be coffee grounds, although he couldn't be sure. He took a tentative sip and grimaced. It was lukewarm and tasted as if it had been allowed to brew for an entire day, cooled overnight, reheated to the boiling point, and then cooled again. It was undoubtedly the worst coffee he had tasted in his life.

"They make it out of dirty dishwater, we think," said the prisoner across the hall.

"How could they make it out of dishwater when they never wash dishes?" chided his cellmate.

When the trays were retrieved, a guard sauntered down the hall. Clave called out to him, "Please get in touch with Edward, WOC General Director for Sector 44. Edward will vouch for me." The guard strode past without acknowledging him.

Just before lunch the guard came back and led Clave out of the cell. As he walked past the prisoners, instead of the taunts and curses that greeted him yesterday, a few prisoners raised their hands in salute. "See ya, Doc." "Take it easy, Doc," they called after him.

"I'll pray for you. I mean it," Clave answered.

"What, do you have a fan club here now or something?" asked the guard.

Upstairs, at the main desk, stood a solemn-looking Edward. The guard removed Clave's handcuffs and he rubbed his wrists.

"I'll be sure to keep an eye on him," said Edward. "You will be notified of any unstable behavior."

Clave looked at him, mouth agape. Maybe Edward and the Community knew best, but why couldn't the Christians just come out and say who they were? Clave had done so last night and hadn't been struck dead. In fact, during the entire time not one guard had even walked down the hall.

A seed of an idea wended its way into the corners of Clave's mind as he sat next to Edward in the passenger seat and watched heavy snowflakes splotch against the windshield. When he climbed into Edward's hovercar, the only thing on his mind was a shower and a good meal. Now there was something else.

It was sirens which brought Clave out of his reverie. Edward pulled the hovercar to the side of the road to let two hover fire trucks and a police van pass.

Clave craned his neck but saw nothing. As they inched closer to Clave's living quarters, traffic slowed almost to a standstill. Cresting the hill, they saw swirls of black smoke ascending skyward.

"Must be something big," said Clave.

Edward nodded.

Twenty minutes later they were within a block of Clave's mansion. It was consumed in flames.

"Wait," said Edward, reaching across to Clave, but Clave was already out of the door, staggering toward the blaze. Police had cordoned off the gate and grounds, but Clave ignored the ropes and tapes and blindly wove his way through the wet snow. He was only dimly aware of the noisy confusion and the troop of robots armed with canisters of fire retardant gliding in and out of the blaze.

Clave slumped against a marble statue of the goddess Venus which stood near his front gate. The heat from the blaze burned hot on his face. The front part of his living quarters had already succumbed to the flames. A loud crack and a crash sounded and Clave watched his master bedroom plunge to the ground—bed, dressers, robots, end tables. Why, God? All of his possessions, all of the things he had worked so hard for. Why? The intense heat reddened his cheeks. His eyes burned and watered and he held tightly to the statue for support. Spectators huddled in groups and muttered among themselves. Mercifully, over the roar of the blaze he barely heard their conversation.

"Probably did it himself. I wouldn't put it past him."

"His wife left him, that should tell you something."

"Did you hear what they said about him on the news last night? He's in jail."

"The High Priestess says he is a menace."

He felt Edward's arm on his shoulder. Edward embraced Clave and held him while he sobbed. In the foreground the face of the marble Universal Trinity glinted in the flames. Soon, it too would topple.

On the far side, a lone, hooded figure in a long cloak stood motionless. Clave recognized her immediately.

"Diona!"

He tore away from Edward and ran around the perimeter of the activity, dodging equipment and robots and fire fighters, leaving them yelling after him. He ignored a police officer who called, "Dr. Hammill, can we talk to you a minute?"

When Diona saw him, she ran to him; they clung to each other. They stood that way a long time until Edward put his hand on Clave's shoulder.

"An officer wants to see you. Said it can't wait."

"Dr. Hammill!" It was the paunchy little cop who had been at his office break-in. "We found something curious, something very curious. We were hoping you'd be able to shed some light on it."

He motioned and Edward, Clave, and Diona followed him around to the back of the grounds. The snow was coming down harder now. Clave could hardly see. With one hand he kept wiping the wet snow out of his eyes and with the other he held tightly to Diona's waist. Her face was covered, barely visible behind her hood. At the back side of their grounds, the officer stopped and pointed to the rear gate.

At first, it looked as if four black cats had jumped up onto the metal grillwork, paws apart, spread-eagled, and had somehow stuck there. Leaving Diona, Clave walked slowly forward. Revulsion like a hammer blow to his stomach hit him. All four animals were impaled, face down on the grill work, their paws nailed right into the heavy metal. With his long club, the policeman reached underneath one of the lifeless bodies and lifted it up slightly.

"Now I find this real curious," he said. "Their throats were slit; blood was drained, looks like."

Clave felt Diona take hold of his arm. He held her.

"Now, you got any ideas about how that could've happened, Dr. Hammill?"

"We never owned any cats, just our dog, Dos. In fact, we've never even seen any cats roaming around."

"Now I think it's real strange," the officer continued, "that the writing on your office wall was cat's blood, and that now we find dead cats on your property here." He prodded the lifeless bodies with his stick. "Dr. Hammill, we're not taking you in for questioning about this because we have released you into Edward's custody, but you should know that you are under suspicion for arson, and we hold you directly accountable for what happened to these animals. We don't know how you did it being in prison last night." The officer shook his head. "But we know that you're somehow responsible."

The chubby little officer strutted away.

"Why don't we go?" said Edward.

Clave nodded, barely able to speak. "You know I wasn't even here. Why didn't you defend me, Edward?"

Silently, Edward picked up Diona's bags and the three of them trudged back through the snow, climbed into Edward's hovercar, and took a zigzagged path through the city, finally coming to a stop in front of a neon-lit restaurant called "Joey's Pizza Emporium."

They followed Edward past checkered, cloth-covered tables where noisy groups of people sat in front of plates of lasagna, rigatoni, and deluxe pizzas. They passed waitresses with handreaders clipped to their belts, and past the kitchen out back where Joey, wrapped in a tomato sauce stained apron, grinned and gave them the thumbs-up sign.

The tomato apron made Clave look away. He saw not the day's pasta offerings, but an upside-down cross scrawled in brown-red blood; cats, murdered, their blood drained; and a boy lying in a pool of blood on a brightly lit Mars walkway.

Edward opened the door to a body analyzing booth and led Diona and Clave inside. When the door to the booth closed, another on the opposite wall opened, and the three of them rode down two elevators and three escalators until they arrived at the Safehouse.

28

It was evening. Twenty people sat at a long, cloth-covered table laden with bowls and plates of food, eating their evening meal. There were parents and their children, babies, single people, some elderly, working people, academics, handicapped.

Diona was conscious that mothers were trying to shush their little ones in deference to her and Clave. A few hours earlier, when they had entered this labyrinth of twisting tunnels and corridors, these strangers had welcomed them warmly. A couple of older women had bustled about getting tea and cookies and blankets and extra clothing, smiling warmly. A small woman with white curly hair, which fit her head like a bonnet, took them down a corridor to a cozy, country-decorated guest room.

Diona moved the little synthetic peas and carrots around her plate with her fork. She couldn't eat. Even the smell of the food was making her feel ill. Usually a regimen of Morag's healing herbs rejuvenated her and had little effect when she went back to eating meat and vegetables, be they genuine or synthetic. This time, however, her stomach hurt, and she felt nauseous. The counselors at Morag's had put her on more healing drugs than usual. She didn't know why. Maybe that's why she felt so tired.

Across the table a small boy was smiling awkwardly at her. She tried, but she couldn't get the corners of her mouth to move up. Maybe after she slept a while.

Why had Edward whisked them here? Shouldn't they have stayed and talked with the police and fire fighters, and filled out forms or something? And that policeman accused Clave of setting the fire! A dreadful thought nagged at the back of her mind. Might he have done it? Sister Morag said that Clave was on the brink of a dangerous nervous breakdown. Because Clave is the kind of person he is, Morag told her, his nervous breakdown would undoubtedly have violent repercussions. "When a small man falls, no one notices. When a strong and mighty and wise man falls," said Morag, "the world feels it."

Diona looked at the faces around the table, Clave's friends. Were the whole lot of them crazy? Morag had told her that entire groups were drawn together by the aura of their poor psychosis. This entire community could be a dangerous, radical faction. Not only were they threatening to upset the balance of universal energy on the face of the worlds today, but they were undermining the entire political structure according to Morag. Clave could well be capable of burning down his own house and even killing little cats.

She had so many questions. Who are these people? "Friends" was all Clave had said. Why is Edward here? "He is a friend too," answered Clave, who then began reading to her strange words from his handreader. They were from the Bible, he said.

She didn't know where she was or why they had come here after the fire, why they were eating an evening meal with these people. The girls! They should call the girls. She leaned over to talk to Clave when a blinding pain struck her between the eyes. Her fork clattered to the floor. She rubbed her forehead and winced. Diona rarely got headaches. This was Clave's department.

When she bent down to pick up her fork she could hear Hirsch and Edward whispering, talking about things, "gearing up for the end times."

The end times of what? she wondered. The Universal Mind of God was like a circle, no beginning, and no end. She had been taught all her life that time was a human commodity and the more we allowed ourselves to see past, present, and future in one vision, the closer we would be to God. What strange beliefs these people had.

She ate very little. The pounding in her temples finally gave way to a dull, throbbing ache.

She looked over at Clave now. He was spooning himself a second helping of noodles and gravy. She marveled that he could smile and eat when their lives were turned so upside down.

She thought of her studio then, all destroyed, her state-of-the-art kiln, her brand new chalice. All gone. Her hands shook. She felt numb. She folded them on her lap. She remembered being told once that when great tragedy strikes the only thing to do is to live one minute at a time; get through one minute and then on to the next, and then the next, and then you'll have found that you have gotten through a whole day, and then a whole week. She tried to focus in on the god-mind, but she couldn't. She couldn't see past, present, and future in one vision. She couldn't. She longed for the past, was disoriented in the present, and feared the future.

She whispered to Clave and he smiled at her, "Yes, I spoke with the girls earlier by special message phone. I told them to stay where they are. That we would be fine and that we would see them during the Earth Day vacation. I think it's too dangerous for them to come here. I told them the insurance money would take care of anything they had lost in the fire."

During dessert Diona excused herself. She felt rotten, she told Clave, and needed to go back to their room to lie down. Leaving the brightly lit, noisy room, Diona decided that what she really needed was some air. Her head still hurt and her skin felt clammy. She walked down the hall toward the front room she had seen before supper. Earlier she had admired the sculptures and artwork displayed there, but now she just felt tired and achy. She tried the door in the far wall. Locked. Not really hoping for much, she placed her palm on the computer sensor. It remained locked.

Desperate, feeling that she would choke without fresh air, she ran her trembling fingers over the lock. She saw a series of numbers scribbled on the wall next to the sensor. She bent down and peered at them. She memorized them, then walked over to the room's computer console and punched them in. She heard a click. The door was unlocked!

She stood for a long time at the bottom of the stairwell gulping in the night air. Her headache lessened. Secure in the knowledge that the others were still in the dining room, Diona left the door open and walked up the cement stairs. At the top she was surprised, stunned even. It was a street she knew, a street she had walked down numerous times. Their living quarters, or rather what used to be their living quarters, was immediately to the right up the hill. Through the night she could see a few fire trucks and robots still parked by skinny plumes of black smoke. To her left was the lit spire of the WOC. Close. So close, right in her neighborhood, yet it had taken Edward so long to drive them here.

Back down the stairs, Diona shook the snow from her cloak and stepped back into the front room. When she looked up she saw the strange little boy they called Tommi standing in the hallway staring at her. When he saw her, he turned and ran back down the hallway toward the dining room.

After supper the small group made their way into the front room where they grabbed chairs and pulled them into a crude semi-circle. Simon, the one who had been introduced to her at supper as the artist, tried to engage her in conversation, but she looked down at the floor. She loved talking art with a fellow artist. She could see that he had great talent, but not tonight. She wasn't sure her mouth would work right, that words would come out in one piece.

A smiling, bearded man grabbed a guitar and a young boy picked up an electronic stringed instrument and together they began playing and the group began singing. The words to the songs were automatically accessed onto each person's handreader, but most of the group seemed to know the words without having to look down at them. Diona stared at the far wall. Clave held her hand. What was she doing here? she asked herself.

And then she remembered. Like a bomb blast in her head, she remembered! She rose. If I love Clave, then I must do it, she thought. If I ever want any help for him, any help for us, then I must do it. Grabbing her satchel, she excused herself and walked rapidly down the hall to the bathroom and locked the door behind her.

She pulled out a hand held message screen from her satchel. Whispering, she voice commanded the special number Sister Morag had given her.

29

When Diona returned to the front room twenty minutes later, she didn't look well. The group was standing and singing, some were clapping their hands, but when Diona entered, Clave dropped his handreader into his pocket and took her icy hand.

She didn't speak, but stood rod-straight, staring, unblinking, past him. What had they done to her at Sister Morag's? She had told him that Sister Morag had put her on a drug treatment, but what kind of drugs? He chided himself for not flying down to Morag's so-called Retreat and bodily removing her from the premises.

The group sat down, and Diona sat and folded her hands primly in her lap. Peggy, a young woman in a wheelchair, was speaking now. She was paralyzed from the neck down, her hands fixed in wrist supports and crossed in her lap. Because of the WOC's philosophy of Elevation and reincarnation, technology for the handicapped hadn't progressed much in the last two centuries. What she used was constructed for her by those in Christian Communities across the three worlds.

"A couple of months after I had my accident," she said, "when it was determined that it would cost more to keep me alive than I was worth to society as a wage earner, I was counseled about dying with dignity. Day after day nurses and doctors would come in and talk to me, pressuring me to consider Elevation—telling me that I could be reincarnated into a well body. But I was afraid. I don't know why; I was just afraid. When Star came in, I thought she was just another one of those counselors of death. Instead, she told me that I didn't have to die and that she would bring me to a place where I could live. And that there was Someone who loved me just the way I was and could make good come out of something even as bad as my accident. Then Star brought me here. The good He has given me is a peace and joy that I never knew before. And all my new friends," she paused and looked around the room, "I want to thank you all for being my friends. The people out there," and she pointed toward the window, "don't love you if your body is broken. There's a verse that means a lot to me. Psalm 119, verse 71, says, 'It is good for me that I have been afflicted,/That I may learn Your Statutes.'"

The next person to speak was Zig. He cleared his throat and began. His voice shook. "This is the first time I've told my testimony, but here goes." The group smiled encouragingly. "Most of you know that I used to play the keyboards in a Nova music band. At first it was great. I got to travel and meet what I thought were all these exciting people. After a while, it wasn't so neat anymore. I don't think any of you have any idea of what really goes on behind the scenes with that kind of life-style. I don't care what anybody says, I think drugs are wrong. They destroy. They almost killed me. I really think they should be illegal."

For a moment, Zig's eyes seemed to settle on Clave's wife. Diona didn't seem to notice when Zig went on, saying, "I was finding I couldn't do anything, couldn't even get up in the morning without drugs. I was sick all the time. I really wanted to get out but I didn't know how. And then I met Simon. He was doing some posters for the university where my band was playing. Well, I guess the Lord must have had something to do with it, because one morning Simon found me drunk and on drugs, sleeping it off against a doorway. Simon took me home to his apartment and took care of me. Then he brought me here. And then I found the Lord, and like Peggy, God has given me a deep down peace, too. Even when things go wrong in my life, I know He's there and that He loves me. I have a verse too, but I don't have it memorized like Peggy." He fiddled with his handreader, "I just have to find it; here it is, Romans 8:38 and 39. It says, 'For I am persuaded that neither death nor life, nor angels nor principalities nor powers, nor things present nor things to come, nor height nor depth, nor any other created thing, shall be able to separate us from the love of God which is in Christ Jesus our Lord.'"

From the back of the room Hirsch said, "Amen!"

Clave looked down at Diona. Was she listening to any of this? He took her hand again. It was trembling. "Diona," he whispered, "are you all right?"

She gave him an odd look, grabbed her satchel, got up, and fled down the hall, staggering from side to side as if she were drunk. Clave followed. He entered their room in time to see her fall onto the bed, her head in her hands.

"It hurts so, it hurts," she sobbed.

"Diona, what's wrong?"

"It's my head." She reached into her satchel. "Clave, get me a glass of water, please?"

He went quickly into the adjoining bathroom and came back a few seconds later with a half-filled juice glass. Diona washed down two pink pills, and then lay back on the pillows.

"Morag will help us now," she said in a hoarse whisper.

"Diona, how will she help us?"

"She will come through like she promised. Now I can rest. Now my part is done."

"What are you talking about?"

Diona sat up on the bed then and looked at Clave, looked through him as if she really didn't see him. She fumbled in her satchel for a cigarette. With a few nervous tries she got it lit. Clave had seldom seen her smoke. Now didn't seem to be the time, he reasoned, to question her about it.

"I can rest," she said, rising. "Now everything will be all right." She looked at Clave and tried to smile, but it looked more like a painful little grimace.

Something was wrong. Diona had never behaved so strangely before. She was usually the level-headed one—at home baking bread while Clave went off on various spiritual searches.

Diona carried her cigarette and walked over to look at a picture on the wall, a pen and ink drawing of two children kneeling, their palms pressed together, their eyes upturned toward a cross. Her back was to him when she said, "I don't like that picture. That's a bad picture."

"Diona." Clave stood up, hesitated, then sat down heavily on the bed, his action spilling out the contents of Diona's satchel. He glimpsed the corner of an unfamiliar message screen. He picked it up. She turned and grabbed it from his hands.

"That's mine. You've no right!"

But Clave had seen the last number. The last number keyed in was for Morag's Retreat for Spiritual Wholeness. Dread knifed through his belly. For a moment he couldn't speak. Then he said, "What did they tell you at Morag's?" His voice was quiet as he struggled for control. "What did they promise to give you if you told them where the Christians were? What, Diona?"

Diona sat down, covered her face with her hands, and began to cry.

"I'm your husband, and I love you. No matter what, I'll always love you. Those people at Morag's, they lie. They're liars. They don't love you. They only love themselves."

"No, Clave. They said they would get help for you. They promised to help you and me. They said you were endangering the flow of universal god-energy."

"How do you even know where we are? Edward took a circuitous route to get here."

"I went outside," she answered. "Right through the front door. I saw our living quarters and the WOC."

"That was your 'fresh air.' What did you tell her?"

"I told her about this community, about you, and about Edward. Sometimes my mind gets so muddled. I can't think straight. Morag gets quite angry with me."

Clave's mind was reeling. If Morag knew, then the High Priestess would know, and if the High Priestess knew, then Vaney Stodge would know.

"They'll come right away to help us, won't they?"

Clave sat beside her on the edge of the bed. She leaned into him, her head on his shoulder. He could breathe in the clean smell of her hair, disarrayed now and coming loose from the braid. He held her close. Despite everything, it felt good to have her back.

"We just have to wait," she said faintly. "And they'll come and give us a new place to live, new living quarters, more grand and more majestic than the one on the hill. That's what they said."

Clave looked down at the deep circles under her eyes, at her slightly reddened nose, her colorless cheeks. She looked tired and worn out like an old woman. He took the cigarette from her and snuffed it out in a coffee cup by the bed.

She shivered; the skin on her thin arms was goose-fleshed. Her thin arms! What had she eaten at Morag's? He reached behind them and pulled up the patterned quilt which lay neatly folded at the end of the bed, wrapped her in it, and held her until her shivering stopped.

After a long while Clave could hear her steady breathing. He lay her down gently on the bed and tucked the flowered quilt around her. She was sleeping.

By the time he got back to the front room the meeting was over and the group was beginning to disperse. Clave motioned to Hirsch and Edward; they followed him into an adjacent prayer room.

When he told them that Diona had called Morag, Edward ran his hand through his stubbly hair and looked concerned, "I think she was drugged," offered Clave.

Edward said, "I've spoken already with the leaders in a few of the other communities. I'll call a general meeting for tomorrow. Tonight, if need be. Between us we'll come up with a strategy."

"Prayer might be a good strategy," offered Hirsch. He placed his hand on Clave's knee. "How is your wife now, Clave?" he asked.

"She's sleeping. She's not herself, that's for sure, but so much has happened." He paused. "She went to Morag's to try to sort out her life. We were having some problems in our marriage. She's been there before—we've both been there before. But she's never come out so disoriented."

Hirsch kept his hand on Clave's knee as he bowed and prayed, "Father, we thank You for bringing Clave and Diona to us. We ask You to heal Diona now, help her to understand just how much You love her. Amen." Then he looked up and said, "Maybe this is just what we need to come out of hiding."

His comments brought to mind the idea that Clave had been turning over before the fire. "I've been thinking about that, too," he said. "I wonder what you would think about holding a few public meetings in the near future."

"Public meetings?" asked Edward.

"Right. Maybe we could find a place to meet and then invite the public. We need to tell them about Jesus. The old stone church would be ideal." Clave looked over at Hirsch, who was smiling broadly. "Too bad it belongs to the WOC." Clave then told them about prison and about his conversation with his cellmate.

Hirsch said, "Good idea. A very good idea. If Morag knows, then everybody is going to know, anyway. We might as well be the first to tell the world and not Morag."

Edward scratched his head. "I just don't know. We still have to wonder—who will she tell? Maybe no one for now. Maybe we can lay low for just a little while longer," he urged. "We have the families to think about, the disabled, and the children. I'll bring this up at the meeting with the leaders. But I, for one, think the wisest course is just to lay low."

The three of them discussed the issue for nearly half an hour. In the end they decided to keep things as they were for a little while longer.

"Once again the church is on the defensive, rather than the offensive," muttered Hirsch as he wheeled himself back into the front room.

30

Vaney Stodge sat across from the High Priestess in her new office at the Presidential Palace. The room was spacious and airy with the latest in computers and robot gadgetry lining each wall. In the center of the room Kiki, in her gilt cage, nibbled on bits of lettuce that the High Priestess pushed through the bars. Dr. Stodge, new High Priest of the World Order Church, pretended to listen while she went on and on about how Kiki was looking peaked, and did he think there might be something wrong with her.

Having exhausted the subject of Kiki, she looked over at Stodge. "I called you in here this morning because something seems to be happening. I wonder if you can clue me in, Dr. Stodge?"

"Happening, High Priestess?"

"You have no doubt heard me mention an old man, an old man who threatens to undermine our power, all of the power of the WOC, all of the power of the NWO. Well, I am getting stronger impressions of him all the time—I've been troubled in my dreams—but I cannot locate him. And then there's Edward. I haven't talked to Edward in quite a while. I've left dozens of messages for him. He just doesn't seem to be around."

At the mention of that name, Stodge smirked.

"And what is so funny, Dr. Stodge?"

"Ah, nothing."

She eyed him warily. "Edward is my faithful servant and has been for many years. I trust him implicitly. If you would get to know him you would see, as I have come to see, that he is an asset to the carrying out of the plan."

So low, almost so that the High Priestess could not hear him, Vaney sneered, "Plan, right."

"One thing I am confused about, however. I didn't authorize the break-in of Clave's office, nor the fire. The only thing I approved was the taking of the Josiah Files, and of course the assassination went well, Dr. Stodge. I must commend you on that. I was a bit surprised to hear from the police that Clave had been imprisoned. I have known, or at least suspected, that Dr. Hammill's emotional health has been extremely unstable.

"It seems too coincidental to me, however, that his office would be ransacked and his house burned all in the space of a couple of days. So there comes to mind a question: If I didn't authorize these events, who did? Dr. Stodge, perhaps you could find out. If there are other powers at work, for or against us, we should know about it."

"Ah, they probably were coincidences."

"I doubt it. The news reports said something about dead cats. That totally baffles me, Dr. Stodge, and I wonder if you could investigate that for me. Why would someone leave dead cats on their grounds? And something else—I cannot locate him—Clave disappears every day. I have had my men following him and they continually lose him."

Stodge laughed. "Those two bumbling idiots who stumble over their own shoelaces?"

"At least they are loyal. They and Edward."

Stodge sneered again.

"And what are you grinning at? A few days ago they followed him into an office building. On the fifteenth floor they ran into a doctor who said that someone fitting Clave's description was washing his hands in the men's room. But when they went in there, he was gone. I don't understand it. I'm afraid, Dr. Stodge, afraid that every day he meets with someone who is undermining our power. We need to make sure we are completely unified before we go after Mars."

Stodge stroked his beard, an inscrutable expression on his face.

"But our plans will come together, yours and mine. Wait and see. They will come together. I will find that old man, get rid of him, and then you and I, you and I, Dr. Stodge, will take control of the universe! Mars *will* come under our authority."

And with that she rose, signaling the end of the meeting. Stodge left. Far down the hall and out of earshot he took out his hand-held messager and voice commanded the number for Sister Morag's Spiritual Retreat. He input the message: "Plan A is underway." Then he folded up the message screen, dropped it into the deep pocket of his black robe, and walked out.

31

Even though Clave was spending all of his time with the Christians at the Safehouse, technically he was still employed by the WOC. So every other day he called in to his office via computer message screen for his messages. It was on the second week after Diona arrived that a robot secretary told him in its clipped computer voice, "Your daughter is seeking to reach you. She would like you to meet her at the grounds of the burned out living quarters tonight at twenty-two hundred hours."

That was the message, the entire message. Clave looked up from the computer message screen in the front room. Which daughter? Dierdron? But that was impossible. She was on the Moon teaching a bunch of little level-fourers. Nori? Highly unlikely. Nori didn't go out of her way to seek meetings with her parents. *Me, I'm trying to escape it.* The remembered words still pained him. No, it couldn't be Nori.

His thoughts were interrupted by Tommi and Dos, who raced through the room. A little girl named Cindy sat in a small wheelchair laughing and clapping her hands at their antics. She was new to the Safehouse. Star had smuggled her in a couple of days ago.

Hirsch was in the prayer room reading his Bible and praying, and Diona was sleeping. Lately Clave's wife seemed to fatigue so easily. Through the walls muffled kitchen sounds could be heard. Aside from them, he was alone in the front room. Quietly, Clave bowed his head.

✝ ✝ ✝

The forlorn figure walking slowly through the ruins, her long cloak dragging through the soggy ashes, seemed oblivious to the pouring rain. Now and then, she bent down, picked up a piece of something, turned it over in her gloved fingers only to drop it again.

Dierdron? Through the rain-soaked windshield of Edward's hovercar, Clave couldn't tell. Gently he set the vehicle down on a patch of cement and grabbed his umbrella from the front seat. He attempted to avoid the largest of the puddles as he made his way out to where his daughter stood.

She looked up. Rain poured down her face and mingled with her tears. She was saturated, soaked to the skin. Her wet hair was plastered to her face. Beside her on the ground was a large fabric satchel. Clave hadn't noticed that before.

"Nori?"

"Daddy!" She rushed into his arms sobbing. "I can't believe it's all gone, burned to the ground. Everything gone."

Clave was taken aback. It had been a very long time since she had called him "Daddy."

She moved away and wiped her face with her drenched gloved hands. Her eyes were red and swollen and her cheeks were smeared with black soot.

"Daddy, this is all so terrible, isn't it? Are you okay? Is Mom okay?"

"I'm fine and your mother, she's going to be fine. She's a little tired now. Nori, let's get out of the rain."

Their feet squished as they ran to the waiting hovercar. Once in the car he turned to her, his mind a whirlwind of questions. Nori threw her hood back and shook her head like a puppy dog.

"I know you're wondering why I'm here, why I'm not in school, why I wanted to see you." She hesitated. "But do you think I could live with you, with you and Mom? I mean I really don't have anywhere else to go." A gush of fresh tears followed this statement.

"Nori, what happened? Why are you here?"

"It was your letters that got me here, Daddy."

"My letters?"

"You remember—the letters you wrote just after Winterfest about how Jesus was so important to you now."

"Nori, that was months ago."

"Well, I got to rereading them the other night, and everything you said seemed to make sense. I just had to come. I've had so many things in my life go wrong lately, so many problems, so many questions. I had to come to see for myself what your new religion is all about."

"That's fine, Nori, I'm glad. But what about school?"

"Oh, Daddy, I had to drop out. Only temporarily, of course. I plan to go back as soon as I get my life together."

It was cold in the hovercar and Clave turned on the heat. Nori shivered. She ran her thumb over a fingernail, and said finally, "May I come and live with you? I really have no place else to go."

Her look was so pleading. She looked so like Diona with that dark hair, her dark eyes, and small upturned nose. Clave smiled.

"Sure, Nori. You're welcome. We've plenty of room."

32

It was late when the Hammills got to the Safehouse. The rain hadn't let up; it was worse. By the time Clave parked Edward's hovercar in the underground garage and the two of them dried off and made their way into the house, most of the residents had gone to bed. When Nori saw the well-equipped kitchen she insisted upon making some hot chocolate.

"Daddy, I made you come out on a cold, rainy night, so the least I can do is to make you something hot to drink. Sit down and I'll bring it to you."

There it was again: *Daddy*. Come to think of it, Clave could remember only a few times that Nori had called him Daddy.

A few of the people who lived at the Safehouse yawned out into the front room in an assortment of flannel nightgowns, flowered robes, plaid housecoats, and fuzzy slippers. Clave introduced them to his daughter.

But Diona wasn't there. Diona was sleeping. Lately, that was all she did. In the two weeks she had been here, her listlessness had grown. She walked up and down the Safehouse corridors in a somnolent haze. Concerned, Clave had asked Star to look at her. After a lengthy examination Star pronounced her okay, just needing to rest and build up her strength. Privately Star told Clave, "I don't know how people can go to that Sister Morag. She starves the body, the soul, and the spirit, and calls it cleansing, while she herself eats like a pig!"

Star could find no trace of mind-altering drugs in Diona's system, but told him that if drugs had been administered at the retreat they would surely be out of her system soon. "But with your permission I'd like to run a few more tests. I don't trust Morag. I'd also like to see Diona get some top-notch synthetic food into her system—good food. Can you manage that?" Clave nodded.

Still Diona ate very little. She took no interest in her artwork, and that grieved Clave the most. The few times Simon had tried to talk to her, she had smiled wanly and excused herself as soon as possible.

"Daddy," Nori said, interrupting his thoughts. "I want to tell you why I'm here, why I'm really here." The house-coated party made excuses to leave, but she pressed them to stay. "You should hear this, too, because you've made such an impression on Daddy's life, because you've been so wonderful to my parents."

They sat down, and Nori began, "Daddy, you just don't know how many times I reread your letters. I've had such a hard time in school. I just can't seem to keep my grades up. Well, I decided to trust Jesus, just once. I had a real hard exam. So I prayed, 'Jesus, if You're there, help me on this one. Just this once.' And you know what? I aced it!"

Nori paused. "I just know that God is real. I came because I want to believe the way you do."

The members of the community smiled warmly. A few reached over and took her hands. One of the older women turned to her and said, "Well, Nori, God loves you, and we'll take care of you. You have a home here."

Nori smiled, a wide, engaging smile, but Clave suddenly frowned.

Nori looked over toward the door to the dining room, rose, and ran, arms outstretched.

"Oh, Mama, Mama," she said, embracing the figure in the doorway.

33

Was that Nori? It was so hard to tell. Diona rubbed her eyes with the backs of her hands. Her eyes hurt. Lately, she was having so much trouble focusing. It was like the part of her brain that had to do with seeing things was wearing out.

"Nori?" Did she say it out loud or only think she did? That's another problem, she thought. I can never remember if I say things aloud or just think them in my head. I can't tell the difference anymore.

"Mama, I'm so glad to see you! It's me, Nori!"

Why was she calling her Mama? Nori never called her Mama.

"Nori. You've come here?"

"Yes, because—oh, Mama, I want to know about this Jesus. These wonderful people have meant so much to you and Daddy, especially Daddy, and I want—Mama, you seem so tired. Are you okay?"

Diona shrugged. She *was* tired. That much was true. She had to sit down. Right now, she had to find a chair or she would faint. She looked wildly around the room, frantic lest she fall before she found a place to sit. A shudder went through her body.

Nori led her mother to the one empty chair and someone else wrapped a bright colored afghan around her. In some dim recess of Diona's mind, she could hear people talking. It kept fading in and out, like a broken HV not quite picking up the signal.

"What about university?" It was Clave and he was talking to Nori. Why had Nori come here?

"I do want to go back and finish someday. I know that education is important, but right now I have to find Jesus."

Diona looked around. There were a lot of people sitting on chairs. Was it meeting time? But then, why were they all in their pajamas? Maybe it was breakfast, time for breakfast.

"Coffee," she said. "Is there coffee?"

Nori jumped to her side. "You want coffee, Mother? We've got hot chocolate, will that do?"

Diona thought about it. "No thank you, but you've been very helpful." And then she looked down at her hands. Skinny hands. Hands like an old woman. Was she an old woman? I couldn't be, she thought. If I am, I can't remember getting here. Clave was her husband. And he looked young. So she couldn't be old. Or was Clave her son? Husband or son? But I don't have a son, no son, just girls, two girls—Nori and—and—I can't remember the other one's name. Clave would know. Clave would remember.

"Clave," she called.

"I'm right here."

"What's the other one's name? Do you remember?"

"The other one, Diona?"

"There was another girl once, but I can't remember her name."

Clave tucked the blanket around her.

"She's like this now," Diona heard him tell the girl called Nori. "She forgets things, forgets who I am and rambles on."

Diona looked into his face. Why were his eyes so sad? Don't be so sad, she thought. Dear Clave. Sometimes he would sit by her chair and tell her about a person called Jesus, who loved her and could make her well. Then he would dig out his handreader and read and read and read to her. It gave her a headache, all that listening, all that trying to concentrate. She couldn't understand it. And when Clave would ask her something about what he had just read, she couldn't remember.

The one thing she did remember, faithfully day after day, night after night, was to take her pills, the pills Sister Morag had given her. Clave didn't even have to remind her. This was something she could do all by herself. Maybe Clave doesn't even know about them. She smiled to herself.

The room was dark. She was lying in her bed with the covers pulled up to her chin. She didn't remember how she had gotten here. Why had they taken her here? She began to cry. She didn't know why, but she cried and cried into her pillow. And then something in her head remembered. It was time for another pill. She rose, shuffled into the bathroom, closed the door, and reached under the sink and into the secret place where she kept them.

34

Diona was up again. Clave could hear her fumbling around in the bathroom. He leaned over and looked at his digital readout—3:00 A.M. The only light in their underground bedroom was the phosphorescent green readout. Exactly 3:00 A.M. Wasn't it 3:00 A.M. last night, too? He pulled the quilt up around him. The blackness tonight was unusually oppressive. It was as if the air was particled with darkness; tonight these particles had combined, creating a thick, viscous blanket, a rug that threatened to smother him.

Diona was getting worse. He had no wife, just this form of a wife who wandered restlessly in and out of rooms. Maybe the sight of her daughter would cheer her. The tests Star had run on Diona were negative. "Something's got to be here," Star had said, hunching over her computerized microscope. "I'll find it, Clave. We'll get Diona back."

Star said that physically Diona seemed fine; she hinted at some deep emotional trouble. Clave couldn't reach her. No one could.

And the insurance settlement on the house was still up in the air. It was unlikely that he would ever see the money he was entitled to, money that was rightfully his. He prayed about it daily. The insurance company's story was always the same; since the fire was set under "mysterious circumstances" and Clave was still legally "under suspicion," no settlement would be forthcoming. What were he and Diona, and now Nori, supposed to do? Live forever at the Safehouse, forever dependent on the handouts of these fine people? "God, why are You so far away tonight?" he cried.

A few weeks ago he asked his publisher to withhold all future royalties on his books. How could he accept money from books that had led so many people astray? As he lay staring at the wall, he wished he hadn't been so hasty. He could sure use some of that money now.

Unconsciously in the darkness he began to rub his forehead. It took him a few minutes before he realized that an old enemy was threading its way into his temple. A headache! But he wasn't supposed to get headaches anymore. God had healed all that months ago. He shut his eyes tightly and faced the wall, but he couldn't shut out the pain, the loneliness, the turbid darkness.

He heard Diona pad listlessly back into the bedroom and climb into her side of the double bed. He reached out for her and touched her shoulder, but she turned away from him. Clave rolled back and faced the wall, his headache worsening. He couldn't sleep. He pulled himself noiselessly from the bed, grabbed the flowered quilt from the chair, and stole silently out into the front room to read for a while. He sat down in an overstuffed chair and grabbed a handreader from the coffee table. The first story keyed in was the daily newspaper and staring up at him was the face of the High Priest, Dr. Vaney Stodge. Clave forced himself to look long and hard at that face—those dark eyes, straight nose, high cheekbones. Stodge was now sporting a new clerical collar and headpiece. Clave switched off the handreader, but the image of Vaney Stodge remained before him. It was a strong face. Some would even call it a handsome face. But something about it seemed almost evil to Clave.

Even with the table lamp on, the darkness was like a blanket, but it was suddenly more than that. Shadows elongated on the wall and danced in the still air. Clave looked up, entranced. He saw nothing in the room that would make such shadows, yet he felt something, a presence. The same presence that had tried to pull him from his bed so long ago. Clave wrapped the quilt tightly around him and massaged his forehead. I am dreaming, he told himself. I am tired, depressed, and so I am seeing things, hallucinating.

But the presence was close to him now. He could feel it all around him, enfolding him, embracing him with its evil claws. And then he heard the laughter. He bowed his aching head into his hands. Fingers of pain began to creep down his head, past his eyes, to his nose, to his ears. His ears began ringing so loud that all other sounds, even the laughter, were drowned out. He placed his fingers under his nostrils. Blood. And the pain; it was like his head was being squeezed in a vice. When the fingers crawled down into his throat, he gasped for air, choking, choking.

"Je—Je—Jesus," he finally managed to say while clutching at his neck.

"Jesus," he said aloud again. Like an ocean wave receding on the shoreline, the pain abated, moving upward from his neck, to his ears, to his eyes, and out of the top of his head. "Jesus," he said again, tearfully, prayerfully.

For a fleeting moment he felt, heard, sensed a multitude of bright beings surrounding his chair, singing, protecting him, comforting him. He sat up suddenly and blinked. The vision was gone. There was only the stillness of the Safehouse front room. But for that moment, oh, for that moment!

He sat for a few minutes more praying, quietly basking in the light of God's Son, the light that banished the blackness of sin from him. "Deliver me from the evil one," he prayed.

And then he made his way back into his bedroom, where he fell into a peaceful, deep sleep.

35

Clave fumbled through the lush bins of synthetic fruits and vegetables at the front of the grocery store. They were expensive, but they were also highly nutritious, in many cases more so than "genuine" produce because no vitamins were lost in washing and cooking. Clave wanted something full of vitamins. Diona was getting weaker. Four days ago, Diona had fallen out of bed and couldn't get up. Clave and Star had helped her into a wheelchair, and she hadn't walked since.

"I just can't understand it," Star had said, shaking her head. "I've run dozens of tests. I've taken blood samples, had them analyzed a hundred ways; I've examined her thoroughly—but nothing. I'm almost out of options. It's frustrating."

"Here are some carrots that look good," said Nori, holding up a small bunch by their greenery. "From Sector 3 Earth labs."

"Those will be great," said Star. "A hearty soup, something with lots of vegetables will be good for her. We can supplement with a synthetic vitamin."

When Star and Nori volunteered to do the weekly shopping, they had persuaded Clave to come along. He was getting too cooped up and exhausted and needed to get out, they said. Taking care of Diona was time-consuming, wearying, and frustrating, especially since there seemed to be no outward cause for her malaise. He balked at first, but then went along. The three of them began their shopping expedition with pasta at Joey's. Nori had paid for them all, although where she got the money from Clave didn't ask.

"I think these will be enough," said Star, placing a small bunch of carrots, a few potatoes, and a head of cauliflower in the grocery cart.

"Diona used to grow all this stuff in her greenhouse," Clave said wistfully. "She will again," Star said, placing her hand on his arm. "Now let's get the rest of the groceries." Clave wanted to believe her. Ever since his experience in the front room the night Nori had arrived, he knew, like Jim Swanson, that his God was powerful, more powerful than the host of demons that would war against him. But sometimes trust was a hard thing.

They pushed the cart over to the frozen foods. Nori grabbed four bags of synthetic peas, two of corn, and one of mixed vegetables plus a large, economy size box of frozen synthetic meat chunks. They wandered up and down the aisles, filling the cart with coffee, sugar, milk powder, bread, flour.

In the beverage aisle Clave looked ahead of him at Nori and Star who were comparing the prices on tins of coffee, their heads together. The two had become fast friends over the past few weeks. Nori followed Star everywhere. She would lounge in an easy chair next to Star while Star worked on what they were now calling the Christian Information Center, digging up Christian literature, sermons, and commentaries from old archives.

Nori seemed changed in other ways as well. She was certainly devoted to her mother now, constantly administering cups of tea, plates of toast, and pushing her wheelchair everywhere she wanted to go. And Nori never missed a meeting—singing and clapping along with the rest of them. The people in the Community, especially the older ladies, seemed quite taken with her. But Nori had always been good with people. When she was a young teenager, Clave's father had remarked to him once that "Nori can play people like a master violinist plays the strings of a Stradivarius." Clave had nodded.

It was crowded in the store. Mothers pushed carts with youngsters swinging their chubby legs and munching on animal cookies. Groups of young people picked out candy bars and movie magazine demichips. They wheeled their cart behind the shortest cash register line. Star and Nori giggled at the tabloid demichip headlines at the counter—"Man with two heads weds alien princess," and "Robot waitress comes to life! Doctors find living heart growing inside."

Finally, it was their turn. Star keyed in a PDN, one she had set up for the Community, and then the three of them began unloading the cart. A robot cashier scanned each item as it crossed its path on the conveyor belt. Clave stood at the end of the aisle watching the robot pack their food in the bags. Out of the corner of his eye he glimpsed something dark. A movement. He turned toward the door. A tall blond man clad in skin-tight black slacks, black turtleneck, and black boots leaned against the wall by the door, his arms crossed. Hanging from his neck was a single silver cross—an upside-down silver cross inside a triangle. The sight unnerved Clave. He had seen that same sign splashed in blood on his office wall.

The man, whoever he was, seemed to be looking directly at him. Clave turned away and nervously watched the remaining packages move slowly down the conveyor belt and into the bags. But he could feel those eyes boring into his back. Nori and Star were giggling and talking, unaware of the stranger and the effect he was having on Clave.

"Ready?" asked Star.

"Sure." Clave's voice cracked. He hurried out the door. When he turned around to wait for the girls he saw that the man in black was staring now at Nori. She looked up at him as she passed him. And then Clave saw something pass between them, a look of recognition. And the faintest of smiles on Nori's mouth. Or did he merely imagine it?

36

Feverishly they worked—two men and a woman. Round the clock they worked. Stodge was paying them well, but that's not why they worked. Something else drove them: Stodge's anger if they failed. His rages were well-known, and they feared, all of them, being on the receiving end.

Empty pizza cartons along with half-filled cups of cold coffee and crumpled bags of chips were strewn all over the tiny computer console room. There was also the smell of their bodies, too long in one place.

It was 4:15 A.M. when the tall blond man turned to the others. "We almost have it. Won't be more than a day or two now."

The woman, who always wore her hair tucked up under a skin-tight silver plastic cap, said, "I never doubted us for a minute. This is a piece of cake compared to Kyzer's palace."

"We don't have it yet. I said *almost*. The locks on their system are quite sophisticated. But with that little bit of help from our source, we're well on our way. All we need is that series of passwords, one from each group."

The other man asked, "Why is Stodge so bent on destroying this book in the first place?"

"No idea. I just do my job, ask no questions."

The woman said curiously, "Makes me want to read it just to find out."

Her companions laughed.

"So, what are you going to do with your bonus?" asked the younger man.

The tall one leaned back in his chair and folded his hands behind his head. "I'm getting out of here, out of this line of work. I figure this'll be my last job. With the money I make off this one, I'm going to buy an anonymous little farmhouse somewhere on a quiet lake on Mars."

"Good luck, but you know Stodge'll find you," said the woman.

"Not where I'm going."

The woman shrugged and the three of them went back to work.

37

The day they made the soup was the day everything changed for Diona. It started off a day like any other day. In the morning, Clave had lifted her out of her bed and helped her with her clothes. A sob stuck in her throat. She didn't want to wear the green sweater today. She thrashed her arms in protest. And why wouldn't they let her walk? She tried to kick Clave when he lifted her into her chair. "Why don't you let me walk by myself?" she said, but she wasn't sure whether she actually spoke the words aloud or not. She couldn't tell the dreaming from the waking, the thinking from the saying.

She was only dimly aware that Nori had come for a visit. The only thing driving her from day to day was her need for the pills Morag had given her. She had to take the pills every day, three times a day, or something terrible would happen to her.

All that morning she sat in her chair in the dining room while Nori and that girl with the long blonde hair, the one they called Star, rattled pots and pans around the kitchen. The sounds were making her head hurt, but she was powerless to move herself away from the noise and back into her own room. She could hear them laughing and talking while she sat in the dining room in her wheelchair, her hands folded on her lap. There wasn't even a window to look out of.

A few hours later, although she had no way of measuring the passage of time, they brought her a bowl of steaming soup.

It smelled good. But after only a few mouthfuls she choked. She couldn't get it down.

"Mama, come on. You have to eat this to build up your strength."

Diona shook her head. Clave walked in and Diona could hear Star saying, "I think we should take her to a hospital."

"Is it safe?" he asked.

"I'm not sure, but what other options do we have? I've done everything, Clave, and I don't know what is wrong with her."

And then Star came over. "Mrs. Hammill, you should really try to get more of this down. You're never going to get well unless you do."

Diona looked down at the bowl of soup and then over at Nori. She waved to her daughter. Nori bent down and put her ear to her mother's mouth. A few moments later Nori was wheeling Diona down the hall. In the bathroom the door shut behind them and Nori turned around and locked it.

"Please . . . hurry," Diona whispered hoarsely.

"Okay, Mama."

Diona watched as Nori reached under the sink and pulled the bottle out from that secret place. At that very second Clave burst through the door, breaking the computer sensor system so that it beeped and flashed and sent a siren warning throughout the entire Safehouse. Residents came running, but Clave didn't seem to care. His eyes blazed. He grabbed the pill bottle out of Nori's hand. The top was off and little pink pills clattered all over the floor.

"Pills, Nori? What are these pills you're giving her?"

Nori seemed genuinely stunned, and then she said, "Just her pills, Daddy, the ones she's supposed to take."

"She's not taking any pills!" His voice thundered through the Safehouse. Why did he have to yell so loud?

"They're mine," said Diona, leaning forward and grabbing at them on the floor. "I have to have them."

Clave bent down and gathered up the pills from the floor. "Why on Earth were you giving her these, Nori?"

"She told me she was supposed to have them."

"If they were something she was supposed to have, why would they be taped up under the sink?"

"I don't know. I don't know." Nori said. "I thought that was just a part of her strangeness, that she hid her pills under the sink. What's wrong, Daddy?" Her eyes were wide with innocence.

"These pills!" Clave's voice trembled. "Where did she get them?"

"She told me Sister Morag gave them to her."

Clave clenched the pill container so tightly that Diona thought it would crack in two.

"I have to have them," Diona mumbled, but no one heard her.

"Nori, Sister Morag, that fat cow, would love to see your mother dead. She would like to destroy my whole family, anyone connected with me."

"I didn't know. I promise I didn't know. I thought Mother was supposed to have them. I thought I was helping her."

Nori turned and left the room then, slamming the door as she reached her room.

Clave carried Diona to bed, carefully lifting her from the wheelchair, "I only hope there's been no permanent damage. Oh, Diona, you have to come back to me."

But Diona didn't care about Clave. She only asked for her pills. All night long, over and over, she asked for her pills. In the morning she didn't feel well. Her head hurt and she needed her pills. Her pills would help. Carefully, gently, Clave dressed her and wheeled her out to the communal dining room. Today she was too weak to protest. One of the ladies set a cup of broth down in front of her. She ignored it. The knot, a pain, like a sharp knife in her stomach was growing. At the other side of the room Clave was waving that little plastic bottle in his hand and talking with Hirsch and Edward. She watched them bow their heads. Why did they always do that?

Her throat hurt. She couldn't swallow. It was like her body was shutting off, slowly, like you turn off a tap. Just a trickle left. At times there was a sensation under her skin, like an itching. She tried desperately to scratch it. But it still itched. She scratched and scratched until her arms bled. She looked at her bleeding arms as if they belonged to someone else. When the itching turned to burning she began to scream. They carried her out and laid her on the couch in the front room. They covered her with a quilt. It was a soft one, but it felt so heavy on her. She screamed and screamed. They placed their hands on her and prayed. It burned her skin where their hands touched her.

Did it go on all day, that praying? All day and all night? One hour? Later they could have told her one hour or one week. She wouldn't have known the difference. Time didn't exist for her.

All Diona remembered was that eventually the pain began to diminish. She fell into a dreamless sleep. She woke once to find one of the ladies sponging the blood off her arms with a soft damp cloth. Then she drifted off again. Finally, she woke limp and spent—but strangely clear-minded.

Hirsch turned to her. "Do you want to trust Jesus to free you from this?"

She nodded, almost imperceptibly. Clave took her hands and they prayed.

The fear left her then; the pain receded at once. She looked up through focused eyes. She sat up on the couch and looked deep into the eyes of her husband.

"Clave, I'm well," was all she said.

38

Early the following morning Diona was up making blueberry pancakes. Clave could smell the coffee and hear her humming in the kitchen as he made his way down the hall. Hirsch was already there, reading from his handreader.

"Diona, don't you think you're overdoing it a bit?" Clave called in to her. "Just yesterday you couldn't even walk. Why don't you take it easy for a couple of days?"

She laughed and entered the dining room, a large tray of pancakes in her hand. "No way! Do you think the man in the Bible who took up his bed and walked would have heeded any advice to 'take it easy for a day or two'? Or how about the blind man? Do you think he would have listened if anyone had said to him, 'Why don't you keep your eyes closed for a few days and gradually work up to looking at things?'"

"Well," said Hirsch, reaching for his coffee cup, "you certainly know your Bible."

"I couldn't sleep last night, so I got up and started reading the book called Luke. There were so many stories of people in it, people like me. I found it fascinating."

Gradually the other residents began arriving for breakfast; they greeted Diona, amazed at the transformation in her. Halfway through breakfast, Tommi, dressed and ready for the day, dashed into the room, Dos close behind wagging his tail.

"Well, the day has begun," laughed Diona. She helped Tommi to pancakes and syrup, and sat down next to him and chatted with him.

Clave watched Diona; tears filled his eyes. Late yesterday afternoon Star had come in and told them that Diona was lucky to be alive. She had secretly taken one of the pills to her hospital and run some tests on it. They indicated that this was a new and very potent drug, probably developed at Morag's. It evaded all known blood tests. It was highly destructive and very addictive. It would have killed her in a week or two.

"It's a good thing she was so healthy when she started taking the pills," said Star. "What she had running through her veins would have killed anybody else."

"That's just like sin," Hirsch had said, "totally destructive, but so addictive. People crave the very thing that ultimately destroys them."

Everyone around the breakfast table that morning praised Diona's pancakes.

"Clave can tell you how much I love to cook," she said.

Moments later, Simon was the first to notice Star standing ashen-faced in the doorway with one hand leaning against the door post to support herself. Her eyes were hollow, and she looked as if she hadn't slept all night. Her normally shiny blonde hair hung in limp, knotted strings down her back. Simon rose at once.

"Star!" he said.

Diona looked up and put the coffee pot down on the table. "Star?"

"I don't know how it could have happened," she said. "All the controls were there. All the system controls. We made so sure of everything. We worked so hard."

"Star, what happened?" asked Edward.

She looked blankly at him. Clave thought perhaps she hadn't heard the question.

Finally, she spoke. "The Bible is gone. All of the copies. Erased from our library system."

"What do you mean?" asked Simon.

"Gone. Disappeared from the system." She ran a hand through her stringy hair. "I've checked all of the access codes, all the secret files I use for copying and storing."

"But I've got it on handreader. I was reading it just last evening," said Clave.

"And I read the book of Luke in the middle of the night," added Diona.

"Check them now. I'll be surprised if you still have it on your handreaders."

Clave's voice commanded his handreader. The screen remained blank. He tried again. Nothing.

"Are you sure?" asked Hirsch. "I know you've been working a long time on this system."

"It was supposed to be foolproof. There's a whole system of passwords and number codes. No one person could have done it. I was working closely with computer programmers in Sectors 23, 37, and 4. We each have a password, and no one knows anyone else's. The system couldn't be opened unless all passwords are working in conjunction. It's an extremely difficult procedure. No amateur computer hacker could just go in there and erase the Bible."

She fought tears. "We originally set it up this way to preserve the Scriptures, to prevent people from just getting in and changing them. It was locked in. That's why I don't understand. I've been up since 5:30 and on the message phone for the last hour with the other programmers. But it just seems to be gone."

"An error on the computer?" ventured Diona.

"Computers don't make errors. There's just no such thing. I've heard that when computers were first developed there could be glitches on them all the time. But with the wireless networks that we use now, that sort of thing is impossible. Back in the early days, computers even got viruses. But nothing like that happens anymore. No, it had to be someone who knew all of the access codes, all of the passwords, and who went in deliberately to destroy the Bible."

"So what you're saying, Star—" The volume of Hirsch's voice was slightly raised, the way it got when he was excited. "What you're saying is that the Bibles everywhere—Earth, Mars, Moon—have been destroyed?"

"That's the size of it."

"What about the Bible Clave found, the bound one?" asked Simon.

"Great, if we could find it."

Edward spoke, "I think the High Priestess still has it and the journal, but she won't tell me where they are. I'm fairly certain she hasn't destroyed them."

Clave spoke. "What about the bound Bible I borrowed from the archives using your PAC, Edward?"

"That robot, unfortunately, was hijacked. The Bible never made it back to the archives after you returned it."

"They really are thorough."

Star slid down the wall and sat on the floor. "It's my fault. Obviously, I missed something."

From the door to the kitchen another form appeared. "Hi guys, how's it going?"

They all looked up to see Nori leaning against the kitchen door. "What's the matter? Did someone die or something?"

"Nori," Clave's voice cracked, "all of the Bibles have been removed from the library system."

"What?" Her eyes widened. "Removed? What do you mean?"

"Someone got into the network last night or early this morning, we don't know how, and destroyed the Bible."

"But, Daddy, oh, that's terrible!" said Nori, her hand flying to her mouth. "That book means so much to you, to all of us. Why would someone do something so terrible?"

"They aren't all destroyed," said Hirsch suddenly from his chair. Nori looked at him sharply. "God will not allow His

Word to be destroyed. 'Heaven and Earth will pass away, but My Word will not pass away.'"

"Oh, but what if they *are* all gone, Mr. Swanson? That would be so awful. Oh, I could cry."

"They aren't gone."

Clave looked at his daughter. There it was again, this feeling that she was somehow acting. He looked across at Diona. Did she sense it too? Diona had gone over to Star and sat on the floor with her, her arm around her. Clave picked up his coffee mug and then set it down again. What was he thinking? It was an awful thing to doubt your own child.

39

It was dusk outside when Clave left the Safehouse with Dos, ostensibly to go for a walk. Just need to get some air, he said.

All day there had been frantic activity. Edward and Star had flown out mid-morning to a general assembly of Christian leaders in the catacombs of Sector 23. Hirsch stayed and organized round-the-clock prayer, and spent the morning praying, talking, singing, and trying to recall verses they had memorized.

By mid-afternoon, Clave remembered a snatched bit of conversation. He didn't tell the group. It might all come to naught, anyway, he said to himself as he led Dos through the empty back streets. Clave buttoned his cloak up to his chin and threw the hood over his head to ward off the cold. He held tightly onto Dos's leash.

His destination was an office mall seven blocks away. Always aware that he might be followed, Clave darted in and out of buildings and alleyways. Being outside and away from the Safehouse always made him feel vulnerable.

The first floor of the office building was empty. When Clave and Dos entered the deserted elevator, the computer voice said, "Floor, please."

"Eight."

The elevator stopped at the second floor. Two workers dressed in blue laughed and guffawed and slapped each other's shoulders and ignored the hooded man and his dog who stood against the back of the elevator. They got out on floor five and Clave and Dos ascended, uninterrupted until floor eight. When the elevator doors opened, Clave turned right and found the public phone booth at the end of the hall. As far as he knew it was the only public interplanetary phone in this part of the sector.

He spoke into the small microphone and the door to the booth opened. He and Dos barely fit inside. In front of him was the orange plastic audio phone with its list of operating instructions printed along the side. He spread the scrap of paper napkin out in front of him on the console.

"On," he spoke into the little microphone.

"Audio phone on," the computer voice replied.

Clave hesitated slightly. "Mars, Sector 7, please." He rubbed Dos under the ears while the machine in front of him flashed and whirred.

"One moment please. Connection being completed. One moment please, connection being verified," a voice told him.

Finally a robot voice came on and in a Mars accent said, "Number, please?" Clave was always surprised that even the robots spoke in the accents of the places they came from.

Clave read the numbers on the napkin, "3-413-217-0911."

"One moment, please. Connection being completed. One moment, please. Connection being verified."

The call was answered on the second ring.

"Hello there."

Clave recognized the powerful voice of the man they called Latz. He remembered a chestful of wildly patterned fluorescent tattoos. "Hello, Latz?"

"Yes, well." The connection was surprisingly clear.

"This is Clave Hammill. I don't know if you remember me or not, but—"

"Oh, but of course, I remember you. The coffee shop, right?"

Clave began, "At that coffee shop you mentioned that you owned a bound holy book. I wonder if you could tell me the name of this holy book."

"Why, yes, it's the Koran." He paused. "No, wait." He put his hand over the receiver and yelled something. When he came back he said. "No, not the Koran. Maeva tells me it was the Bible."

"Ah, the Bible," said Clave.

"Why do you want to know the name of it?"

"So you have a copy of the Bible?"

"That's right. But not me, Anthon does. His grandmother gave it to him, put it in a box and gave it to him with a note. It was in her will when she died."

"Is Anthon there?"

"Can't say that he is."

"I wonder if you could do me a big favor."

"Name it."

When Clave laid out his request, he concluded by saying, "By the way, Latz, have you ever read that book?"

"Can't say that I have."

"You should read it. All of you should read it. It changed my life."

"Funny. That's what Anthon's grandmother said in the note she left. She was a pioneer, Anthon's grandmother was. One of our Mars pioneers. Did you know that? Came over on the first spacecraft to colonize Mars. You know what the name of it was? Mayflower II. And in those days the trip to Mars took almost a year. Can you imagine that?"

Clave said no, he couldn't.

On the way back to the Safehouse Clave thanked the Lord that there were people like Pastor Jim Swanson and Anthon's grandmother who knew the value of the Bible and had the foresight to hide it away against a coming persecution. There must be thousands of Bibles hidden in attics and basements and safe deposit boxes, he thought, thousands of "Josiah Files" waiting to be found just when they were needed.

40

When he got back, Clave motioned to Edward and Hirsch to follow him outside. Clave didn't feel safe in the so-called Safehouse anymore. Anyone capable of destroying the Bible would have no trouble installing surveillance devices throughout the tunnels. Edward wheeled Hirsch out and the three of them squeezed into the dark, cramped stairwell just outside the front room door. When Clave told them that he'd found another bound Bible on Mars and that friends on Mars were sending it out, Hirsch said, "I wasn't even worried."

"They're sending it out on the high speed IPV. It should be here in about five days. I'll see if Star and the other programmers can scan it in and then come up with an even tougher access code to crack, but I'm a little concerned. . . ." Clave paused and looked up. The night was clear and quiet. The Big Dipper sparkled from above. Just say it, he told himself.

Edward looked at him quizzically. Clave went on, "I think we should really stress to Star that she say nothing about this to anyone. To keep it quiet, even from Nori." Especially from Nori, he thought.

"If you say so, Clave," said Edward. "The fewer people that know about this the better."

Clave looked away. "If word gets out that Anthon and his friends have a Bible, you can bet the WOC or whoever is behind this will dash off to Mars and find it, just like they did with the ones we found."

"I agree with Clave," said Hirsch.

Edward shrugged and the three went back into the front room. Nori looked at them curiously. "Out for a walk?" she asked.

"Sure," said Clave.

She looked at Hirsch's wheelchair, but said nothing.

The following afternoon Clave met Star at the hospital where she worked and as they walked the streets toward her apartment he told her of this new development. In her apartment, away from the Safehouse, she contacted the Christian computer programmers from the other sectors. Via video conference, they worked feverishly through the night setting up new, tougher access codes.

Five days later a square, self-refrigerated metal box labeled "Living Human Tissue" arrived at the hospital addressed to Dr. Star. Lou in shipping automatically placed it on Dr. Maury Fitzhugh's robot delivery cart. He was the chief surgeon and had made it clear to her and everyone else in shipping that all human tissue/organs were to be sent to him personally. It was policy.

Lou had a lot of other packages that morning to sort through. Most of them were the little square envelopes that contained demichips. It would be a busy day, she could tell. Absently, she scratched her thigh through her blue trousers and looked again at the refrigerated box on top of Dr. Fitzhugh's cart. Something about it bothered her. Then she glanced at the calendar above her work table. Thursday. Today was Thursday. Dr. Fitzhugh wasn't even in today. Today was the day he took off to go down to Sister Morag's Retreat for inner wholeness, or whatever he called it, to get revitalized.

A lot of the doctors visited Morag. Lou wondered what the attraction was. She'd seen Morag on holovision, and she didn't seem especially brilliant or charismatic. Lately everybody seemed to be talking about Sister Morag. Sister Morag this. Sister Morag that. Lou frowned. She knew it would cost practically her entire month's salary for only one counseling/channeling session, and some of these doctors went all the time, like Dr. Fitzhugh. And what did he get out of it? Did it make him a better person? He still grumped at her all the time. Lou, get this. Lou, you forgot that. Lou this. Lou that, yeah, yeah.

And then there was Star. As far as Lou knew, Dr. Star never went to Morag. And Star was a doctor; she probably could afford it. But Star was nice. She gave things to Lou, too. Like flowers on her birthday. And lots of times Star would bring a cup of coffee down to Lou in the morning. Now that was a switch.

In one moment of defiance, Lou picked up the metal box from Dr. Fitzhugh's cart and placed it on Star's.

"It's addressed to Dr. Star, it's going to Dr. Star," she said aloud. "You can grump at me all you want, mister. It's going up to Star."

In her office later that morning Star opened the metal box marked "Living Human Tissue—Keep Refrigerated," and pulled out a square parcel wrapped in brown paper. She closed and locked her office door, and then sat down at her desk and undid the wrappings. Underneath five layers of paper Star finally unearthed an old, black leather Bible. Engraved on the bottom right in gold, much worn off, was the name Corinna Harris. Lovingly she ran her hands over the cover. She opened to the first page and read the inscription:

Presented to Corinna Harris on the occasion
of her leaving on the Mayflower II for the

Planet Mars, January 6, 2073. We will miss
you. May God go with you.
                    Love, Mother and Father.

Below that a verse was handwritten in neat, precise letters:

There is no one like the God of Jeshurun, who
rides the heavens to help you, and in His excellency
on the clouds.
                    Deuteronomy 33:26

Star allowed herself a moment more to savor the old Bible,
and then she wrapped it up again and placed it at the bottom
of her briefcase. Tonight her work would begin.

After two days of nonstop, mind-wearying toil, the Bible was
scanned into their computer network. Star and the other
programmers added extra security locks. As well, they made a
number of printed copies which were stored away in various
safes and locked hiding places.

A week after the initial disappearance of the Bible, the new
one was up and running on everyone's handreader.

"You're amazing," said Nori, as she carried a cup of coffee
into the front room for Star. The evening meeting was
scheduled to begin in a few moments.

"To think you were able to get that important book back on
track. How did you manage it?"

Star's explanation was silenced by a look from Clave.

"Well, it wasn't easy," she said.

"Amazing," Nori said, walking away. "You'll have to show
me sometime."

Star only smiled.

41

After Nori went back into the kitchen, Clave once more brought up the subject of public meetings to Edward and Hirsch.

"I think it's high time. The Bible was almost destroyed. What are we waiting for?" Clave asked.

"The High Priestess doesn't know our location. I'm still her trusted assistant, you know," said Edward.

Hirsch spoke now. "Maybe, Edward, it's time you left that role, time you became a minister of God rather than a minister for the World Order Church."

Edward nodded and looked down. "I've been feeling that, too. This playing on both sides of the fence is taking its toll on me. I feel I'm not doing either side any good. The Holy Spirit's been dealing with me about that."

Clave said kindly, "There are so many people out there who need to hear about Jesus. If it hadn't been for Simon's brave move in putting up those lights, I would never have known a Christian group existed."

Later that evening they presented the idea to the group.

"I say we go for it," said Sam.

"It's got my vote," Rawn agreed.

And then it was decided. The Christians would invite the residents of Sector 44 to weekly meetings. When the group discussed where they should hold these public meetings, Edward excused himself and went to the Safehouse office. A few minutes later, he returned with two demichips.

"Why not the old stone church?" he suggested. Why not indeed? they asked each other, except for the fact that the stone church was smack on WOC property. Then Edward showed them a copy of a deed he had recently dug up in the archives and had scanned onto demichip. The deed stated that the stone church belonged to the members of Northridge Community Church. Edward clicked in another demichip and ran down the long list of Quadrant 3 churches which had been transferred to WOC ownership. A Norfolk United Church was followed immediately by Northroads Christian Fellowship. Northridge Community Church was omitted. It just wasn't there.

"What happened?" asked a dark-haired woman from the back.

"A computer glitch most likely," said Edward. "Back then computers weren't quite as advanced as they are today. A momentary power failure could have done it, or a power surge, perhaps.

"An astute computer programmer should have picked it up on his printout, but I imagine with the volume of work they were going through, and with the deadlines they were facing, they missed it. Technically, this church still belongs to the members of Northridge Community Church."

Two mornings later two dozen women, children, men, and even some of the handicapped people made their way down the street toward the stone church carrying buckets, mops, and tool kits. A small army of robots followed them.

Using Clave's key, they opened the front door of the stone church and propped it open with a heavy tool kit. It was just as Clave remembered it, vast, cold, echoey. Like Clave, all of them were awed by the interior of the old building. After a few moments of wandering around examining things, exclaiming and touching the wood surfaces, they met in the large sanctuary where Edward led them in prayer, dedicating their efforts to God. And then they got to work. They scrubbed out the corners, cleaned off the chairs, polished the woodwork, and began tearing off the boards that covered the windows.

At noon they broke for lunch. Sharan took out a stringed, harp-like instrument; they sang, clapped, and danced around, holding their mop and broom handles. "Praise the Lord!" they sang. "Praise the Lord!"

Later that afternoon, when the last board was finally removed from the stained-glass windows, a collective cheer went up from the group. Beams of light like laser rays shot in through the mosaics of varicolored glass and filled the auditorium with color and light.

Sam installed computer sensor locks and set up the electrical lights and heating networks. He found lengths of wire coated with rotting plastic in the walls and along the floorboards. "How odd," he said as he held up a piece of wire and examined it. He shook his head until Edward explained that electrical currents used to run through wires and not through power waves.

"How weird," said Sam. "That means you would only have certain places in a room where you could have a lighting unit, say, or an HV."

"Right. People have been using these non-plug units for so long we have forgotten that electricity used to run through copper wires."

"Interesting," said Sam, and he went back to work.

Every once in a while Clave's former assistants and clients clustered together in groups beside the WOC or on the back steps and looked over the work in progress. When Clave or one of the others invited them over, they shook their heads and hurried back into the chrome and crystal building.

Clave marveled at how much his original dream had changed. No more a shrine honoring the achievements of Dr. Clave Hammill, now it would be a monument to Christ.

42

Early that evening, what Clave had been dreading, what they all had been dreading, occurred. Their singing, cleaning, and hammering was interrupted by the sound of clanging doors, heavy boots, and thundering voices. The Christians turned and watched three uniformed police officers stride down the aisle, the heavy inside doors swinging slowly behind them.

Clave recognized the young officer and his paunchy partner. With them was a muscled, mustached man with the chest and forearms of a body builder. They stopped directly in front of Clave. He put his robot controls on the floor.

The paunchy officer spoke first. "Are you Doctor Clave Hammill?"

"You know that I am."

"We have a warrant for your arrest."

"What are the charges?" asked Clave.

Edward stepped down from the platform where he was polishing the cross and hurried to Clave. The others watched in horror. For most of them, this was their first encounter with an antagonistic police force.

"Suspicion of arson, public mischief, harassment, and torturing and disfiguring small animals without a valid musician's license."

"Torturing small animals?" Clave was incredulous.

"The cats, sir. Need I remind you that their throats were slit and blood drained? Not a drop left in any of those little bodies."

Diona gasped.

The body builder spoke next. "And we have an order here to shut down this establishment."

"On what grounds?" asked Edward.

"Trespassing."

"I have a deed here," said Edward. He reached into his inside pocket for a demichip and handed it to the officer who immediately plugged it into his handreader, adjusted the light source, and peered closely at it.

"You can see that the property was never transferred over to the WOC or to the NWO," said Edward. "It belongs to the people of the Northridge Community Church. And we are the people of Northridge Community Church."

"There's got to be a mistake," said the officer, tapping the top of his handreader and shaking it, as if that would rectify the error. "This is impossible. All property was transferred over during Aquarius."

"This little piece of land, gentlemen, was missed."

"Well, it will be checked out thoroughly. You can count on that."

The paunchy officer spoke, "We still have a restraining order on this place."

"A restraining order?" asked Clave.

"There have been complaints all day from the WOC next door that their meditational solitude is being hampered by your loud hammering, singing, and occasional clapping."

Edward said, "I hardly think 'clapping' constitutes a misdemeanor."

"But we can still arrest Dr. Hammill."

"You have not one shred of evidence to keep him."

Now it was Mac's turn. He swaggered up to the front and faced the three officers. "You ain't arresting nobody, no how, no ways. All you got is trumped up charges."

Clave grinned broadly. Since the crusty little former prisoner had joined the Community, life just wasn't the same.

"Where do you find these people?" asked the muscled officer. "Under logs? Pull up a bit of artificial turf? Come on, Dr. Hammill, let's go."

Edward raised his hand. "I believe that an arrest would be illegal, gentlemen."

"Illegal?"

"He was released into my custody, or have you forgotten that? According to a directive issued by the High Priestess, now the President of the NWO, you cannot take him away without my express permission. And I don't grant it."

The three disgruntled officers looked at each other, then turned and sidled out, muttering.

"They're going to hear abut this."

"Someone's head's gonna roll."

"There's going to be trouble."

The door banged closed behind them.

43

Sector 17, Quadrant 1, where the Presidential Palace was located, was normally one of the warmest places in the Northern Hemisphere. That is why Vaney Stodge and the High Priestess could take an evening stroll on the rooftop garden wearing only summer cloaks around their shoulders. His was black. Hers was gold. The High Priestess was clearly agitated. Her face was drawn; her eyes darted nervously around the rooftop.

"I'm glad you could get away. I've something to tell you—something that may change our plans for getting ultimate control of Mars." She scowled and looked up at the sky. Dark thunderheads welled and heaved across the distant sky.

"Go on, High Priestess." Stodge's voice was expressionless, controlled.

"It's Edward. He has betrayed me." She clenched her fists.

"Betrayed you? How?" His face was unreadable.

"He belongs to a little band of Christian fundamentalists. He has belonged to this merry little group for a long time. The whole time he was working for me he was, apparently, working for them, betraying my plans, and my cause."

"Ah, so you've been duped, High Priestess."

"Don't call me High Priestess. You are the High Priest and I am President of the Universe! I have succeeded, Dr. Stodge, succeeded despite Edward's attempts to thwart me."

"Well then, all's well."

She gestured with her hands. "Do you know he came to me yesterday afternoon to tell me personally of his decision to come out and openly admit to being a Christian?"

Vaney scowled and flung the end of his cloak over his shoulder. The inside of his robe was lined with red satin. "Don't say that word in my presence!" he roared.

"All right, all right. From here on we'll refer to this merry band only as fundamentalists. Will that satisfy you, Doctor? I must tell you that Clave, that toad, is also among their number. I received his letter of resignation yesterday as well."

"You still have the Josiah Files?" he asked.

"Yes, Dr. Stodge, I do."

"I would like them."

"I'm sure you would. Never mind; they are safe, and when Mars becomes ours and the Chris—I mean fundamentalists are defeated, then you and I shall rip the Josiah Files, page by page, into an open fire pit."

"How graphic, High Priestess." Stodge was smiling now.

"Do you know that they had the audacity to take possession of and move right into that old stone church building in Sector 44, the one next to the WOC? They've walked right in."

Stodge stopped walking and looked over at her. He seemed genuinely surprised by this news. "How dare they?" he asked.

"How dare they indeed, yet they did."

"We should destroy that church with them in it."

"Vaney Stodge, you're so impetuous. That's not the way at all. I think we should let them go for a while. See what they do—let them feel safe for a while and then bring in the big guns."

"I say we kill them now."

"Oh, we shall; we shall kill them—but *I* will call the shots."

Stodge turned away from her and looked out over the night sky to the lights of the vast city, the city which went on and on in the darkness. All would be his one day. All his and not Morag's, not the High Priestess's. He mumbled something but his words were lost to a sudden chilling wind that surged across the rooftop garden and whipped their cloaks around their legs, molding them to their bodies. Fighting against the sudden squall, they held on to their cloaks and headpieces and made their way to the staircase descent.

The High Priestess took one last look at the sky before the door closed behind them. The storm was worsening.

44 ✝

The Christians' very first public meeting in the stone church would be the celebration of the Lord's Supper. They had wanted to meet on Sunday mornings in keeping with ancient practice but since Sunday was a working day just like every other day, they decided against it. Working people had a choice of two days off per week, and the majority of people, for some unknown reason, had for decades taken Fridays and Saturdays off. Thursday evening after work was chosen as the time for the public meetings.

The group decided that Edward would officiate. Edward was taking more and more of a leadership role in the fledgling church. He had recently moved his robots, computers, and demichips into the office—the office that held so many memories for Clave. A few in the Community had looked to Clave for leadership, but Clave declined. He told them that he was still a baby Christian, still had so much to learn, so far to go. He wasn't ready, he said.

Clave also resigned from the WOC. He sent a written letter to the High Priestess explaining that since he had read the Bible he had come to see that the God of the Bible was not the god of the WOC. Realizing this, he stated that he could no longer fulfill the duties and obligations of the World Order Church and asked to be relieved of them.

It was liberating. No longer did he fear being followed everywhere. No longer were the Christians forced to enter and exit the Safehouse by a dozen different doorways.

It was a curious procession, therefore, that made its way to the old stone church that cool, spring day for the first public meeting. Residents of Sector 44 lined up to watch the strange parade go by. Able-bodied community members pushed wheelchairs and talked amiably to the open-mouthed crowd, inviting them to come along. Very few of them had ever seen a wheelchair, much less the people that sat in them. Tommi and Dos scampered alongside.

"Hiya," Tommi called to the crowd. Most of them turned away from him, not knowing how to react.

Clave and Diona entered the church and walked quickly to the front pew. Tommi sat between them, and Dos curled up on the floor at Tommi's feet. On the platform, Sharan began playing a medley of worship songs.

Clave looked around. The place was filling up fast. Everyone from the Community had come, along with many from Sector 44. Clave recognized his former accountant and his family, Risa from the jewelry store, the lady from the bakery down the street, someone named Lou that Star knew from the hospital, and Mac's daughter. He saw Diona look around a few times. He knew she was looking for her old friend Kara. Kara hadn't come.

Tommi squirmed in his chair, conscious of a strange excitement, and a few times Diona leaned over, a finger to her lips to shush him. Dos remained asleep on the floor at Tommi's feet, which was good, because Clave had said earlier, "The first time Dos makes a noise I'll take him out." No one seemed to mind the gentle dog. He had "attended" so many meetings in the Safehouse that it just seemed natural for him to be there as well.

The service was about to begin. Diona turned in her chair, looked over at Clave, and mouthed the words, "Where is

Nori?" He shook his head. Diona shrugged. She'd been saving the place beside her.

Lately Nori was spending less and less time with Star on the computer and more and more time in the kitchen. This made more sense to Clave, knowing her propensity toward food. Maybe his earlier apprehension had been unfounded. Maybe she really was fitting in here.

A plate of small pieces of bread was passed around first. Clave held the piece of bread in his fingers and bowed his head. As Edward gave the now familiar reading, Clave thought about Christ's broken body, broken so that I can live, he thought. Following the reading and prayer the entire congregation ate the bread in unison.

Dos whimpered slightly and shifted his bulk. Tommi bent down and put a finger to his mouth and said, "Dossy, Dossy, be quiet. Shush, shush."

Clave smiled down at the young boy, a young boy so full of life and love and eagerness to please, one of the most affectionate children he had ever known, and yet a child who according to the law of the land should not even be there. Tommi slipped off his shoes and rubbed his socked feet on the dog's soft furry back.

Diona frowned, but decided to let it go. Next, the group passed around a tray of tiny wine glasses. At the front Sharan played a hauntingly sweet melody.

The tray was passed to Diona and she took one of the small cups. She was passing it along to Clave when Tommi reached out.

"I help you pass it, I help you," he stage-whispered up to Diona.

"Be careful then," she said, keeping a firm hand on one end of the tray.

"I be careful. I be careful," he promised.

But he wasn't careful enough. He took the tray in his two small chubby hands, and when Diona lost control of her side of the tray, crash! The tray with a hundred little cups of red fluid spilled all over Tommi, all over the chair, all over the floor, and all over Dos, who immediately yelped and jumped up disturbing the solemnity of the ceremony. Cries of exclamation were heard all over the church. Diona dabbed red liquid from Tommi's shirt and he went immediately into her arms for a hug. "I sorry," he cried loudly.

"Okay, okay," she said soothingly.

Star and Simon, who had been sitting on the other side of Clave, left discreetly. They returned with wet paper towels which they used to sop up Tommi, the seat, and Dos, but Dos was already licking the red fluid off his coat. Clave and the ushers went about setting the glasses right.

At the front Edward smiled and made a comment about this being a real family and that they'd all get back on track in a few moments. Sharan continued to play while the rest of the congregation was served. All would have begun again except Dos began choking; violent spasms racked his body. Clave, thinking that perhaps he had swallowed one of the small glasses, tried to check the dog's throat.

"Dossy, be quiet, shush, shush," said Tommi.

Clave, aided by Simon and Star, couldn't find any obstruction in the dog's throat, yet Dos continued hacking, whimpering, heaving, and retching. Edward was trying to keep the service from utterly falling apart, and Sharan continued to play, although she herself was clearly more interested in the little drama going on in the corner.

When Edward lifted his tiny glass and urged the congregation to partake of the communion wine, Hirsch bellowed, "No!"

Everyone stopped and looked at him, including Clave, who held the dog's head in his lap. At that "no," Clave felt the life leave his old friend. The dog's eyes rolled back, the head sagged. Clave laid the yellow, furry head down and looked helplessly at Diona who held Tommi in her arms.

"Dossy's sleeping," said Tommi. "Wake up, Dossy. Time to get up. No more sleepy head." As Diona clung to the child, she lowered her head onto his little shoulders and began to cry for a lumbering old friend. Clave stroked the furry head and wept, too.

"Don't drink it! Don't drink the wine," Hirsch waved his hands in the air and wheeled himself to the front. After a brief conversation at the front, Edward turned to the congregation.

"Something may be wrong with the wine," he said. "Clave's dog just died after drinking it."

A gasp went up from the group. "He may have died from something else, and we'll check that out, but at this point we don't want to take any chances." Ushers quickly retrieved all of the full wine glasses from a confused congregation.

Edward dismissed the group, and Sharan played softly. A few left, but most preferred to stand together in groups and talk. A few came forward to talk to Diona, who sat on the front seat still crying and hugging the little boy.

Star and Simon carried Dos's body out, while Hirsch sat at the very front of the church and began to pray. One by one people joined him until the entire congregation was raising a single prayer toward heaven.

✝ ✝ ✝

At the Safehouse that evening, Star exposed a droplet of the wine to various tests. Then she told Clave, Hirsch, and Edward that it wasn't just a bad batch of wine, but that the wine had been poisoned, deliberately, with a new drug that instantly kills.

"It's basically in the same drug family as the pills Diona was taking," she said. "The molecular configuration is only slightly different. It looks like it was probably manufactured by the same company."

"Morag!" shouted Clave, clenching his fists. "First she tries to kill my wife and then she kills my dog." Edward placed a hand on Clave's shoulder.

"The question is," said Edward, "how did someone from Morag's camp sneak in here and poison the wine?"

They called in the two women who had prepared the communion elements. Both of them shook their heads, their eyes wide. They had seen no one, heard no one.

Betta, a woman with a mopful of steel gray curls and thick, dark eyebrows said, "But I think you should talk to Nori."

"Nori—why?" said Clave, but a knot was already beginning to twist in his stomach.

"Well, she was the last one with the wine glasses. She'd be able to tell you if she saw anybody."

Sara, a small, round woman who always wore a faded pink apron, added, "I haven't seen her since the service started. I don't know where she went."

Nori was gone. Everyone said they saw her just before the service, but no one had seen her since.

"Maybe she's been kidnapped by the people who poisoned the wine," suggested one of the women.

"If that's the case, we'd better start looking," said another. "She could be in danger."

But Clave had a different idea. Quietly and alone, Clave made his way down the hall to Nori's room, telling himself it couldn't be, it just couldn't be. But it was. Clave entered her room. Empty. All of her clothes, all of her things—gone. Suddenly he couldn't breathe. A deep sob originated from somewhere in the depths of his being. She had done it. He groaned and fell to the floor beside her bed, her empty bed. She had even taken the sheets and blankets. No, she hadn't quite taken everything. She had left one thing behind. On her end table Clave noticed the Bible demichip he had given her the day after she arrived.

"Oh, Daddy, how wonderful," she had said and hugged it to her chest. "I'll cherish it always." She deserves an Academy Award, Clave thought wryly.

It was unthinkable that she would want to kill them all. Her own parents. Her own dog. Did she even know that he was dead? Clave covered his face with his hands and began to cry, great wrenching sobs. An idea came to him then of just withdrawing, taking Diona and quietly fleeing, like Nori had. He and his family had caused nothing but pain from his arrival. How could he face the members of the Community again?

"Oh, God," he cried. "How could Nori do this? How could Nori not see? After all those months how could she not see the wonderful difference that Christ makes?"

He remembered the night Nori had come, a rain-soaked, solitary figure walking forlornly amidst the rubble of their burned estate declaring that she had so many questions, so many problems, and she wanted Jesus to fix them. That was her final exam in Drama 101 and she had passed. Clave believed her and had taken her back to the Safehouse shelter.

"Oh, God," he prayed through his anguish. "You've got to make her come to her senses." He paused then and bowed beside her stripped bed. "I command, in the name of Jesus Christ, that wherever she is right now that You will turn her around and have her walk back here and repent, walk back and become Your child." He rose then, confident that God would answer his prayer spoken in faith.

Images of the prodigal son returning and Clave watching, ready for the great bear hug filled his mind. He had all power, didn't he, through the Father? He clenched his fists and walked around the small room. If he had enough faith, she would come walking back. He just knew it.

But then another image wandered into the corners of his mind. That same Father, the perfect Father, letting the child go, letting her go even though He knew the child would grovel in hog's food. He began to realize the senselessness of his demanding God to physically turn Nori around. That is not how God deals with us, he thought. It's not how He deals with me, forcing me, commanding me to obey Him. He gives me choices. Nori has choices too, and Nori has made her choice.

He knelt beside her bed again, "I can only pray that You lead people into her life who will help get her turned around, so she *wants* to come back."

Clave also realized something else. A long time ago he should have gone to Hirsch and Edward about his suspicions about Nori. It could have saved everyone a lot of grief. But he chose to keep them to himself because of some pride that they would think less of him if they could see what kind of a family he had. He purposely "hid" his misgivings and his head filled with pride when Betta or one of the ladies would say to him, "She is such a wonderful child. You must be very proud of her."

Clave picked up Nori's little Bible demichip. Underneath it, drawn in crimson ink on the fiberglass desk was an inverted cross inside a triangle. That symbol again. He didn't know what it was, but he knew it represented something evil. He groaned again and fell on her bed. Clave stayed that way for a long time, cradling her Bible handreader and praying, praying and crying out before the Lord.

45

The faces around the room were solemn when Clave returned, still clutching Nori's demichip. He stood before them for a moment and said nothing. Edward broke the silence.

"We all think Nori may be in some kind of danger," he said. "We've been talking about it and feel that a few of us should go out and try and locate her."

Clave remained still. Diona looked at him hopefully from across the room. Clave walked over and stood beside Diona.

"If Nori's in danger, she put herself there," he said slowly, articulating each word. "Nori is gone. All of her things are gone. Nori is the one who poisoned the wine."

A collective gasp went up from the group.

Diona rose from her seat. "How can you say that? How can you say that, Clave?"

Others nodded in agreement.

Clave put up his hand. "Think about it—Nori was here when Diona was poisoned. In fact, she made *sure* her mother took her poisonous pills three times a day."

"But Clave, she didn't know. She—"

"And," said Clave, "when the Bibles disappeared, Nori was here; she just happened to take this very real interest in Star and our computer network system before it happened."

"But Nori couldn't have done that, she couldn't have," protested Star. "The job was far too technical."

"I'm not saying she did it all by herself, but she was here and by carefully watching she could have found out the password. If all of the communities had someone on the inside—all of the passwords could have been known. And now, when the communion wine is poisoned, Nori is suddenly gone. Oh, and I should tell you, she took almost everything, including the bed linens, which don't even belong to her. But she left two things—her Bible and a little drawing she scratched onto her desk, a symbol in red of an upside-down cross inside a triangle."

The group was silent. No one knew what to say.

Finally, Edward spoke, "The symbol of the Alliance of Dagon."

"What?"

"The Alliance of Dagon."

"Who is Dagon?" asked Diona.

"He was an ancient Philistine god. He's mentioned in the Old Testament."

"And he's still worshiped today?" asked Clave.

"It looks that way," answered Edward. "Although we've never been completely sure of just how big his following was."

"I've seen that symbol before," said Clave. "It was painted on my WOC office wall in blood. I also saw it on a necklace."

"I'm sure I've seen it at Morag's," Diona told him. "I can't remember where, but I'm sure I've seen it."

"His followers are everywhere," said Edward.

"But I don't understand how Nori could have gotten mixed up in a group like this," said Star. "She was so nice."

"Dagon deceives. There are a lot of cult activities these days, hundreds of legal and illegal orders, but may I say that Dagon is probably the strongest, the most vicious, and the most evil. Its leaders want complete control of the universe, and we Christians stand in their way. We pose a very real threat to them."

"So the High Priestess could well be involved in the top echelons of this group," said Clave.

"That I'm not sure of," said Edward. "I've known her well for six years. She has her own reasons for wanting control—greed and power—but I'm fairly sure she's not mixed up with the Dagon Alliance. But I feel Stodge is, and this union of the High Priestess and Stodge has me worried."

"So Stodge could be the leader of the Alliance?"

"That's one of their best kept secrets—who is the supreme leader of the Alliance of Dagon. It could be Stodge. I just don't know."

Hirsch looked up from his chair. "Why didn't you tell us about this before, Edward?"

"I didn't know the Alliance of Dagon still existed. We thought it had died out. Also, we were underground. There was no need to know. No one in the Alliance even suspected that there were Christians around."

"But now they know," said Hirsch.

"And that puts us in danger."

"Not if the Lord is on our side!" thundered Hirsch.

"What does the symbol mean?" asked Simon.

Edward answered. "The triangle is a parody of the Father, Son, and Holy Spirit, the upside-down cross is a travesty of the Cross of Christ. It's meant as a symbol of disrespect."

"I still don't see how Nori could get involved with such people," said Betta. "She was such a sweet girl. I thought she was my friend."

"I thought she was my daughter," said Diona, with tears in her eyes.

46

Morag was sitting on the large chair Stodge normally used. It was the only one in the room which would contain her bulk. Today she wore layers of pink and mauve chiffon, what looked like miles and miles of the stuff draped around her large body. Translucent scarves streamed around her face and hair, but it wasn't enough to hide her multiplicity of chins.

Without the candlelight beaming out from the skulls, and the blood and dancing, the room looked like any ordinary warehouse, like an airjet hangar, or a garage used for servicing hovervehicles. The little brown spots on the floor could just as easily be fuel stains. The heavy wooden table could be someone's work bench, the gouges made by clumsy robots dropping their tools.

"The Master is not pleased," Stodge said. He was pacing back and forth in front of Morag.

"You're right about that," she said. "Dagon is not pleased."

"The hosts are not pleased. I can sense it. I can sense all of the armies in disarray."

"Cut the gibberish, Stodge, and tell me what went wrong with our little ace in the hole." She flung a pale piece of chiffon around her neck.

"I don't know." He stopped suddenly and looked at her. "I don't know. For some reason they just didn't drink it. I waited with the HV on, surely it would be on the HV, I told myself; something of this magnitude would make the evening news, yet nothing. So I called over to the WOC. I got this little freckle-faced kid on the screen, I told him, I said 'Go over next door and see what's going on.' So he does, and then he calls me back. You know what he says? 'Dr. Stodge,' he says, 'Dr. Stodge, there's a whole bunch of them in there meditating or something.' " Stodge raised one fist toward heaven. "Nothing makes me madder. Nothing!"

"So they didn't drink it."

"Right, Morag. They didn't drink it."

"They are becoming a powerful force, Vaney, and I don't like it."

"We've got to get rid of them."

"You mean *you've* got to get rid of them. My hands are clean."

"Me?"

"Or I blow this little operation of yours sky-high," she gestured with a sweep of a flabby, draped arm.

"What about your little operation, Morag?" he protested.

"My hands are clean, Vaney. Or have you forgotten? I run an innocent little New Age Retreat for spiritual wholeness. Now have you figured out what to do with the High Priestess?"

"It's already in the works."

"Don't fail me, Vaney, my son, don't fail me."

47

The following afternoon all was quiet within the Safehouse. In the front room Diona sat in a chair with the newspaper on her handreader. Clave sat across from her, a book keyed up on his handreader, but he wasn't reading. He couldn't concentrate. Others sat quietly reading or trying to. Meals that day were subdued affairs. No one felt like talking. Though it wasn't voiced, everyone realized just how close they had all come to dying, as Dos had died. Even normally boisterous Tommi sat in a corner with a couple of his toy hovercars around him on the floor. Every once in a while he would look up and say, "Where's Dossy? Where's Dossy? Nori gone, too?"

In the far corner of the room, the HV was turned to the all-news channel with the volume low. Clave felt that some of the people, including Diona, carried a faint hope that Nori had been kidnapped, and that the story of her abductors would soon be aired. But Clave knew this was not the case. He didn't know how he knew it, but he knew it.

The quiet was shattered in the late afternoon when Sam yelled, "Hey, look at this! Louder," he shouted into the volume control.

"—and that Vaney Stodge has done what no other leader in the history of the three worlds has successfully done."

"What has he done?" called Clave.

"Shh, they'll tell us," said Sam.

On the screen, hundreds of reporters were buzzing around the presidential palace. The group in the front room moved their chairs to face the HV.

A slim, blonde reporter, clad from head to foot in shimmery gold, spoke into the microphone. "The High Priestess, who has been in office for more than two decades, is deposed in what some analysts are calling the biggest religious coup in history."

The group in the front room sat stunned. They watched as the scene shifted first from the grounds of the presidential palace to its massive Grand Office where Stodge himself sat proudly behind the crystal desk saying to the cameras, "It's the will of the people. It's what the people want."

Then the scene shifted back to the HV studio where various political analysts and psychologists were interviewed, one by one, as to the political ramifications of the event.

The little group in the front room of the Safehouse watched in bewilderment, silent as the broadcast went on and on through the night, interrupting soap operas, nova music concerts, scent-vision movies, and sitcoms.

Finally Edward spoke. "So he has finally done it." He rose then, a grim expression on his face.

48

The High Priestess sat on a low stool, her knees tucked under a thin robe. She faced a fireplace where sizzling artificial logs wafted heat into an already stuffy room. Even though the place was stifling, the High Priestess shivered and clutched a faded, woolen shawl tightly across her thin shoulders. Kiki's gilt cage was on a round glass table next to her.

The Priestess looked up into the faces of her guests. "So you have heard the news and you have come to gloat," she said.

"No. We haven't come to gloat," Edward said.

This was the first time Clave had ever seen her in person. As she shrugged beneath her threadbare shawl, she looked smaller somehow than he had always imagined her; shrunken and drawn, the flesh on her face was pinched and tight over the protruding cheekbones. She wore no makeup today, leaving a gray cast to her skin. Gone were the red lips and the high penciled eyebrows, arched in defiance. She wasn't wearing her headpiece, and sparse black hair stuck out all around her head in no particular style.

"How dare you come—you betrayer!" she snapped. Edward sat there and looked into her eyes. She continued, "And you, Dr. Hammill, will be happy to know, will be *pleased* to know that I have been invited, imagine that, *invited*, to take the directorship of the WOC in Sector 44. Your old stomping grounds, I believe."

Clave moved closer. "We didn't come to gloat," he said gently. "We came to help you. We came to offer you a way out."

"A way out, hmmm, you mean like join, perhaps, your merry little band of fundamentalists?" She pulled the faded piece of wool around her more tightly and spat out the words, "I'd rather be reincarnated as a garden slug!"

Sweat beaded on Clave's forehead, yet the High Priestess shivered. "I am surrounded by betrayers. Even my servants have betrayed me, have gone over to Vaney and Morag."

"Jesus loves you. He would never leave you." Clave wiped his brow with his handkerchief.

The High Priestess ignored him, rose, and walked with slow, mincing steps, like an old woman, to a wall safe. Pressing her palm against the lock, the door opened. She reached in and pulled out two books, and with a sudden show of strength flung them across the room. Clave caught one; the other fell to the floor, its pages fluttering.

"Take these books. Get them out of my sight," she said, squatting back down on her stool. "Vaney, the slime, is pestering me for them. I'll tell him I destroyed the Josiah Files. Oh, and I'd advise you to watch out for him. He'll kill both of you on sight."

Clave bent down to retrieve the old Bible. "Come with us," he said. "You'd be welcome at the Community. You'd be safe there."

"Kiki and I will stay here, won't we, Kiki?" She opened the cage door and reached in for her pet. As she lifted the little ball of fur out of the cage her mouth twisted into an expression of horror. She screamed and screamed and screamed until Edward reached out and put his arms around her shoulders. She pushed him away, and Clave saw the lifeless little furry body fall to the floor. She flew to pick up the animal, shrieking at Edward and Clave to leave her alone, to please just go away and leave her alone.

And they left her then, sobbing on the floor, wrapped up in a dingy shawl and cradling a dead hamster.

49

Persecution was stepping up. Without being told they all knew it. Sam had been fired from his job at Venus Reclamators for "theft." When some highly sensitive and expensive machinery parts were "found" in Sam's work locker, he was fired on the spot. Management was told that Sam was a member of that growing group of radical fundamentalists and that they were planning to use the parts to build bombs. Sam, his wife, and their two small children moved into the Safehouse, along with Star, who had also been "released from her duties" at the hospital.

According to rumor, someone spent a lot of time checking back-hospital records and "discovered" that Star had been running an "illegal baby-selling operation." Allegations were that she had kept poor handicapped souls from being "released" into a better life, and instead "sold" them to families of a cult group. The story devastated Star; she had received no money for the infants, but often spent vast sums of her own money caring for the babies until a Christian family could be found somewhere on the planet.

Money at the Community was becoming scarce. Those who still received salaries shared them with those who didn't, but the Safehouse residents were eating more and more of the grade B or C variety of synthetic vegetables.

Periodically, police raided the stone church hoping to find some reason to shut it down. Health inspectors arrived always during the middle of a service demanding to examine the refurbished kitchen. After hours of tedious inspection, inspectors and police would walk out disgruntled and bad-tempered when they couldn't find anything amiss.

The WOC next door still attracted crowds. One of Clave's former assistants, an energetic red-haired woman, had taken over the directorship. The High Priestess had said, "thanks, but no thanks" and following the coup and the death of Kiki, had gone into seclusion.

Clave and Edward had presented the Josiah Files to Hirsch, who eagerly read through his great-grandfather's journals. With the help of Edward and Clave, Hirsch began working on the history of the Northridge Community Church.

Vaney Stodge, now the head of the combined NWO and the WOC, was gradually bringing in changes the Christians feared. Elevation was now, of course, mandatory. His troops were cracking down on drugstores that sold prescriptions to those over the age of 65. Through her work, Clave's sister, Katron, had connections and was still able to secure medicines for their parents, but Clave knew that it wouldn't be long before Katron and people like her would be investigated. Already Christians were investigating a couple of new Safehouse locations, places that the disabled and elderly could flee to.

Stodge was also seeking ways to outlaw the new, growing Christian church. "Dangerous, radical fundamentalists," he called them. Some speculated that the real power behind the throne was Morag, that somehow she called the shots, but no one could be sure.

The one bright spot was that Tommi seemed to be slowly coming around. After Dos died, the little boy had become withdrawn and difficult, but the influx of many more full-time residents with children cheered him up. Sam's two children spent a lot of time with Tommi, reading to him, playing computer games with him, or playing tag or ball in the covered courtyard.

They still held their Thursday evening public meetings in the stone church, but Sam, Rawn, and a few other men stood at the back and kept an eye out for ominous-looking strangers.

It was on a Thursday evening that Vaney Stodge tried for the last time to destroy the Christians. Tensions that evening were high as the faithful ascended the steps to the stone church. There seemed to be an electricity in the air; they spoke to one another in hushed tones.

"I heard on the news that he's after Mars next," Rawn said.

"He'll never get Mars; there will be a war first," Clave told him.

An older woman nodded. "Marsians will never stand for Earth rule. I've got a cousin on Mars. She says they'll never condescend to him."

"Still—" Rawn said sadly.

"How can he do this?" Diona asked.

Simon glanced back at Diona. "He's building up troops, that's for sure."

A bald, sixty-six-year-old pharmacist spoke up. "Do you know they came into my drugstore the other day and demanded to see all my prescription reports and the ages of the recipients?"

"I wasn't the only Christian fired," Sam said wearily. "I heard that the silicon factory in Sector 4 is firing all those who admit to being Christians."

"We've just got to stand up for our rights!" the pharmacist said.

"We've just got to pray!" Hirsch told them as they crowded into the sanctuary for pre-service prayer. As he began the meeting, he said, "A year ago, and for many, many years before, I prayed for this kind of persecution to come upon our churches. We were so well-hidden that no one knew about us. You had to know five secret passwords and take twenty-five elevators to even get down to the Safehouse."

A few faces smiled.

He continued, "But we weren't in the real world—yes, maybe there was a time, back during Aquarius when we had to go underground for a time to regroup and plan our strategy. But we were never meant to stay there. And not for 150 years!"

A few heads nodded.

Clave sat at the back with Sam. It was their turn to keep watch. At first Clave thought the noise came from the front of the auditorium, a fluttering sort of sound, like the leaves of those large artificial trees—the ones they put around shopping malls—rustling in the breeze. He looked across the room, but everyone was sitting as still as he was, faces turned toward Hirsch. Clave went back to listening to the man in the wheelchair.

"And now that we are no longer underground, but have opened our windows, opened our doors, opened our hearts, have we been decimated? No! Our numbers have increased! We have doubled in size. So many more hungry and needy people have come to know the Lord. You know what this tells me? This tells me that we don't need a Safehouse with twenty-five different doorways. Jesus is our Safehouse!"

A few amens were heard throughout the room.

There it was again, that fluttering sound, only louder this time, almost like a flock of birds. Clave was sure now that it was coming from somewhere outside. Trying not to attract too much attention, he got up and walked to the front door and opened it a crack. Nothing. Nothing but blackness in the street outside.

He wondered if anyone else had heard it, but back in the sanctuary all of the faces were either looking down at their handreaders or up at Hirsch. It was probably nothing. Clave sat down again.

The third time he heard it, Clave slipped quietly into the foyer. It had a clear window to the outside. He lifted the blind and looked outside. Still nothing.

"You heard it too?" Sam had walked up behind him.

Clave nodded. "What could it be?"

"I don't have a clue, but I thought I'd better find out. I don't trust anybody these days."

They stood side by side for a few moments in the darkened foyer staring out into the empty street. Even the WOC across the alley was dark and quiet. But the sound was unmistakable now. Something or many things were flapping, whirring, buzzing. Or singing? And then stillness again.

"What's out there?" Clave asked.

"I'm going to get the binoculars," Sam said.

When Sam left, Clave moved closer to the window. As he gazed out into the night, a black hovervan crept silently on its cushion of air down the deserted alley. Its lights were out. It settled down directly across from them, right next to the back stairs of the WOC. No one emerged. It just sat there. Watching?

Sam returned with two sets of high-powered infrared binoculars and gave one to Clave. They stared at the van.

"Look, Clave, into the front of the van. The front window."

Clave directed his vision through the front window of the van. Both the driver and the passenger's seats were empty, but along the dashboard he saw a variety of dials and graphic readouts. "What's all that?" he asked.

"I don't know, but it's definitely not your ordinary family van. Clave, can you see the steering wheel?"

Clave directed his binoculars until he could see what Sam saw. The insignia in the center of the wheel was that symbol again—the Alliance of Dagon.

"Sam, what should we do?"

"Look, Clave—" The side door of the van opened and three black hooded individuals with large laser guns and rocket launchers stepped out onto the pavement. As they watched, other vehicles began pulling up behind the van—armored cars, tanks, vans, and robotic tanks. Clave couldn't see around the corners, but he suspected that the entire stone building was being surrounded.

"We've got to alert the others, Sam." Leaving Sam to keep watch, he rushed into the sanctuary.

". . . and clad in the armor of God, the full armor of God, we will come out victorious," Hirsch was saying.

"Hirsch!" yelled Clave as he ran forward. "We're under attack. Get these little ones to safety. The place is surrounded by Stodge's men. Do we have any weapons?"

"A few," answered Edward. "I'll get them."

Horrified gasps went up from the congregation.

Mothers picked up their little ones in blankets and carried them down the stairs to the basement rooms. Wheelchairs were pushed quickly down the newly installed ramps to safety.

"What's happening?" Clave asked running back to the foyer.

"I don't know. Nothing, it seems," answered Sam.

Clave picked up his binoculars again. Edward came in with two small laser handguns. "This is all we have." Besides the three standing outside the van, there were dozens, no, hundreds who stood outside of the vehicles, their weapons by their sides.

"Talk about David and Goliath," Sam said.

"They must be waiting for some central command," said Clave.

Sam nodded grimly. "We should be better armed. We never expected anything like this. A few strategically placed high-power lasers and we could be rid of them now. I wish we were armed."

"We are armed," said Hirsch. He had wheeled himself into the foyer. "We have the most powerful armor in all the worlds—the armor of God."

He turned toward the sanctuary. "I will be up at the front, praying."

He bowed his head. One by one, others joined him, pulling up chairs or kneeling right where they were. Mothers returned with their blanketed babies. Fathers came back holding the hands of their older children. Wheelchairs were pushed back up the ramp; the elderly, some with walkers, some with canes, slowly made their way back to the circle. And in one accord, they began to pray.

They prayed for a quarter-hour, half an hour, while Sam kept watch. Every five minutes or so Sam whispered down to Clave, "They're just standing there."

About forty minutes later, Clave heard it again, that light, gentle flapping sound—fluttering like the wings of a hundred butterflies. It was odd, but it reminded Clave of singing. It must have had that same effect on Sharan because she grabbed her harp and began to play. Softly, quietly at first she played and sang, "I will praise Your name forever and ever." Gradually the others joined her, "I will exalt You my God, the King. I will exalt You, my God, the King."

Finally, the entire community was singing, dancing, and praising God. It was a joyful song, a lively song.

> *I will exalt You*
> *I will exalt You my God the King*
> *I will praise Your name*
> *I will praise Your name forever and ever.*
> *Every day I will praise You*
> *And extol Your name*
> *And extol Your name forever.*

As they sang, it seemed to Clave that the very angels in heaven were singing with them.

"They're leaving," called Sam from the window.

"What?" Edward exclaimed.

"I don't know what happened." There was joy in Sam's voice. "They're all getting in their vehicles and just driving away."

"Praise God!" Clave shouted.

"Praise God!" Diona whispered behind him.

"What happened?" Tommi asked.

Tears formed in Star's eyes. "Why didn't they attack us? Surely they outnumbered us."

"Does the word *miracle* ring a bell?" asked Hirsch.

"But miracles were things that only happened a long time ago," said Simon, an incredulous look on his face.

"Maybe it's about time they started happening again," said Edward.

And then Hirsch voice commanded his Bible handreader and scrolled to 1 Samuel 5. He read:

> *Then the Philistines took the ark of God and brought it from Ebenezer to Ashdod. When the Philistines took the ark of God, they brought it into the house of Dagon and set it by Dagon. And when the people of Ashdod arose early in the morning, there was Dagon, fallen on its face to the earth before the ark of the LORD. So they took Dagon and set it in its place again. And when they arose early the next morning, there was Dagon, fallen on its face to the ground before the ark of the LORD. The head of Dagon and both the palms of its hands were broken off on the threshold; only Dagon's torso was left of it.*

He paused and looked up. "We serve a mighty God, One who can totally crush the enemy."

"Amen!" said Edward.

"Praise the Lord!" Clave cried.

"Hallelujah!" said a chorus of voices.

50

Splintered shards of white-gray skull and fragments of wax candle lay in haphazard piles all over the floor like debris washed up on a beach. A heavy silver scepter in his hands, Dr. Vaney Stodge raged through the cavernous room systematically smashing the skulls. Their toothy grins finally died as they shattered on the cement floor.

"It's all come to nothing," fumed Stodge. "Nothing! There is nothing left."

He smashed the wand down on the wooden table. The sheer force of his fury dented the heavy surface. Then he picked up the silver chalice and hurled it across the room. It clunked hollowly against the far wall.

"It was almost happening!" he bellowed. "We have never been this close before. Never before in all of the centuries have we been this close to defeating the hosts of heaven in annulling the prophesied Word!" He raised the silver stick high in the air. "We could have done it. We would have done it! And now—" He took the scepter in both hands and smashed it against a crystal and silver candelabra with all the force of a baseball player winding up for a grand slam. It shattered to the floor in a thousand pieces. "And the Master is not pleased with me. I hate it when the Master is not pleased with me."

"He's not alone," said Sister Morag. "I'm not pleased with you either. But I've told you that before."

Stodge dropped the scepter to his side and whirled around. A mountain of airy yellow chiffon stood in the doorway.

"Why do you keep coming in here uninvited? What do you want, Morag?" he demanded.

"It's too bad I need you," she said, gliding into the room, clouds of fabric following her. She stood in the middle of the wreckage and looked around.

"Tsk, tsk, my dear. Such a violent temper for a universal leader of church and state. As I said before," she picked up a piece of jawbone with teeth intact and studied it, "it's too bad I need you. If I didn't, I'd have you terminated." She placed the jawbone on the wooden table and looked at him fully. "The only reason I need you is because you're such a perfect specimen of a man. With that body, my dear, you could have been a movie star—or a political leader." And then she laughed. "And that's why I need you, my dear."

"Morag—"

"I just want to know one thing, Vaney," she said, walking around him looking him up and down as she did so. "What happened *this* time?"

Stodge scowled and looked away from her.

"I don't know, Morag. I just don't know."

"Try, Vaney, my boy. Try telling me in your own words exactly what happened."

"I sent in my best people, my *best* people to destroy that entire building and all the inhabitants."

"And then what?" She scratched her bulbous nose with a chubby ringed finger.

"They took rocket launchers and grenades. I'm not talking small stuff."

"Right, you're not talking small stuff. Go on."

"Well, all they told me was that they couldn't get past."

"Get past what?"

"They merely said they couldn't get past a huge army of trained and equipped bodyguards with glowing face visors."

"Glowing face visors?" she mocked.

"Glowing face visors. Their words exactly."

"I'm not impressed, Vaney."

"There's more."

"I can't wait."

Stodge looked away. "The bodyguards were singing."

"Singing."

"That's what they said, Morag, singing, standing all over the church, on the gables, on the window ledges, on the roof, and singing."

"So tell me, Vaney, my boy, why didn't your army just destroy that military choir? I mean, you've been telling me all along that you have the firepower—not to worry, you were building up your troops."

"They said they couldn't get past the singing."

"Incredible."

"That's what I said."

"So, the fundamentalists hired highly trained bodyguards?"

"It would seem so. They are very resourceful." Stodge laid his scepter down on the wooden table and faced her, his palms open. He tried a half smile, "I'm afraid I'm out of options."

"You'd better not be. I'm counting on you, my boy. Dagon is counting on you."

"So what do we do now?"

"Your plan is obviously not working."

"So what do we *do*?" he repeated.

"The question is what do *you* do? Change tactics, I should think. These bombings and firings are only making them stronger. Look how the fundamentalists have grown in recent months. I think it's time you went from Plan A to Plan B."

"Which is?"

"That's for you to figure out."

With that Morag turned and swished out of the room. The door clanged shut behind her. Even though it was cool, cold even, in the dungeon-like room, Dr. Vaney Stodge was covered in sweat.

51

Clave sat at the kitchen table and looked out the window at the late afternoon summer sun. He was alone. Diona was at the university attending a demonstration in color laser sculpture. Spread out in front of him on the kitchen table was a letter which had come by interplanetary robot courier just a few minutes before. He got up and walked around their three-room apartment.

He and Diona had moved into it four months ago, just after the attack on the stone church, the attack that went nowhere. It was small, "cozy," Diona called it, but with the fire insurance still unsettled, they really had no choice. They didn't want to live forever at the Safehouse, although they had been assured many times that they were welcome there. So they had dug into their savings account and decided to rent a small place.

Clave sat down again and absently ran the edge of the letter between his thumb and forefinger. Its contents excited and frightened him. "Is this what You mean, Lord, about going?" he asked.

The Hammills had been through a lot in the past year. Clave had seen his life radically change from a self-assured WOC director into a Christian, dependent solely upon God. They had gone from living in a twenty-room mansion to a three-room apartment. Despite it all, they had come through. He couldn't believe the change in Diona. She whose mind, whose spirit, whose body was almost broken by Morag's so-called treatment, was now a new person.

A few weeks ago she had told him about her latest project. She was working her way through the Gospels and decided to start a series of paintings depicting the life of Christ. But she wanted to picture Christ as He might look in the cloaks and garments of the twenty-second century and not in the robes of thousands of years ago. She spent almost every waking hour on her new project. A few nights of late, Clave had awakened to find the other side of the bed empty. When he padded bleary-eyed into the kitchen, there would be Diona hunched over her sketch book.

As he sat there holding the letter, he thought about the stone church, Northridge Bible Church, as it was called now. There was a growing nucleus of people committed to serving Christ, committed to be a force, clad in the armor of God. He still could not walk into the back office, now Edward's office, without reliving how God met him there on a cold, wintry day, and how a man from 200 years ago had led him to Christ.

Clave flattened the letter out on the desk. For a number of weeks now, he had felt a restlessness in his soul. He knew Diona felt it too. Late at night they would sit in their small living room and sip cups of tea and talk. Is there something the Lord would have us do? Shall we move somewhere? But where? Since the Christians in Sector 44 had come out in the open, many more Christian communities had come forward. Did any of them need help? But Clave was such a young Christian, he hardly felt capable of ministering, but what else was he trained for? Speaking and writing were what he did best. Then they would take each other's hands and together ask God to show them what He wanted them to do.

A curious excitement began to build within him as he went through the letter's contents once more. Is this where Diona and I should serve? *Mars?*

He got up again and walked to the large open window that let in the warm summer air. Diona had planted bunches of colorful flowers in the window box; they seemed to be thriving despite the pollution. Petals of gold, red, and blue fluttered in the breeze. Clave thought of other flowers, then: wildflowers. Jim Swanson's wildflowers. "Let me be a real flower, too," Clave prayed.

In the street below, half a dozen children dressed in customary white were jumping rope and chanting a childhood singsong ditty. He couldn't catch the words. A couple of young teenage boys rode by loudly on bright orange hoverbikes. A young couple dressed in blue working class outfits licked ice cream cones and pushed a sleeping baby in a stroller. And then he thought of Mars, cultural worlds away from this place. Could they live there? Should they go there?

He picked up the letter. The governor of Mars's simple question was, "Where are you?"

"The WOC in Sector 7 is constructed, and we are waiting for a director," the letter read. The governor made it clear that since all WOC property in the universe had been recently transferred to the NWO, the Sector 7 WOC technically was now under the control of Mars's governor. The letter continued, "We on Mars have strong reservations about current WOC philosophy; therefore, if you decide to come, you would have free reign in all lectures and policy decisions which affect the church in Sector 7. Come," the letter pled, "and direct this WOC any way that you wish."

Clave recalled the crime, the murders, the squalid neighborhoods in Sector 7, but he also remembered a fiercely independent people who clothed themselves in vivid colors and were passionately proud of their land.

A quick interplanetary call to Orbit Realty on Mars confirmed that the apartment they had put a down payment on, but then had to let go, was still available. Still available after all this time. Another miracle of God? Yes.

Bowing his head, Clave prayed and waited for Diona to come home.

EPILOGUE

Dr. Clave Hammill, his plain purple robe falling in neat folds about him to the floor, picked up the loaf of bread. He tore off a piece, then stepped down from the low platform and served the people, one by one, walking in between rows and reaching across the tops of chair backs until everyone had taken a piece of the bread.

As he moved among them, he said, "The Lord Jesus, on the night in which He was betrayed took bread, and when He had given thanks, He broke it and said, 'This is My body which is broken for you; do this in remembrance of Me.'"

Back on the platform Clave repeated, "This is My body which is broken for you." Then he ate the bread and the people sitting in front of him did likewise.

Like a brilliant patchwork quilt, the little congregation of Sector 7 Mars Christian Fellowship spread out in front of him. No one, not even Diona, wore the plain occupational robes of Earth anymore. But even Diona in her most outlandish costume paled in comparison to Mars's styles. She had told him laughing the day she came home with a blue streak in her hair and gold pantaloons decorated with eyelashed eyes that winked when she walked, that this would be the day everyone would know she had finally arrived as a Marsian.

Following the example of Jim Swanson, Clave prayed for his people daily. But at times he worried for them, too. So far, the governor still supported Clave, but the political situation on

Mars was volatile. A change in leadership could mean the end of their church. Of late, Stodge and his supporters had been strangely quiet—too quiet. But Clave knew that Satan wasn't finished with them, and he prayed fervently that Christians worldwide would be ready for his next attack.

As Clave walked to the front again and readied the wine glasses, he remembered the service that their friends at Northridge Bible Church had held for them the Thursday evening before he and Diona had left. They had called it a Commissioning Service. It had been a Communion Service where the bread and wine were distributed. Then, all of their friends had come forward, laid hands on them, and prayed for them. He and Diona were daily conscious of that prayer support.

As Clave passed around the tray of miniature wine glasses, he thought about his family. Star had recently moved to the Moon and had looked up Dierdron. The two were becoming fast friends, she wrote. But Nori? He didn't know where she was. She had not gone back to the university, and no one had heard from her or seen her since the day she walked out of the Safehouse. Tommi had been adopted by Sam and his family, who were still living at the Safehouse while Sam continued to look for work.

Clave and Diona had made new friends on Mars. By day they went out into their community and walked from living quarters to living quarters, inviting people to church. During the evenings they held Bible studies in their home. Their church was growing. Clave was especially concerned for the inner-city core of Sector 7. He never forgot the brutal murder he had witnessed there.

In their customary place in the front row sat some new friends: Maeva, Latz, Nikke, Anthon, and Roderick. Latz winked at Clave. Anthon gave him the thumbs-up sign. Only on Mars, thought Clave smiling. Only on Mars.

At the front of the church Clave picked up his cup, smiled down on his small congregation, and said in a voice deep with emotion, "This cup is the new covenant in My blood, do this, whenever you drink it, in remembrance of Me. For whenever you eat this bread and drink this cup, you proclaim the Lord's death until He comes."

ABOUT
THE
AUTHOR

Linda Hall grew up in a pastor's home in New Jersey. She graduated a Communications-Writing major from Moody Bible Institute, Chicago, where she met her Canadian husband, Rik. They were married in 1971 and moved to Canada where they have lived ever since.

Linda has worked as a freelance writer, a news/feature reporter for a daily paper, and an English instructor. She also coordinated a community adult literacy program and has written six books for adults who are reading at a grade 4 to 6 level.

The Halls have two children and make their home in Barrhead, Alberta, where Rik works for the Alberta Department of Education.